The  tween
he and rably.

"Ma only if I
start now," Virginia said.

He looked toward the woman. Her intense gaze met his directly.

"I see what I see, Jack. There are great things in store for Virginia as an artist," Madeline said.

Was this woman some important art critic? Perhaps he was judging her too harshly.

"You've seen her work?"

"I don't have to."

"You don't have to see her work?"

The woman shook her head, offering a cool, thin smile.

"Listen, Jack," Virginia said. Was there a note of pleading in her voice? "I'm not taking this action lightly. It's what I believe as well." She looked toward Madeline and nodded.

"It's perfectly natural," the woman said to Virginia, as if he weren't in the room.

"What the hell is she talking about?" His testiness was beginning to spill over.

"A true Capricorn," Madeline said calmly.

He turned to Virginia. "You're not serious?" he said hoarsely. It had finally dawned on him. *Oh, my God,* he thought, caught on the razor's edge between laughter and shock. A gauntlet had been thrown down and he was very much aware of his inability to react.

Muttering a perfunctory good-bye, he left the room. It was either that or exhibit his frustration and impotence.

WARREN ADLER

MADELINE'S MIRACLES

LYNX BOOKS

New York

MADELINE'S MIRACLES

ISBN: 1-55802-348-8

First Printing/April 1989

This is a work of fiction. Names, characters, places, and incidents are either the product of the author's imagination or are used fictitiously. Any resemblance to actual events, locales, or persons, living or dead, is entirely coincidental.

This book is published by Lynx Books, a division of Lynx Communications, Inc., 41 Madison Avenue, New York, New York, 10010. The name ''Lynx'' and the logo consisting of a stylized head of a lynx are trademarks of Lynx Communications, Inc.

Printed in the United States of America

0 9 8 7 6 5 4 3 2 1

Dedication

To California, a State of Mind.

MADELINE'S MIRACLES

·1·

It was the last sentence the woman uttered before she left the beauty shop.

"Don't worry. He'll come home."

Virginia Sargent looked at the fragile Vietnamese girl sitting across from her at the manicure table. Intense in her concentration as she put the finishing bright cherry glaze on Virginia's right-hand nails, the girl hadn't moved a hairbreadth in reaction. *Of course*, Virginia decided, *the language barrier*. During the entire extraordinary conversation between the woman and Virginia, the doll-like manicurist had remained, except for her diligent nail work, impassive.

Well, then, Virginia wondered, to whom were the woman's words directed? A panning glance in either direction of the beauty shop did not reveal anyone who reacted to the remark. And since neither Jack, Virginia's husband, nor Basil, their dog, were among the missing at last roll call, Virginia dismissed any thought that the words were meant for her.

Then why did the woman's words trigger a

sense of ominous expectation? *Face it,* she addressed herself, *that woman knows more about my personal life than it's possible for a stranger to know.*

Virginia had met the woman only a short while before.

She had been sitting at the manicure table, her nails just finished by the same girl who was about to do Virginia's nails.

The woman had remained seated, waiting for the polish to dry while Virginia, obeying the marching orders of the tyrannical shop owner Mel, had planted herself on the chair next to her.

In a beauty parlor women engage each other in conversation. It is commonplace, coincidental, banal. When the woman had said, "You have beautiful hands," Virginia was flattered, of course—her hands were, indeed, one of her greatest assets—but not surprised.

"My grandmother's legacy," she had replied.

"I'm sure she wanted you to have them," the woman said. It was an oddly original remark that sparked interest.

"She was a lovely lady," Virginia had said. "Beautiful in every way."

"Yes," the woman said, "she is a grand lady."

Surely, Virginia decided, she had misunderstood the tense. Often people made little slips in describing time. Her grandmother had died nearly a decade ago.

"She certainly was," Virginia said, noting that the woman continued to observe her hands. In the brief silence, she felt a strange sense of intimacy.

Virginia studied the woman. She was impressive. Big brown eyes flecked with bright yellow

that did not waver when she spoke, two intense
beams, hot with the kind of observation that
might make a woman press her thighs together.
God knew what a man's reaction might be.

Her face was miraculously unlined, barely a
squint wrinkle to be seen and her teeth were
the kind of sparkling pearl white Virginia hoped
her dentist could equal through the bonding
process she was undergoing. Physically impressive, yes, but just short of exquisite, Virginia
had concluded with her artist's eye. Neck too
long. Lips not full enough for dynamite sensuality. On a scale of one to ten, only a solid nine.
Only? she sighed, repressing a giggle.

It was the kind of judgment befitting the time
and place. After all, in a beauty parlor one
judged beauty.

But the woman's real seductive power was in
her voice. It seemed to come from deep inside
her. No twangs or high pitches. It was perfectly
modulated and rhythmical, as if the words she
uttered were accompanied by background music heard only by herself.

Virginia broke the brief silence. "Do you come
to Mel's often?" she had asked.

"Occasionally," the woman had answered.

"Mel's is very convenient for me," Virginia
had felt compelled to explain. Living on Rising
Glen in the hills above West Hollywood, she
could be home in ten minutes barring traffic.

"Probably wise," the woman said. "Not that
the twins are a problem. Especially during the
soccer season."

"I'm thankful for that." This said, Virginia
paused abruptly. Had she mentioned that she
had twin daughters who played soccer?

"You know them?" she had asked.

"Not exactly," the woman had replied, offering a smile.

"Are you one of the teachers at their school?" Virginia had asked. Even in the asking, it seemed far off the mark.

The woman shook her head gently, keeping her smile.

"You've seen us around?" Virginia had asked.

"I suppose," the woman had responded.

The woman's answers had been vague and the puzzle persisted in Virginia's mind.

"I know," she had said, as if it were a game, "you're a client of my husband's." A picture of Jack's office flashed in her mind. On his desk was a photograph of her and the kids. Two peas in a pod, they were unmistakably identical.

The woman threw her head back in a throaty, sophisticated laugh. "I don't buy stocks," she said.

"So you do know he's a stockbroker?"

"Yes."

Virginia wondered if she might have met the woman before at Mel's, although she could not remember even the most casual encounter. On her part, Virginia had a standing appointment at the beauty shop every Friday afternoon. For the past month she had scheduled her bonding appointment at her dentist's earlier to dovetail with her hair appointment. Keeping up appearances, after all, was an important part of the California life-style, wasn't it?

She had a secret agenda, as well, she assured herself. It gave the weekend a certain aura, as if she were preparing herself for some romantic interlude with Jack.

Lately, he was too distracted to participate. Their brief couplings took place on Sunday mornings and were hardly memorable. Still, the Friday ritual, if anything, kept hope alive.

Virginia felt a momentary shiver. Did this woman know about her sex life as well as everything else? She dismissed the idea. Perhaps the woman was having a joke at her expense. She searched her mind for some other explanation. "We've met socially."

"No, we haven't."

"Ever?" Virginia had asked.

"Not even in Connecticut," the woman had said.

"Are you from Connecticut, too?" Virginia had asked. She and Jack were rooted there. Connecticut was home. Forever home, she sighed, feeling once again waves of loss and nostalgia. It was one of the secret afflictions of her new life.

"Afraid not, but I hear it's a pretty place."

"It wasn't easy to leave," Virginia had said, her voice no louder than a whisper. Pain radiated through her psyche. The move had been a traumatic yank, but Jack's company had made an offer impossible to refuse. "I'll make it so special, Connecticut will fade faster than autumn flowers," Jack had assured her. The poetic promise seemed to set the stage for the fantasy. "Wither thou goest, we goeth," she responded finally, hiding her New England sense of terror at being tossed among strangers.

"And out there in the sun, you'll be able to paint at last," Jack had promised, a tantalizing prospect. When she and Jack married, Virginia had postponed her one burning ambition, working instead as a commercial artist for an advertising agency. Then the twins had come.

"You're one helluva salesman, Jack," she had responded.

"And two fifty a year guaranteed ain't chopped liver," he had emphasized, a compelling argument. To Jack, upward financial mobility was an article of faith. Not that she was against it, but for him it was, after the family, the ultimate priority.

He had assured her that the move was the only way to really pile up enough money to set up on his own.

She had trouble reconciling her artistic goals with his monetary ones. But only in theory. Early on, she had accepted his single-minded drive to accumulate wealth. Wasn't it an admired trait? A good husband and provider were a cliché of the American experience. Who was she to argue with that? Nor could she deny to herself her own pleasure in possessing creature comforts.

"I am as committed to the good life as you are," she had reassured him.

"I certainly hope so," he had replied.

She told herself that more money would mean more freedom and more freedom meant she would be able to give up her commercial illustration jobs and pursue her art. The reality had been somewhat different. The fantasy life cost more that they had dreamed.

"It takes time to adjust," the woman said, as if she were reading Virginia's thoughts.

Turning away from the woman's face, Virginia had watched the manicurist deftly file her nails, impervious to the odd conversation going on around her.

"But I'm not sorry," Virginia had said with a flash of belligerence.

"No, you mustn't be."

"Jack was transferred, the money was impossible to refuse." Virginia had been surprised at herself. This was completely out of character. Why had she needed to explain herself to a stranger?

She resented the woman for dredging up all the pain and uncertainty of leaving Connecticut. And guilt. How was Virginia expected to know that her widowed mother would develop pancreatic cancer and suffer a painful descent to death?

Only the day before, she had received a letter from her sister Kate, pressing little guilt buttons. Kate, after all, had been left with the real burden.

"You can't blame yourself," the woman had said, startling her. It was as if she had thrown a dart with deadly accuracy, a bull's-eye into Virginia's most vulnerable target.

"Blame?"

The tightness in her stomach began, always the first sign of her tension. She was here at Mel's to feel good about herself, for crying out loud. Then, it occurred to her that this woman might be a friend of Kate's. How else could she have learned so much about Virginia's innermost turmoil?

"You must be a friend of my sister Kate," Virginia had said. She had not posed it as a question. "You've heard all about us from her."

"I've never met your sister," the woman had replied.

"I assumed—" Virginia began, then stopped abruptly.

"California is a remarkably fertile place," the woman had explained, as if she sensed Virginia's sudden anguish. "People sink roots here faster than almost anywhere."

"I'm waiting for mine to take," Virginia had replied with a note of frustration.

For a brief moment she considered the peculiar emotion she was feeling. Was it vulnerability? Or relief that someone understood her? She looked toward the woman again. She was inspecting her nails. Suddenly, she gazed up at Virginia and flashed a broad, perfect smile.

"They do excellent work here," she said, "and your hair looks lovely."

Virginia reflexively stole a glance at herself in the mirror. Actually, she had not been fully satisfied with Mel's work that day. Too teasey. She was growing tired of the curly-mop style. No longer individual enough or was she getting too old for it? And lately she had spotted tiny sprouts of gray among the blond. In her family, gray came early.

"Not too young for me?" she asked, wishing she hadn't vested the woman with so much authority.

"Thirty-six isn't old," the woman said, locking her brown eyes onto Virginia's. They seemed to engulf her. "Not for a Cancer."

"A Cancer?"

"The sign, not the disease," the woman said, her head swinging back, revealing her long swanlike neck. "Cancers persevere."

If Virginia hadn't been startled by the comment, she might have put her usual brand of put-down on the exchange. Astrology was, to her, like all pseudoscience, a sop for the weak-minded. Hadn't she lectured the twins on the subject ad infinitum? Their response had always made her cringe. "We're twins and we're Pisces."

"Pure coincidence," she would counter. "Your daddy and I got carried away on the Fourth of July." By the time they understood, it was old hat. Now all she got for the explanation was an "Oh, Mommy," always in unison.

Astrology aside, the woman's comments were unnerving and, worse, suspicious. Virginia's mind groped for some logic in the exchange. *Calm yourself*, she urged herself, searching for an explanation for the woman's uncanny knowledge. None came to mind. Surely she was missing something, she told herself.

And why was the woman still here? Virginia wondered. Her nails had long since dried. Virginia forced herself not to allow the mystery to deepen into bafflement. She opted, instead, for an aggressive counterattack.

"How did you happen on Mel's?" she asked pleasantly.

"A client recommended me."

A lawyer, perhaps, Virginia thought, or maybe she was an investigator of sorts. Stockbrokers and their families were always being investigated. She waited for a further explanation. None came. The woman certainly kept a lid on herself.

"Are you married?" she asked the woman.

"No."

She was attractive and stylish enough to interest men. Indeed, most men would find her looks exceptional. In a brief inspection, Virginia's eyes wandered to the woman's figure, which, under her smock, looked curvaceous and well-proportioned. Her legs, which were

crossed, seemed particularly lovely and graceful.

"Are men that blind?" Virginia asked, offering the compliment with some calculation.

"I've often wondered," the woman said.
"Perhaps the single state is my destiny."

The remark seemed to open a small chink in
the woman's protective armor. Yet, Virginia
could not bring herself to exploit it.

She speculated that the woman must be
deeply discontented. Or did she not require the
blandishments and comfort of a man? The
thought triggered a flash of anxiety in Virginia.
California was changing her marriage. Was it
mere financial overextension or something
more? The fact was that something seemed to
be happening beneath the surface of her relationship with Jack.

In his effort to give the move an aura of high
adventure, Jack had insisted on purchasing a
house that made a personal statement. They
were on the way up and why not tell the world?
Unfortunately, the cost of California real estate
raised the ante on such a statement. The house
had cost just over a million. Then had come
taxes, furnishings, the works.

"My income can only get better," he had assured her. "In two years it will seem like pea-
nuts." A brave prediction, but it did not
completely hide his anxiety.

She, of course, had also agonized, but the
house on Rising Glen, with its breath-stopping
view of Los Angeles, did have all the earmarks
of a dream house. At night it was like riding on
a cloud in the sky, exhilarating and romantic.
In the end, money be hanged, she, too, had been
swept up with the idea.

"And I'll go back to work," she had promised. "This town is a mecca for free-lance commercial artists, especially good illustrators." It was an enterprise not without its own special deadline pressures, but better that than feeling the guilt of not contributing to what in her heart she knew was an obscene pleasure, very much against her New England grain.

"You don't have to," he had told her, but she knew he was pleased. And the money had come in handy. Her work was in demand and already they could count on an additional fifty thousand a year from it. They had agreed that whatever she earned would be used to cover the household expenses, freeing his salary for the bigger items.

It was comforting to blame her little stab of anxiety on what they both jokingly referred to as the "Yuppie factor," but marriage, after all, does not live on bread alone. Once, their marriage had been highly physical. The old wheeze about poverty making love fly out the window had an ironic twist to it. Living too high off the hog might be having exactly the same effect on them. Suddenly, she did not like the way her thoughts were heading She brought herself back to the present.

"I assume that you're a workingwoman?" Virginia had asked the woman.

"Yes, I am."

Virginia was not a natural solicitor of information, an old throwback to her New England reserve. As part of her upbringing she had been taught that prying was a violation of another's privacy. She felt embarrassed by her questioning.

"Do you enjoy what you do?" the woman

asked, as if she needed to deflect Virginia's interrogation.

"I do, as a matter of fact."

"You should get on with your painting," the woman said sweetly.

"Someday," Virginia whispered. Now, how could she possibly know that? The idea made Virginia's lips tremble. She stilled them with her teeth.

"Creative talent is a gift. It was given to you for a reason."

"Perhaps when the children grow up," she muttered after recovering from this new surprise.

"It could go dry," the woman said. "I've seen it happen."

The woman had exposed most of the fears that Virginia, by a superhuman exercise in mental gymnastics, usually avoided. Who needed this?

"I have other priorities," she said, suppressed anger rising to the surface. The skin on her face grew hot.

"A true Cancer," the woman said, "always sensitive to the needs of others." Virginia had no chance to reply, for the woman rose and, standing over her, extended her hand.

"It was wonderful meeting you, Virginia," she said. As a reflex Virginia took the woman's hand which was firm and warm. Looking up, she again experienced the power of those penetrating brown eyes. "Perhaps we can see each other again. I'll give you my card before I leave."

"Yes, that would be nice."

Virginia's anger dissipated, thawed by the woman's obvious solicitation of her friendship. It felt good to be wanted in that way, Virginia thought. She hadn't made many friends in California. At the same time, she would not lower her guard. Perhaps the woman, out of loneliness, had made a conscious effort to befriend her, had picked her out of the pack, so to speak. What harm would there be in taking her card?

The woman moved gracefully to the dressing room and reappeared again in a tight-fitting yellow slacks outfit that flattered her tall, well-proportioned figure. Virginia's artist's eye marveled at the elegance of her movements. Perhaps she had once been a model. She came back to the table and placed a card on it.

"I hope we can get together," she said pleasantly. "Really."

"I'm afraid my cards are in my purse," Virginia said apologetically.

"Well, then, I'll await your call. Perhaps lunch."

"Yes, that would be very nice," Virginia had replied, with some surprise at the eagerness of her own response.

It was then that the woman had made her eerie pronouncement. She had hesitated in the doorway, her tall, slender figure framed in a halo of afternoon light, her jet black hair softly curling. Her figure, in a soft *S*, seemed to sway, as if it were a willow branch gentled by the wind.

"Don't worry. He'll come home," she had said.

When the woman was gone, her farewell image, in the full glory of its dramatic pose, was, unavoidably, permanently engraved on Virginia's mind.

But wasn't that the objective? Virginia asked herself, with a note of cynicism. This Southern California compulsion to be memorable. Yet, considering the extent of the woman's revelations, Virginia still felt some discomfort. Who would come home? Who was supposed to be missing?

Jack had rolled out of bed that morning at five, one of the penalties of brokering stocks on the West Coast. The New York market bell sounded at seven Pacific time and his sense of responsibility demanded that he prepare for his impending frenetic day in the quiet time before the avalanche of activity began.

He never left without a parting kiss on her forehead and a whispered "Bye, sweetheart."

Always, this farewell triggered in her a brief stab of guilt. Poor Jack, busting his chops to make the West Coast move right for her and the twins. The pressure to support their life-style was taking its toll.

Remembering, she sighed, then rebuked herself. *No gloom and doom, Ginny baby,* she cajoled, telling herself for the trillionth time: *You're living in paradise in a smashing house with a drop-dead view and your kids are taking to it like little piglets in swill. So stop bitching and moaning, woman.*

As for Basil, she had heard his pathetic goodbye yap less than an hour before as the electronic gate closed in front of him. She always waited until the door completed its full cycle. No, her men weren't missing, she concluded.

Her nails dry, Virginia proceeded to the dressing room, put on her blouse, retrieved her pocketbook and paid her bill. She did not completely dismiss the exchange with the strange woman from her thoughts, but she was already contemplating her next chore which was to finish an illustration for an important advertising client. It was still on her drawing board and was due in the morning.

"Ma'am, you forgot."

The manicurist had followed her to the parking lot holding a card in her birdlike hand. Virginia took it and thrust it into her pocketbook.

In less than ten minutes she had angled through the traffic on Sunset and rolled up Rising Glen Road to their house. It was of traditional design which suited her Connecticut upbringing. Except for the electronic gate, it might have fit just as well into the New England landscape. Indeed, nothing in California seemed indigenous, as if its destiny was to make do with the jetsam and flotsam of other states and other cultures.

The house sat on a high knoll in the Hollywood Hills, and both her studio and their master bedroom had a commanding view of the city. Lying in bed at night gave her the sensation of floating in space in the midst of the star-studded sky.

With a cozy crackling fire in the bedroom fireplace, and the sensational view beyond the windows, she and Jack had, at least during their first few months in the house, spent a great deal of time in bed, savoring the romance of their new surroundings. Sometimes in the wee hours, when the twins had long since gone to bed, they had skinny-dipped in the pool which was set behind the house in such a way that it, too, had a spectacular view of the city.

Making love frequently had been an integral part of their marriage. It was, as Jack put it, "the whipped cream of life." At the moment, a lot of the whip had gone out of the cream.

Yet, she could not bring herself to confront

Jack on the subject. Nor herself. No need to increase the tension in either of them. Surely marriage, like most things, had its peaks and valleys. Besides, as Jack had assured her, the market was booming. Soon, they would be able to put financial pressures behind them.

Still it wasn't easy to watch Jack crawl out of bed in the darkness of dawn and slip quietly out of the house.

"It's the reality of the time zone, had explained. "If I'm not on tap at the bell, then I'm not doing my job. In this business, fortunes can be lost in the first minute of trading."

Of course, she accepted that and everything that went with it, including his having to go to bed a couple of hours before she did. Invariably, that meant he was asleep before she got to bed and she was barely conscious when he awoke. In purely practical terms, it was not an arrangement conducive to making love.

She was barely inside the courtyard. The electronic door had completed its closing cycle. Something was not quite right. It took her only a few seconds to realize what was amiss. No yapping from Basil.

"Basil," she called.

No answer.

She inspected the grounds. Tight shrubs made the periphery secure. It was one of the reasons that they had taken the house. Basil could be safely imprisoned behind the shrubs which were too high for him to jump. The electronic fence completed the closure. Perhaps, she speculated, he had somehow gotten inside the house.

She dashed through every room looking into

all his special bunks: behind chairs, in closets, under beds. No Basil.

She went out onto the patio and called his name, imagining she could hear an echo as it bounced back from the city. No Basil.

Just because she could not find a point of exit didn't mean that Basil hadn't found it. He was a clever little bastard. Half sheepdog, half poodle, he had a natural wanderlust. He was also sneaky. If there was a way out, he would find it. It was ironic, too, that he had chosen to escape on Friday, which was the maid Maria's day off. Maria was far more solicitous of Basil's welfare and would never have let him out of her sight.

"Where the hell are you, you little beast?" she cried out as she rummaged through the house again. Her mind vacillated between anger and worry.

She conjured up an image of him splattered on the asphalt of Sunset Boulevard, all but obliterated by the mass of rolling rubber. She was suddenly assailed by guilt. Had it been her fault? Had she left the gate ajar? Whatever, the blame still fell on her. She was the last to leave the house.

In desperation, she hopped into her car and drove to the top of Rising Glen Road, periodically calling his name. Those few neighbors who were outside at that hour contemplated her with some puzzlement, then turned away. Occasionally she stopped to confront a rare pedestrian, running or walking purposefully in jogging clothes.

"Have you seen a lost dog? Looks a little like that movie dog, Benji," she would ask. Invariably the response was sympathy but little information. Finally, after searching for nearly two hours, she returned home. There was a message on the telephone answering machine. "Soccer practice late, Mommy." It was Bobbie's voice. "We'll be home for dinner. Love and kishes from your two little fishes."

A surge of sentiment brought tears to her eyes, blurring the words. Then came another pang of guilt. The girls had wanted two dogs, a natural wish since everything they owned invariably came in twos. It was she who had objected. Jack, who was no dog lover, had maintained a stoic neutrality, which convinced the twins that he was an ally.

"I'm the one who's home all day," Virginia protested. "I don't need the responsibility of yet another life to worry about."

She had been adamant and, after a hard-fought struggle, they had finally surrendered.

"When she gets like this, there's no moving her," Jack had sighed in resignation, as if he was an ally in defeat as well. Actually, he detested the idea of one dog, no less two, and he and Basil had developed a healthy mutual antagonism.

And now there were none, she thought sadly, contemplating the twins' impending reaction to the news.

She made herself a cup of coffee and sat at the kitchen counter trying to think up a next course of action. It was essential, she knew, to call the public animal shelter and give them Basil's description. And there was hope in the fact that he wore a name tag on his collar with their telephone number engraved on it.

When she had come into the house, she had casually thrown her pocketbook on the kitchen counter. Now it loomed large in her thoughts, reminding her of the encounter a few hours before at Mel's.

Opening her pocketbook, she fished in it for the woman's card. She found it among the clutter.

"Madeline Curran Boswell," she read. And under the name, in script, the word, "Psychic." There was a telephone number but no address.

"Damn," she said aloud, angrily. "Hustled by a quack psychic." So that's how they pick up business. She laughed and shook her head, appalled by her naïveté. Jack's response to the incident would be sarcastically snide, setting off ridicule that would be good for a year's run. *Stupido. Stupido*, she repeated to herself.

When the flush of humiliation receded, she remembered the missing Basil and called the animal shelter. No. No sign of Basil. She gave her name and address and hung up.

She sat for a long time at the kitchen counter, the coffee cooling in front of her. She could not get the woman out of her mind. Her come-on was certainly compelling. The clever bitch. But where on earth had she gotten the information? Then Virginia remembered the woman's parting words.

"Don't worry. He'll come home."

Despite herself, Virginia felt oddly relieved.

·2·

Jack Sargent, his mind on the cusp of consciousness, drifted upward out of the pit of
sleep. He squinted at the face of the illuminated
digital clock. Five minutes to five. It was unusual for his sleep to be interrupted before the
sobering rasp of the alarm, but he did not dwell
on the anomaly. There were still five precious
minutes before it was necessary to whip his
body into action.

Beside him, his wife Virginia slumbered in
her classic embryonic position. The first time
he had ever slept with her, her sleep had been
so deep, her breath so shallow, that he had put
an ear to her heart to see if she were still alive.
It crossed his mind briefly that, rested now, he
might caress her awake, make love. No time, he
decided. Thus deflected, his thoughts drifted to
the events of the previous night.

His arrival home had been greeted with tears
and hysteria. The twins often seemed to feed
each other's emotions, heightening their responses to even the most pedestrian catastrophe. But this was a major trauma. The beloved

Basil, that mischievous mutt whose every yap set Jack's teeth on edge, had disappeared.

Secretly, he rejoiced. The dog knew he despised him and, with good reason, kept his distance. But the twins worshiped Basil, shared their food and beds with him, pampered and fussed over him. He was spoiled rotten.

Ordinarily, when any of Jack's family was unhappy, his heart would melt. That was especially true of the twins. And they were wildly unhappy, vociferously unhappy. Besides, he hated to see women cry and these little women, being identical, increased his anguish by double. But he had determined that this period in his life required a hassle-free environment. He was under enormous financial pressure. He did not need any disasters, especially those that he viewed as trivial.

"He'll be back," Virginia had said with a confusing air of certainty.

"He's dead," one of the twins whined, "I know he's dead."

"Of course he's dead, he's not used to traffic. And it's dark," the other said.

It was true. Basil had had the run of a large plot of ground, a fenced-in yard, when they lived in Connecticut. The new house offered a similar environment. The chances of his survival outside were, at best, spotty.

"He'll be back," Virginia reiterated.

"Mommy knows," Jack said supportively, although he was not inclined to take short odds on Basil's chance for survival. He dreaded the moment when the worst-case scenario had to be confronted as reality.

The twins were uncommonly pretty: blue-eyed, blond, dimpled, pink and rosy-cheeked,

just beginning to round out in the right spots.
Soon they would start their menstrual cycles,
turn into women. He shuddered. He wished that
they would be small, cuddly and worshipful
forever. He missed kissing their little butts.

They were even rebelling over his nicknames
for them. Officially they had been named Ro-
berta and Wilhelmina, two old family names,
one for Virginia's side and one for his. But they
had evolved into Bobbie and Billie, which the
girls had begun to detest. To mitigate that distaste he had instead called them One and Two,
based solely on chronology. Bobbie had a minute on Billie. Or sometimes he called them A
and B, which these days also sent them up the
wall.

"You don't understand. Joking is part of
affection," he had told them.

"We are people, not numbers or letters." Billie
was unable or unwilling to fathom the concept.
Indeed, they were swiftly turning into individ-
uals, although they had their own all-inclusive
pet name for themselves: "Little Fishes."

"I'll just die if Basil is gone forever," Bobbie
cried. "Everything will be ruined. School. The
team."

The team was their finest achievement, despite Jack's and Virginia's trepidation that soccer was too rough a sport for girls. But they
were superbly coordinated and aggressive. They
were the stars of the school team, which was
coed, and there was every indication that they
were heading toward the finals.

It was Virginia who took the brunt of their
ire about Basil. It was she who was accused of
somehow being responsible for his getting out.
It was she who didn't care, was thoughtless and

selfish and always worrying about her dumb deadlines. The twins had both dumped on her and the more she persisted in being calm, the more they attacked her.

"Don't you care, Mommy?" Bobbie had asked.

"He's a living creature," Billie had added.

"If you cared, you would have been more careful," Bobbie had pressed. As the "oldest" by one minute, she seemed to take it upon herself to be the more aggressive.

"Yes," Billie echoed.

"Now, that's enough of that," Jack interjected. "I will not allow you to be disrespectful to your mother." He glanced at Virginia. Virginia and he had long ago resolved to show a common front. Even if he secretly agreed with the kids' assessment. Like now.

"You're home most of the day, Mommy," Billie whined.

"I told you I don't know how he got out," Virginia said defensively. She apparently had decided to excuse their brattiness on the grounds of extreme grief. "I can't understand it. I stayed until the gate closed."

"Poor Basil, I just know he's in trouble," Bobbie said.

"You're all overreacting," Virginia told them. "He'll come back, I know he will."

"How can you possibly know that?" Bobbie asked, making no effort to hide her skepticism.

"I know, that's all."

"Well, then, when?" Billie asked.

"I can't be sure, but I know it will happen," Virginia said with firmness. At times, when she felt something deeply, she could be quite intractable. Unfortunately, her confidence did little to mollify the twins who remained teary-eyed and gloomy.

After dinner, Jack had taken the twins on a futile drive through the neighborhood to find Basil. Later the twins locked themselves in their room, ready to cry themselves to sleep.

"I think maybe you raised their expectations too high," Jack said later to Virginia as they sat in the den watching television.

"I guess, I did." She was suddenly tentative, distant, as if she were chewing over some disturbing thought. Fourteen years of marriage had made them both mildly telepathic.

"Spit it out, Ginny," he insisted. He was, as usual at this hour, tired, edgy.

"I'm not sure how to put it," she said. "You'll think I've gone 'round the bend."

"Nothing surprises me anymore," he sighed, checking himself, thinking unexpectedly of Jane Meyers, a colleague of his at the office. With a flash of guilt, he quickly dismissed her from his thoughts.

"This psychic seemed to zero in on me at the beauty parlor," Virginia began.

"Oh, God," Jack groaned, "California, here we are."

"She seemed to know everything about me. Us."

"And you bought it?"

"I'm not sure," she stammered. "Her last words to me were that he would come home."

"Who?"

"That's the scary part. I didn't know Basil was missing until I got home."

"Precognition. Is that the word?"

"If it means knowing about something before it happens."

"Did she actually say that the beast had flown the coop?"

"No."

"Did she even say it was a dog?"

"No. Only a 'he.' There are only two 'hes' in this family. And one of them is a dog."

"And she said 'he' would come home?"

"Yes."

"No charge for this brilliant bit of precognition?"

Obviously feeling restless, Virginia got up from her chair and began to pace the room. "I swear she knew everything. Little details. About my feelings concerning mother's illness. My wanting to paint. The twins. You being a stockbroker. She even knew my sign."

"Naturally, she knew that," Jack said. Despite his cynicism, he felt vaguely troubled.

"But how could she know?" She stopped pacing abruptly and turned toward him. "Jack, I swear the woman knew. I'm sorry, but it's true."

"Well, then, where is the mutt?"

"The point is that she didn't say when he would come home."

He could see she was agitated. Reaching out, he took her hand and drew her down on his lap. He stroked her cheek in an effort to soothe her.

"That's the way they draw you in," he whispered. "They look for suckers, try to hook you so that you can't live without them. She . . . she took a shot." As he reassured her, his mind groped for an explanation. "She must have had prior knowledge."

"I never saw her before. Well, never really noticed. She said she had been to Mel's before."

"There's a clue there somewhere."

"I can't place her. . . ." He watched her struggle with memory. "At first she did look well . . . vaguely familiar. It's the beauty parlor environment. A little like Chinese waiters all looking alike."

He ignored her effort at humor. "She might have made inquiries elsewhere."

"A possibility," Virginia said. "But why me?"

"Good question."

Although he tried to put a calm face on the revelation, he was not comfortable with this element of mystery. It implied danger and set up in him a conscious effort at defense. Above all, his family was his life, his reason for existence. Virginia was obviously upset by the experience. He continued to search his mind for some credible explanation, anything to chase away the thought that the situation was supernatural.

"She could have gone through your wallet, seen your driver's license and gotten your vital statistics."

Virginia grew thoughtful, tapping her teeth with the nail of her forefinger.

"There's a dressing room where we put our pocketbooks and blouses, change into smocks. But I always take my wallet out and carry it with me. Besides, she knew more than just what was in my wallet."

He felt her shiver and he became aware that her hands had suddenly turned cold. He stroked them.

"You're actually believing it," he said, "and it's frightening you."

"You've got to admit, it gives one food for thought. Some people are supposed to have this gift . . ." She broke off abruptly.

"You're a victim of the power of suggestion. Somehow she got to you. That's her business."

"It wasn't like that," she insisted.

"Get it out of your head," he said firmly.

"Easier said than done."

"They have ways for making you believe, *mein Frau*," he said, exaggerating a German accent, goading a smile out of her. He stroked the curve of her buttocks, kissed her earlobe and nudged her off his lap.

"Enough psychic phenomena for one night," he said, getting up from the chair. "Now for beddy-bye. I'm bushed."

She stood up, calmer now, but before he left the room, she turned again. "So what about Basil?" she asked.

"Two possibilities. He'll get home some way or he won't. We'll go out and get another dog. Maybe the two we probably should have gotten in the first place. Then, if we lose one, we've still got one left."

He smiled and gave her a mock punch to the chin, looking into her eyes. Although she laughed, he detected a tremor of doubt.

"It's so easy to be taken in," she said. "Clever the way she did it, offering friendship. You should have seen her. Quite beautiful, really. And yet . . ."

"So she charmed you, too."

"Yes," she agreed, "she was quite pleasant."

"But scary."

"And puzzling."

He gathered her in his arms, kissing her neck, patting her hair. He pressed her close, feeling the outline of her slender body. Again he had to turn away comparisons with Jane Meyers, a

persistent image of voluptuousness and temptation.

"I've got to sack out," he said.

"Need company?" she asked saucily, grind-
ing her hips against his.

"I think I'll keep you at bay for the time being." He smiled and released her with a tweak
at her nose. He knew it was a cover for guilt.

Lately, his erotic mind was focused elsewhere
and it bothered his sense of fidelity. Not that he
hadn't had fantasy feelings about other women
before, but this one seemed different, more
compelling. At times he felt under attack by it,
tempted beyond endurance.

In bed, he found himself too fidgety to sleep.
Ginny's encounter with the psychic was both-
ersome. No denying it to himself. How, indeed,
had she known that Basil would be gone?

It was certainly unsettling to be confronted
by someone who professed to know your innermost thoughts. God, he hoped that no one saw
inside his head. They'd see lewd images of Jane
Meyers, who was tantalizing him with a body
that could raise an erection on a dead Indian.
He was in that state now.

With an effort of will, he forced himself to
think about his wife, the steady, loyal, sincere,
sensitive, artistic, sometimes stubborn, loving
Virginia. Trim, slim-hipped, small-breasted, her
blondish hair done in a curly mop, a cute nest
of freckles running over her nose and cheeks,
she was best described as "pert." Fourteen
years of marriage had not dimmed that image.
She had hazel eyes that changed color from
brown to deep green depending on the light.

There was a fragility about her that had triggered his own need to have someone or some-

thing to protect. And yet, she was anything but fragile. Certainly not in body or mind.

They had met in college at the University of Connecticut at Storrs. She was an art major and he was studying business administration. They might never have met if he hadn't answered an ad on the bulletin board for a male model.

In those days, he had had to scrounge for bucks, taking on any odd job he could to pay his way. His father, a glorified insurance salesman specializing in pay-by-the-week insurance was not exactly a breadwinner, forcing his mother to act as resident manager for the small apartment building where they traded out her services in return for half-rent.

Well-meaning, but economically bungling and forever arguing about money, the vision of his parents' plight was a great motivator in his desire to become financially independent. He hadn't taken a dime from them since he was twelve years old.

He got the job posing for a group of students working on the human figure. Virginia was one of the students. Wearing a jockstrap, he earned two dollars an hour. He kept his mind busy by contemplating Virginia as she worked with great intensity and concentration, seemingly oblivious to anything but the lines of anatomy.

"You're a very interesting subject," she told him one day after a session. He had dressed and she was packing up her paints.

"So are you," he said. By then, he was intrigued by her good looks and air of dedication. She blushed at his remark, but it seemed to signal more than passing interest on her part.

"Are you an artist?" she asked.

"Business major," he answered.

"Oh." She seemed disappointed.

"Sort of balances us out," he had responded. In a way the remark characterized their relationship, a balancing out.

He remembered when love first emerged between them. He supposed that such things often happened in memorable "moments." For them, this moment came when he posed for her in the room of her off-campus apartment.

She had not been fully satisfied with the picture she had painted in the classroom, although he liked to speculate secretly that she had ulterior motives in inviting him over. He was hopeful that this might be the case, but he doubted it. She was enormously concentrated and serious about her work.

By then, he had transcended any feelings of discomfort in showing his body. In those days, he was trim and lithe. Posing seemed a remarkably natural vocation.

He had joked about giving her a "freebie," which amused her more than he had expected. By then their relationship had blossomed into friendship, just on the threshold of more aggressive attraction.

Perhaps it was the sense of privacy that posing in her apartment suggested, or something devilishly pressing in himself, but he chose to pose bare-ass naked.

"All or nothing," he told her, aware that she was trying to keep from showing her embarrassment.

At first, she refused to be drawn into his playful banter.

"You're only interested in one thing," he had said. "How about looking at the real me."

She had burst out laughing.

"You have me at a disadvantage," he had said, deadpan. "A naked person is very vulnerable."

"Are you suggesting that I paint you while I'm naked, too?" she asked.

"Only fair," he had said.

It was a silly little dare. Nevertheless, throwing Yankee conservatism to the wind, she began to undress, although she had the advantage of the easel to hide at least part of her body.

"Better?" she had asked.

"Fairer," he had replied.

This time, he realized, he was truly at a disadvantage. He was developing a massive erection.

"You're going to get more of me than you bargained for," he told her. No point in denying it, he had thought.

"I can always paint it out," she told him.

She had continued to paint, but soon he could not pose comfortably. Besides, he had other things on his mind. He moved toward her. She did not resist, submitting and responding to a long, sublimely erotic kiss. Indeed, it was the kind of memorable "moment" that time actually enhances.

"Be gentle," she had whispered, and he knew then that he would be her first lover.

"I'm not sure whether to celebrate or apologize," he had told her after the deed was done. Actually, it had been a difficult and painful experience, especially for her. She was smaller than any other female he had known, but she had gamely insisted that he not stop.

"I thought tightness was supposed to have its advantages," she had said.

"I didn't like bringing you pain." He had felt as if he had violated her.

"Somebody had to," she had whispered.

"Why me?" he had asked aloud. By then, he knew that he cared for her, deeply, passionately. It worried him to think that he might merely have been a handy instrument for the overdue taking of her virginity.

"Because I love you," she said boldly, directly, firmly. "I have from the first moment I saw you."

"And you kept me in the dark," he had said with mock resentment.

"Maybe I was waiting for the right moment."

"You've got to admit, we found it."

She did not respond, except to hug him closer to her. He gently pushed her at arm's length and looked deeply into her eyes. They were deep spring green, appropriate to the season.

"I do appreciate your love, Virginia, and I return it unconditionally."

He had wanted to say something that would, along with the moment, linger in memory. He hoped it had. It certainly was a scene that they had recalled time after time. In the early days of their courtship and marriage he had often posed for her, but they had never again attained the level of passion and mystery of that first encounter.

From then on, they operated on the notion that they were joined together for a lifetime. They had decided on marriage as soon after graduation as possible. He needed to get on with it, he told her, to pursue success without the distractions of worrying about the dating grind. Besides, he had found his girl. And she had found her man.

He pointed his nose to where the money was and got a job as a trainee with a prestigious

Wall Street firm. Within a year he was making
enough money to get married, a situation that
spurred him on to even greater heights of risk.
After all, he was now responsible for a family.
When the twins came two years after their marriage, he and Virginia bought a large house in
an upwardly mobile neighborhood of Stamford,
within easy distance of both sets of parents.

His steady climb gave him the confidence to
work the further edges of the financial firma-
ment. He discovered leverage, took chances,
built a good clientele and, by the time he left
for California, had the confidence to plunge on
a million-dollar house and all the other accou-
terments of the good life. He bought a Jag, but
Virginia resisted a Mercedes for herself. He
knew she would. Finally, she settled on a
top-of-the-line Honda.

Virginia wasn't much for jewels and expensive clothes and her Yankee work ethic compelled her to help out with her own marketable
skills. She was good for over fifty thou freelancing for ad agencies. Certainly it came in
handy, although he knew she would rather be
pursuing her own artistic goals.

Occasionally he would assure her that they
could do without her earnings, but the assurance came with his subtly injected insinuation
that it would be a tight squeeze without it. Besides, try as he might to explain his various financial strategies, she was never quite comfortable with the concept of leverage. She did,
however, understand the concept of debt.

"Part of the game," he told her. "Greater the
risk, greater the reward."

"Go too far out on the limb, the limb breaks,"
she told him often.

But he, too, had his secret agenda, which was to make it before he was forty, now three years ahead. This meant having enough fuck-you money so he would never have to kiss anyone's ass again. Crude, yet picturesque and, above all, accurate. Money was power and freedom. The more money, the more power, the more freedom. Was he reacting against his father's failure? Probably. But he was not one to try to unravel his own psyche. Money was success . . . period.

He was dead certain that it would all come to pass. With prudent assurance, he margined his own accounts and was able to roll over notes without losing a moment's sleep. He considered such behavior a sign of his inherent "rich man's mentality."

Vaguely, he defined his ambition as "a pot of gold at the end of the rainbow fantasy." Central to the fantasy was his little family in their gold-plated little nest, protected, secure, loving, happy. It took single-minded dedication to pursue such a fantasy, a commitment requiring iron self-discipline and the recruitment of every personal and emotional resource he could muster.

All this determination had not prepared him for his reaction to the aggressive onslaught of Jane Meyers.

She was a divorcée who also worked as a broker in the firm and their proximity had a great deal to do with their situation. Often, they worked as partners in various deals. Aside from her physical arsenal, Jane had a good head for business.

"Only two things turn me on, Jackie, baby,

money and men. In that order," she had told
him soon after their initial meeting.

Jane was a California native, just on the
wrong side of forty, childless, with two broken
marriages. She was tough-guy-cynical and sexy.
It was her blunt edge, her inability to suppress
whatever came into her head, that made her appear somewhat coarse. But the shock value of
her remarks, salted by foul language, gave her
an entrée into the male world of stock hype
where she was a trusted member of the frater-
nity.

She exuded experience and wisdom and conveyed a sense that she had somehow managed
to survive psychic plagues, mysterious sexual
wars, failed love affairs, an abused childhood
and an economic bashing.

The fact was, she was an exotic bird in the
firm, a sexy object to be ogled with salacious
longing. But few, if any, among her colleagues
had the temerity to put their fingers, or whatever else, in her cage.

"You'll discover that there's a lot more to me
than big tits," she had told him one day as they
lunched at the sidewalk tables of Chin Chin.

The purpose of the lunch was to declare a
salesman's truce. They had both oversold stock
in an underwriting to their respective clients,
each exceeding the quotas the firm had set.
Worse, the stock had gone up and Jack's cus-
tomer had demanded profits on a stock that he
did not own.

A hot blush rose in his cheeks at her comment, embarrassing him. It wasn't at all cool to
blush in front of this tough California woman.
He felt he was undergoing some kind of test.

"I guess I've shocked you. But take comfort, I only talk dirty to my closest friends."

"It took me by surprise," Jack mumbled.

"I'm sorry," she said. "I sometimes overlook the eastern sensitivity. Actually, it was a defensive remark."

"I understand," he had responded, sounding stupid even to himself.

"How can you? It's a woman's thing."

They had settled their business difference at lunch, but her remark had planted something disturbing in his mind. With keen interest, he searched for the promise of her big tits under her proper business suits. He imagined them, thought about them. Occasionally, she caught him ogling her and smiled knowingly. Whenever this happened, he blushed.

For reasons he barely understood, he found himself in her company with greater frequency. Often, they worked in tandem on various transactions. It became commonplace for them to react to each other's buys and sells in dealings with their own accounts.

Increasingly, after the market closed, they would repair to one or the other's office to discuss the transactions of the day. Sometimes, they discussed a lot more than that.

"The fact is," she admitted one afternoon, "men have always inflicted pain on me. Now that the dating environment has become physically dangerous, I've got a good excuse to cease and desist."

"You're not lonely?" he had asked. They had just completed an underwriting and he had brought a bottle of wine into her office. He had poured drinks into paper cups.

"Lonely as hell, Jack," she told him. They

were sitting on her nubby upholstered couch. Her legs were crossed, her dress hiked to mid-thigh. She had turned to him suddenly. "You are one lucky bastard. Two beautiful kids. A lovely devoted wife. How many years has it been?"

"Fourteen," he said.

"Ever stray?" she asked.

"Never," he replied, almost embarrassed by the admission.

"Ever want to?" she pressed.

"I'm only human." He shrugged.

She stretched and held out her glass, gesturing for more. He obliged and also poured himself another.

"A woman alone has to devise different strategies to get around the male mine fields. My antenna is always up. Don't think I like going home to an empty bed. . . ." She checked herself and watched him.

"It's all right, Jane." He had smiled, determined not to let her know that her talk was arousing him.

"Slim pickings out there, I can tell you," she sighed. Her emotional guard was getting lower. She looked up at him, her eyes moist. "I picked two lulus," she said. He could see that she wanted to talk and he kept his silence.

"The first was an actor. Christ. The worst. His life was waiting for the telephone to ring. His income in the last year of our marriage was thirteen hundred and sixty dollars and twelve cents. Imagine remembering something like that. I finally said take your thirteen hundred and sixty dollars and twelve cents and shove it.

"Then I married Harold. Harold had big bucks. But Harold was a paranoid. Possessive.

If I stayed too long in the john he would kick in
the door. Toward the end, I had to keep it open.
I couldn't work. I couldn't go out of the house
without him. I was a prisoner in my own five-
million-dollar home. Actually, it wasn't my own
five-million-dollar home. I had signed a pre-
nuptial agreement, which got me zippo after the
split.

"After Harold, I spent five years mooning
about life being shit. Then I booted my ass up
and said to myself: 'Jane, fuck 'em. You live
your life for you.'"

She looked up at him. "Real original." The
wine had loosened her tongue. "I can't say I've
gotten all the fuck-you money I need yet, but
I'm well on my way if the market doesn't go to
hell. Money may not put a dent in loneliness,
but it's better to be lonely with it than without
it."

"I'll drink to that." They tapped paper cups.
Then her eyes locked onto his and she moved
her face closer. He could see the ridges in her
lips.

"God, you are something, Jane," he said,
turning away. He knew his desire was stretched
as taut as piano wire. He wanted to take her in
his arms, undress her. Fuck her.

She reached out and touched his chin, gently
nudging his face toward hers. Leaning closer,
he kissed her, deeply and passionately, his
tongue groping for hers. Shifting his weight, he
stretched forward on the couch. She reached
out and put her hand on his erection.

"No conscience here," she whispered.

But there was. He sat up abruptly.

"Guess I found the spellbreaker," she sighed.

Her face had flushed and she primly pulled down the hem of her skirt.

"Maybe betrayal takes a little practice," he said.

"That seems a rather brutal way to put it," she said, pouting. "I'm not a housebreaker."

"I hadn't meant . . ."

"I know what you meant."

She stood up and began to pace the office, running her fingers through her hair. "You know what it feels like to be odd man out? The fucking truth of it is that there's not enough to go around. It's so damned frustrating . . . and humiliating." Her eyes were moist with tears of anguish.

He stood up and came toward her, reaching out. She backed away.

"I don't need your fucking pity," she said, her shoulders heaving as she fought to control herself.

"It's my fault, too," he said. "I wanted you . . . but I . . ." He groped for some way to put it right. "I don't want anything to louse up our relationship."

"Shit," she whimpered, "that's the woman's line. Next comes: 'We can still be friends.' "

"We have to be," he said, "we're colleagues. We work well together."

"I feel like such a fool."

"So do I," he said. Much to his relief, she was calming.

"You never get what you want exactly at the moment you want it."

"That's life," he said. They were back to the old banter now. He knew, of course, that it would never be the same between them.

She turned away, gathered up some papers

on her desk and stuffed them into her briefcase. As she breezed toward the door, she turned. "There may come a time . . ." she said hesitantly. "I'm not closing the door on the possibility. But if you ever put your chips on the table again, you better be prepared to play."

It was taken as delivered, a warning, a come-on, an offer. He knew even then that it would trouble the hell out of him. Not a day had passed since that incident that he hadn't debated the point with himself. Where lay the greater satisfaction? To be a saint or a sinner. Always, he came out on the side of "saint." Resistance was a form of self-discipline, he assured himself. Nothing must threaten the family fortress.

Always, lately, in the private precincts of reflection, the subject arose in his thoughts. Like now. He looked at the digital clock again. In less then twenty seconds the alarm would go off. He wondered why he had awakened so early.

It was then that he heard the sound, certain now that he had heard it before on some subconscious level. A muffled scratching noise from the direction of the front of the house.

He bounded out of bed and raced to the front door. Opening it, he found a bedraggled Basil looking up at him with limpid grateful eyes.

"Hope it was worth it, you dummy," Jack said, leading Basil by a pinch of neck muscle to the twins' room where he jumped into Bobbie's bed and licked her awake. Billie was up in another second and they were both cuddling him while his ardent tongue bathed their faces in moist gratitude.

"Oh, Daddy," Bobbie said, grabbing Jack

around the neck. Billie quickly joined them, kissing him on each cheek.

"Mommy told you he'd come back," he said.

In the distance he could hear the buzzing of the alarm. Rushing back to his bedroom, he shut it off, but Virginia was already up, rubbing her eyes. He knelt on the bed, bent down and kissed her cheek.

"The little bastard has returned," he said. "I popped him in with the girls. All's well that ends well."

She reached up, pulled his head down, pressed her lips to his and offered a big smacking kiss.

"Might be something to it?" she said, releasing him.

"To what?"

"Psychic phenomena," she said.

"Might be," he replied grudgingly. "But what would life be without unpredictability?"

"Maybe better," she said, slipping back onto her pillow, closing her eyes as he headed for the bathroom.

"I doubt it," he muttered. But he wasn't exactly sure where his doubts lay. He looked at his unshaven face in the mirror through which he could see her reflection, a mound of curly blond hair sunk in the pillow's indentation.

"Just don't get hooked," he said. She hadn't moved. He guessed she had already fallen back to sleep.

·3·

They had established on the phone earlier that she would be delighted to be called Madeline. Virginia was uncomfortable with it at first, but now that she was face-to-face, basking in the woman's bright smile and superb brown eyes, she felt her anxiety receding.

"I hope you like this place," Virginia said.

"I adore it."

"You've been here before?"

"Never."

Virginia had chosen La Scala for its quiet and leisurely setting. A trifle pricey, true, but she wanted to illustrate that she was not cheap and that this was to be a social not a business lunch.

Virginia noticed that the woman's beige outfit matched perfectly with the surroundings. "Wonderful how your outfit blends with the place. It's lovely."

"Why, thank you," Madeline said.

"You knew the decor," Virginia said playfully after a long pause. "Of course, that's what psychics do. They know in advance."

The woman threw her head back and laughed.

It was a gesture that seemed incongruous to her normally cool persona. Makes her seem more human, Virginia decided.

They ordered Perriers with lime and sipped lightly.

"About this thing with Basil . . ." Virginia began, the sentence trailing off into silence. It was a characteristic of hers when she had something on her mind to plunge ahead, eschewing stage-setting small talk.

"I told you not to worry," Madeline said.

"It was so . . . so eerie," Virginia said. "I became certain that he would come home. My husband was skeptical."

"Perfectly natural," Madeline said.

"But then he hadn't had the . . . the experience. It loses a lot in translation."

The woman was watching her with such intensity that Virginia had to avert her eyes.

"I hadn't intended to cause any friction in the family," Madeline said amiably.

"It wasn't exactly friction," Virginia said defensively, although anticipating his disapproval, she had not told Jack about this luncheon. She had some difficulty explaining it to herself. Gratitude, perhaps. Or curiosity. Weren't there, after all, mysterious unexplained things out there? Back in Connecticut, they would think her bananas.

"The important thing is that everything turned out right as far as Basil is concerned," Madeline said. "The twins, I'm sure, are happy, and I know it's a relief not to have to carry the blame."

"You know that?"

"Of course I do. And your husband's feelings about Basil."

"You might say that it was hate at first sight."

The waiter came and stood over them as they scanned the menu. Madeline was deep in concentration. Virginia considered the broiled swordfish or an angel hair pasta with mushrooms. Always figure conscious, she attended aerobic classes three times a week and did a daily set of sit-ups to keep her abdominal muscles tight.

"The swordfish sounds fine," Madeline told the waiter.

"You must have read my mind," Virginia laughed. She nodded to the waiter. "Same. And a cold white Ggigrich," Virginia said.

"My favorite, too," Madeline said, "but so expensive."

It hadn't occurred to Virginia that such a well-groomed beautiful creature could possibly be concerned with money. Intimacy was making Madeline less awesome and Virginia's comfort level was increasing rapidly. She had approached this luncheon with some trepidation. It was not every day that one lunched with someone who might have access to her inner thoughts.

The waiter came with the wine, uncorked it and poured a sample. Virginia sipped it.

"Delicious," she said, giving the waiter permission to pour.

It was Madeline who lifted her glass.

"To our growing friendship," she said, tapping her glass with Virginia's.

"Yes," Virginia said. She hadn't expected the toast to be so personal. Looking at Madeline, Virginia considered the possibility of friendship with this unusual woman.

The fact was that she had no "strong relationship" with any women in Los Angeles. Most of her small circle of so-called intimate friends were back East. And even those friendships had faded since she had moved.

In any event, she had learned that the sharing of confidences was inevitably watered down by life's distractions. People married, had children, became self-involved. The friendship of youth was often spoiled by maturity. As one got older it was more difficult to find what in adolescence one called "a true friend."

Besides, despite her efforts to be engaging, the truth was that she did not make even casual friends easily. In that sense, the woman had struck a chord.

Often she had yearned for a sincere and loving woman friend to whom she could pour out her heart, share confidences that she couldn't possibly share with Jack. Or any man. At first, she had assumed that marriage offered such a possibility. It didn't. Men were different. Their perspectives were on a different plane.

But to consider this elegant, mysterious woman for such a role seemed farfetched. Talk about differences.

"Has it always been, well, like this for you?" Virginia asked with some degree of hesitation. The wine had begun to warm her and she could feel the first flush of euphoria.

"Afraid so," Madeline sighed.

"I detect a note of regret," Virginia said cautiously. She watched as the woman sipped deeply on the wine.

"The visible world is quite limiting to people like me. Also cruel." The woman averted her eyes for a moment, then lifted her chin and fo-

cused them on Virginia. Her gaze was overwhelming and Virginia had to turn away.

"When . . . well, when did you know that you
had this, this talent?"

"In the womb," Madeline said with disarming
ease. "I was born with five veils. They had to be
peeled off within a minute of birth, otherwise I
would not have been able to live in this world."

"But how could you know then?"

Madeline reached out and patted Virginia's
hand, leaving it on hers for a long moment.

"There is only one way to explain it without
being patronizing," Madeline said pleasantly.
The waiter had come and refilled their glasses
from the opened bottle in the ice bucket. Virginia sensed that Madeline was making every
effort not to appear "superior."

"Think of radio waves, bands of vibrating
waves in the air. Take an FM signal. It's in the
atmosphere in this room right now. All it needs
is the proper receiver to pick it up. Now carry
it one step further. We are all emitting certain
signals. In many ways the atmosphere is like
the Tower of Babel. Some people have the ability to receive these signals." With her long del-
icate fingers, Madeline picked up her glass again
by its stem. "Think of me as a receiver."

"Like telepathy?" Virginia asked.

"Exactly. Except there is the notion of time."
Madeline smiled, sipped her wine and deli-
cately replaced the glass on the table. "Time is
an infinite circle. Past, present and future are
all one. And all the people who have ever lived
are still alive in spirit, recycling and reappear-
ing in other genetic combinations."

"Reincarnation?"

"If it needs a word, that's as good as any."

"And you can pick up these . . . these signals . . . from the dead?" Virginia shivered and her lips began to tremble. To still them she gulped the remaining wine in her glass.

"From the living, too," Madeline said firmly.

"Do you do what they call channeling?" Virginia asked, hoping Madeline wouldn't think her too naive. She knew little of these matters. California, she had read, was awash with this phenomenon, but she had never run across anyone who was into it.

"Rarely," Madeline replied. "Only when it's called for."

"And when is that?"

"When one has to sort things out in the spirit world."

Virginia waited for more explanation. None came. She thought suddenly of Jack and his skepticism. The woman struck her as totally sincere and credible, yet her mind groped for still more questions to buttress her assurance.

Madeline smiled and patted Virginia's hand again. A shaft of warmth suffused Virginia's body.

"Nobody dies Virginia. Nobody."

"You talk to people in the future as well?"

"At times. . . ." The woman hesitated, her gaze burning.

"And you know things that will happen before they happen? I think the word to describe that is clairvoyant. Jack called it precognition."

"True by any definition," Madeline sighed. "A gift, but also an affliction, I'm afraid."

"Affliction?"

"It has its drawbacks on a personal level in this life," Madeline whispered. Her statement had the air of a confession and a pall of sadness seemed to fall over her eyes.

"I hadn't realized," Virginia said, lifting her glass and drinking to mask her confusion.

Madeline continued to hold her hand over Virginia's. It felt comfortable, secure.

"As a schoolgirl I was a real worry to my mother and father. One time I begged the parents of one of my little friends not to take her on a trip to Vermont. They asked me why. I told them. They forbade me to play with the little girl again. Of course, it was moot. The girl was accidentally killed on the trip."

"And you knew?"

Madeline nodded.

"How awful," Virginia said. The wineglass trembled in her hand, and she put it down.

"I learned quickly to avoid telling people about impending tragedies."

"Even if by telling them they could be averted?"

The woman pondered the question for a moment. "Only then," she said. "Except that most of the time the result is inevitable and irrevocable."

Virginia felt somewhat relieved. Yet it still troubled her. "Would you tell a friend or only a client?" It embarrassed her to ask such a probing question.

The woman did not miss a beat. "Both," she said. "I have a moral obligation to tell clients what I see. Joy, tragedy, success, failure. They pay for such information. A friend receives it from the heart."

Virginia, feeling the squeeze on her hand, lifted her head, forcing herself to endure the intensity of Madeline's gaze. This time she did not turn away.

"And are you always right?" Virginia asked. She owed it to herself to be fully convinced of the woman's sincerity, at the very least.

"I see what I see," Madeline said. "It would be immoral to communicate information that's not fully formed. Sometimes, I see nothing, draw blanks. I accept that limitation. I don't impart information based upon hints, clues or feelings."

"What you see is what they get?"

"Exactly."

"I . . . I don't know how to react," Virginia said, "nor can I truly buy it on a rational level."

"You're an artist, my dear. Surely, what you create on your canvases does not come from anyplace that you can explain on a rational level. It arrives via your eye, your mind, your other senses, and is translated by brush and paint. It's a message received from somewhere. Don't you see?"

"This is getting too heavy to absorb," Virginia said. She placed her other hand on top of Madeline's. The waiter arrived with their plates of swordfish and poured two more glasses of wine.

"I quite agree," Madeline said. "Time to enjoy the pleasures of this world."

They started to eat the swordfish, which tasted delicious, and washed it down with their wine. Virginia's euphoria was increasing and she noted that a flush had risen in Madeline's cheeks. *She seems so very human*, Virginia thought. A question rose in her mind.

"May I ask you something . . . I hope you'll forgive me, but it's something I have to know,"

Virginia said. She felt drawn to the woman, despite her distrust of hocus-pocus.

"I'll be as open as possible with you, Virginia," Madeline said. "I only hope I know how."

For a brief moment, Madeline seemed vulnerable and Virginia's heart filled with compassion. She juggled the question in her mind, fearful it might go too far. But it was too compelling to withhold.

"If you have this gift, Madeline," Virginia began, trying to clear her throat of a desperate tightness, "then why . . ."

"Why am I not wealthy beyond imagination, happy beyond reality?" She paused and shook her head. "If I know everything in advance, then why do I have to sell my talents like some storefront gypsy? Is that it?"

"Well, yes, although I wouldn't have put it that way."

"The fact is, Virginia, I can do it for everyone but myself. You might call it a flaw in the system." She took a deep breath. "When it comes to me, personally, I'm totally powerless."

Madeline suddenly grew distant. She put down her fork and held her hands in a pose of prayer, forefingers bisecting her lips. Her large brown eyes grew moist, limpid with sadness.

"My gift hasn't made me very happy," she said, unfolding her fingers and reaching for her glass again. The glow in her eyes seemed to fade as if she had turned their power inward. When she had taken another deep sip of the wine, she put the glass down.

"It's not easy to be different, Virginia. Few can understand. My parents . . ." The muscles in her throat seemed to contract. She grew hoarse and quickly cleared her throat. "Only my father believed me." She paused then added quickly, "But that came later."

"And your mother?"

"She died." Her thin lips pursed, turning bloodless under the faded lipstick.

"I'm so sorry," Virginia said.

"Don't be," Madeline said, obviously forcing cheerfulness on herself. "I've been an orphan so long, I've learned how to cope."

Her remarks had the mysterious air of revelation. Virginia waited patiently through a long silence. Finally, unable to control the compulsion to know more, she asked, "Have you ever been married?"

Madeline shook her head. "Not for me, I'm afraid. I'm not very good with men."

"You've never had a relationship?"

"From time to time. Stunted, unnatural."

"I can imagine. Always knowing what they're thinking."

Madeline blushed. The remark seemed to break the tension and she suddenly laughed.

"I'd give anything to know what Jack really thinks," Virginia said. It was a concern that had waited a long time to be voiced. At last, Virginia thought, she had found the trusted confidante.

"You might not want to know," Madeline replied.

"Oh, I do want to know. The big question is, will it hurt or help our relationship?" Virginia said.

"Whenever I knew too much . . . well, it wasn't very helpful to the relationship," Madeline said thoughtfully.

"Yes, I can see that. But in our case . . . I mean fourteen years of marriage. We edit out things that could hurt the other." She paused. Was she going too far? She left the question unanswered and pressed on. "Like, I'm not telling him that I'm afraid that we've gone in over our heads on the house, the life-style. I don't want to add to his pressures. I don't tell him how disappointed I am that I can't get on with painting. And I'm sure he's keeping back things, trying to spare me pain, too. Who knows . . . maybe he hates the idea of living here . . . maybe he's as homesick as I am. . . ." She checked herself. Definitely going too far, she decided.

"Secrets are one thing, sharing them quite another."

"In marriage, there mustn't be secrets. . . ." Virginia was uncovering emotions in herself that she had never been aware of. Of course, she had secrets. This very luncheon was a secret.

"Do you believe there are . . . any serious secrets between you?" Madeline asked.

"Serious secrets?" What did she mean? Was there something ominous in the question? "Like what?"

Madeline became completely serious. "Things that might threaten your happiness."

"What things?" Virginia persisted. "We've had a good marriage for fourteen years. Two lovely children . . ." An onslaught of insecurity discomfited her. "What more can one ask?"

Virginia could not escape a rising sense of danger. Should she ask Madeline to be more specific? No, she decided. She knew the definition of danger. Another woman, perhaps?

Jack? No way. She searched her memory for signs. He's under pressure. He has other things on his mind. He has poured all his energies into a drive toward success. One simply cannot judge the temperature of a marriage by the frequency of sex. Her sudden bout of insecurity puzzled her.

"I'm not saying it's all peaches and romance," she said defensively. "Adolescent girls running around the house put a lot of the fun parts of marriage on hold. I suppose that Jack and I will have to mark time until the girls get older."

"I've never had children," Madeline replied. "Really, Virginia, this is far beyond my frame of reference."

Virginia sighed and said, "The girls are enormously demanding. I try to be fair, apportion my time so that each relationship gets its fair share of my attention, but Jack probably gets shortchanged." Her thoughts seemed to fly in other directions. "Yes, I would like to devote more time to my painting. But you see, there's no market in that, not at first. With my commercial art, I'm actually in business and can still continue my responsibilities as wife and mother. Besides, the money is useful."

It had been a long breathless speech and she realized that she was running at the mouth. Despite that, she did feel unburdened.

The waiter's return silenced them both. He proceeded to show them the dessert tray.

"Raspberries look delicious," Virginia said, forcing away the last vestige of her disturbing thoughts.

"I'd love them," Madeline said.

When the waiter went away, Madeline again put her hand on Virginia's.

"I want you to know how much I adore this heart-to-heart. You've quickly become very special to me, Virginia."

"I'm glad," Virginia said. She felt comfortable, connected.

The waiter brought the raspberries, which they ate with gusto while their conversation followed a less emotional line.

Virginia searched for things that she and Madeline might have in common. Like her, Madeline apparently liked movies and music, books and art, long walks and animals. Virginia was delighted by the responses.

She still wanted to know more about Madeline's life, but resisted giving way to her curiosity. Being too nosy could turn off a budding friendship.

"I know we'll be great friends," Madeline said after Virginia had paid the check and they rose to leave.

"I hope so," Virginia responded and both women exchanged cheek kisses.

The idea of their impending friendship was not without a tiny tremor of anxiety for Virginia. To have Madeline as a friend seemed protective and reassuring, yet Madeline was not easy to understand.

Would Madeline be compelled to tell her of some impending catastrophe in her future? Or would she tell her only of good things ahead? Or tell her nothing?

Virginia dismissed these thoughts from her mind. Surely it was enough that she had finally found a friend.

·4·

Although Jack had been tempted by Jane Meyers, he had, after all, maintained the integrity of his marriage. In the face of his other pressures, he felt there was something to say for a clear conscience.

He knew the attitude was old-fashioned and, when he confessed his resistance to his male colleagues, they were skeptical. Indeed, most of them thought that he and Jane were having an affair anyway.

"Strictly business," he had protested when confronted with the sly wink and knowing smile. Even the manager of the office, Al Conway, had raised an eyebrow.

"Just friends," Jack had assured him.

"Be smart," Conway had said, showing him his disbelief. "Best keep it out of the company inkwell."

"She's a buddy," Jack insisted. "We both get off on making money."

"Man does not live by bread alone," Conway smirked.

"Think what you think," Jack had shrugged.

No point in protesting too much, a sure tip-off of guilt.

Lots of relationships paraded under the guise of friendship, Jack decided. So what if they shared a bit of sexual tension? It made things more interesting, gave them a lascivious kick. Who knew, maybe he would fall someday. The suspense was titillating. Meanwhile, he and Jane could shift some of that energy into the main object of the enterprise, maximizing their personal profits.

In some ways their relationship was therapeutic. They shared confidences, articulated problems, exchanged intimacies. On her part, Jane was a sympathetic listener, which encouraged him to confide in her more and more and to invest her comments with a special incisive street wisdom. Because of this her feedback became an integral part of his decision-making process.

He also became convinced that she satisfied a need in him that Virginia could not. Certainly there was some guilt in that for him, but not the debilitating kind that would have come from actual infidelity.

He could barely wait to tell Jane about the incident with Basil. Over coffee in the little shop in the basement of their office building, he sketched in the details.

"This is California. Weirdos everywhere," Jane replied, shaking her head. "Everyone gets hit on."

"I told her that," Jack said, encouraged by her comment.

"People are always trying to manipulate co-incidence," Jane continued.

"I put it down as lucky guesses," Jack said

with confidence. "But I think Ginny has another view."

"You say the woman predicted Basil's disappearance and his return?"

"Right on the money," Jack replied.

"Dogs are smart as hell. If there's a way out, they'll find it."

"Not our dummy. We've got him hemmed in and the gate shuts tight. He's never even walked the neighborhood."

"All dogs have a homing sense," she countered.

"Not this one. He got lost once in Stamford. Someone found him in Greenwich."

She smiled and winked. "When a bitch is in heat, a horny dog finds a way." She looked at him pointedly.

"Not one without balls."

"Case closed."

"That's the point. I'm sure there's a perfectly logical explanation. I just haven't thought of one yet. But that's not the nub of it. Ginny said this woman knew a great deal about us . . . me and Ginny . . . our lives."

"Couldn't Ginny have misunderstood? I mean, the circumstances are suspect. Two ladies meet in a beauty parlor. People gossip. Maybe the woman had prior knowledge from a third party."

"Could be. But that wouldn't explain Basil. My inclination is to write it off as pure hogwash. Hell, California is the nut case capital of the world."

"Inclination?" Jane said. "That implies a sliver of 'maybe.' "

"That's ridiculous," Jack said with some indignation.

"But Ginny's inclination to believe is apparently a lot more than 'maybe,' " Jane said. "In the face of unexplainable phenomena, people take the easy way out."

Was Jane trying to denigrate Ginny in some way? he wondered.

"Don't get me wrong," Jane said as if *she* was reading his thoughts, "I'm not putting her down. It's just that I've never had an experience like that. Wish I had. Might have saved me two marriages. Hell, might even have made me rich."

"Now there's a good use for a psychic," Jack said, smiling. "Imagine knowing in advance which stocks were going up and which were going down."

"A lot more in it than predicting lost dogs. Anyway it's been tried and I don't think it got good notices."

"If she's that good at it, she should be as rich as Croesus."

"Maybe she is."

"Then what the hell is she doing in a beauty parlor like Mel's?"

"Jesus, Jack, this has got under your skin."

"It's a flimflam. I'm sure of it."

He knew he was giving the impression of a man trying to convince himself of something.

"There's got to be a logical explanation. You must have missed something," Jane said.

"I'm working on it. I hope Ginny is as well. Next thing you know, she won't be able to go to the john without first checking with her guru."

"You mean you don't have a guru?" Jane asked saucily. "I think it's time you gave up your narrow back East ways."

"Frankly, I prefer the suspense of not knowing things in advance. I like the adventure."

"You mean you wouldn't want to know what the price of a stock will be tomorrow . . . any stock?"

"Call that an exception," he laughed.

"It's no joke. We could make a fortune," Jane said.

"Even if she could just call two out of three. . . ." No question about it, Jack acknowledged to himself, the idea was loose in his head.

A week later the market closed up seventy points on the Dow, one of the largest gains in recent history. Jack got a call from Bob Singer, who administered the pension fund that was Jack's most lucrative account.

The day had been frenetic, with the speculators among his private clients keeping him hopping all day. He had barely time to crunch Singer's numbers on the computer.

Singer worked out of his company's office in Pasadena and his relationship with Jack had been one of the main reasons that Jack's firm had transferred him to Los Angeles. Singer came from an old family of Connecticut Yankees, which gave them enough of a geographical context for Jack to snag the account. So far, it had worked out quite well. Jack had suggested investments that had helped the fund beat the national comparables, the equation that determined the success of investment advice.

With the increasing financial pressure of life in Los Angeles, some of their forays had been into the speculative stock arena, resulting in a subtle churning that had also worked out well.

Jack had recently put a portion of the fund's assets into Compulaser, a start-up electronics firm that he calculated had great potential. It had already risen fifty percent and Jack was certain it would soar upward even more when conditions were right. Unfortunately, he wasn't sure when that would be, but his gut told him to hold.

Jack had also taken a personal position with Compulaser, using borrowed funds. He and Virginia had cosigned a note.

"No sweat," he had told her when he put the paper in front of her. Her inquiries were always perfunctory. "Just trust me," he told her.

It was not the first time he had done it. As a matter of fact he was considerably leveraged and had borrowed from a number of banks. Sometimes, when it was more convenient, he would copy Virginia's signature on various notes and documents, although he never felt comfortable about it.

A quick number crunch on his computer assured him that Singer's fund was up in relation to the market.

"Good day, Bob," he said breezily as he took Singer's call.

"Scary," Singer said. Any wide shift in the market triggered anxieties in fund managers. Singer was no exception. At such times he needed lots of reassurance.

When the market went down, it seemed to confirm Singer's subjective validation that the Wall Street colossus had feet of clay. When the market went up, it sparked his New England Puritan strain that characterized his good fortune as ill-gotten gains. Jack was used to dealing with these insecurities, although at times it tried his patience.

"Steady on the tiller," Jack said. Singer, a yachtsman, liked the use of nautical terms.

"How high can it go?"

"How high is up?"

"The winds change, old pal."

"You could always take the money and run."

"Run where?" Singer asked.

"Nice safe Treasuries."

"If it were mine that's where I'd put it." Singer sighed. "They keep pushing to stay with the comparables."

"We've got those in our wake," Jack said.

"Squalls come up fast."

"That's when we batten down the hatches and trim sails."

"Just checking the compass, old pal."

An idea struck Jack. "We could siphon off some profits elsewhere and take a deeper plunge in Compulaser. Could be ready for another surge."

"You think so?"

Jack could sense good old Yankee greed in Singer.

"We're way up. Might be a good time to take some profits on some stocks. Be a little defensive on the upside. What say I pick up another fifty thou of Compulaser at five."

"That will make how much?" Singer asked.

"New buy will make it twenty-five thousand shares."

He sensed Singer mulling it over.

"I'll put it in the buy. No more than ten, okay?" Jack pressed.

He waited through a long silence, itching to hit the computer for his own buy of another ten thousand. He was holding out for a four-time gain, dead certain that Singer's buy would boost the stock a quick point.

"Do it," Singer muttered.

"Smart move," Jack said.

Their little chat over, Jack put in his own order. Then he called Jane.

"Singer is going for more Compulaser. I'm buying ten thou for me. You might spread some around for your clients and take a bit more for yourself."

"I'm in it up to my kazoo," Jane said.

"Just sharing," Jack said.

"Your order in?"

"Just now."

"Goes down, they'll be picking up the pieces from the Palisades to Pasadena." She hung up abruptly.

He gave her a half hour, then put in Singer's order. Tomorrow he would sign another note. In for a penny, in for a pound, he told himself. If ever there was a moment for psychic help, it was now.

When he got home, he was tired. He planned to take a swim and a nap. Normally, he made himself scarce while Ginny worked on her assignments. He rarely went down to her studio.

It was midafternoon, for him, a rare quiet time. Virginia would be in her studio, the twins at soccer practice.

When he thought of the twins and their soccer, he always felt a warm sense of irony. Soccer had never interested him as a sport, either as player or viewer. Because of the twins, he had become an avid fan.

He had been a well-coordinated athlete, but

he had never made the varsity teams. Once it
had been a source of deep disappointment. Perhaps the twins success at soccer was a kind of
generational revenge.

He pictured them on the field, two blond ga-
zelles, never more beautiful than on the offensive, aggressively advancing, their strong young
legs flying as they connected with the ball. God,
they were good, although there were times
when, heart in mouth, he would watch their
devil-may-care movements as they advanced on
stronger, more muscular male players, overwhelming them with greater cunning and speed.
So far they had received no more than mild
bruises.

What amazed him, too, was the way they
shared their teamwork, as if they were one person operating as two halves, yet protective of
each other. As a father it filled him with pride.
He wanted them to love each other forever, to
share their triumphs and their dreams.

Virginia, on the other hand, feared that too
much sharing would suppress their individuality. Only on rare occasions would she yield to
Jack's wishes to dress them identically. But on
the soccer field, they did seem identical, inter-
changeable.

As he crossed the living room to his bedroom,
he heard low voices. Probably one of Virginia's
clients.

"That you, Jack?" Virginia's voice called from
the studio. He hesitated briefly. Ginny rarely so-
licited interruptions. Besides, after a frenetic
day he was in no mood for conversation.

"Come here a moment and meet Madeline,"
she pressed.

The name was not familiar. He went down a

small flight of steps and came into her studio.
She was sketching the face of an attractive live
model in charcoal on a canvas. The woman
turned toward him as he entered and offered a
broad radiant smile. Her eyes, peering out from
under a head of jet black hair, were extraordinarily intense.

"This is Madeline Boswell," Virginia said
with an air of pride.

The woman extended her hand. He took it in
his, felt its pressure and an odd warmth. He
thought it lingered in his a moment longer than
called for by mere politeness.

"Ginny has told me a lot about you, Jack," the
woman said.

"Really?" Jack was mildly surprised at her
easy familiarity. Could she be more than a business acquaintance? He looked toward Virginia
who shrugged and avoided his gaze. But the
woman's eyes did not quit their inspection of
him. He felt uncomfortable, as if he had been
called in to be exhibited.

"You're not keeping the pose," Virginia said
in mock reproach.

"Sorry." Madeline turned her head in the direction of a shaft of sunlight.

"The light has to be just so," Virginia said as
she put additional strokes on the canvas.

"A portrait, is it?" Jack asked. "What are they
selling?"

As an advertising illustrator, Virginia often
did full-color portraits for her clients. "Cosmet-
ics, right?" The woman was immaculately
groomed and carefully made up.

"This one's for me." Virginia spoke softly,
locked in concentration.

Jack was puzzled. Virginia was always under

the pressure of deadlines and normally had more work than she could handle. But he kept his silence.

"Doesn't she make a wonderful subject?" Virginia asked as she sketched. "Great bones. The facial lines are sculpted."

"You're embarrassing me," Madeline said. "I've never done this before."

Neglecting to answer, he, nevertheless, agreed with Ginny's appraisal. And more. Madeline had a charismatic aura about her. He speculated that Ginny had been taken by the desire to paint her and had cajoled her into sitting. Earlier in their marriage, she had done this with various people.

He looked around the neat studio, noting some half-finished work on a drawing board.

"I hope I do her justice," Virginia said.

"Hard not to," Jack concurred.

"She's inspired me," Virginia said, fleshing in lines and shadows.

"Encouraged," Madeline corrected.

"No talking," Virginia commanded.

"That's the hardest part for me," Madeline said, her head retaining its position, "keeping my mouth shut."

"Loves to talk, that one," Virginia said, working furiously now. It struck him that there was more than casual friendship between them. Definitely not a business relationship. He wondered vaguely why he had not met her before.

The telephone rang and a button blinked on Virginia's desk phone. He noted that it was her private business phone.

"Don't worry, the machine will pick it up," Virginia said, not missing a beat in her work. It was her habit to keep the machine on the mes-

sage mode and pick it up when the caller identified himself or herself.

He heard Virginia's very businesslike an-
nouncement, then the beep, followed by the
message.

"Hey, Ginny, Bob Krause here. I've been trying for two days. Are you out of town? Have
you forgotten the deadline? That was yesterday. My ass is on the line. You've got to call me
back . . . pleeeze." The receiver at Krause's end
slammed down.

Virginia seemed impervious, continuing to
work. Jack was astonished by her reaction. Bob
Krause was her biggest client and she prided
herself on never missing a deadline.

"Have a problem with Krause?" he asked.

She ignored the question, put down her charcoal and started to mix paints on her palette.
Perhaps he had missed something. He looked at
the woman she was preparing to paint. She had
relaxed from her pose and was looking out of
the window at the panoramic view of Los Angeles.

"You don't seem very concerned," he said in
a tone that one used when a stranger was present.

"I'm not," Virginia said pleasantly, continuing to mix her paints.

"You really should call the man back," he
said. "He seems agitated."

"In time," Virginia said, testing the colors
with her brushes, barely reacting. She turned
to Madeline, whose eyes had drifted from contemplating the view. They exchanged glances.

"That's the way to lose clients," Jack said. It
was a redundant remark. Ginny, too, knew what
running a personal-service business was like.

"Probably all to the good," Virginia said, although he detected a tentativeness in her tone. "It's about time." Again he noted how they exchanged glances, their eyes meeting for a moment like some secret intimate embrace.

"I'm not getting it," he said testily, the puzzle deepening.

"I'll call him when I'm free, Jack," Virginia said with uncommon aggressiveness, her gaze shifting from the woman to him and back to the woman again.

He paused, trying to understand the situation. It was very unclear. "It's your business," he said, annoyed by her reaction.

"That it is," Virginia agreed.

He felt a surge of temper, but the woman's presence kept it from erupting. As he stood there trying to comprehend what was going on, the telephone rang again. He watched it, waiting for the answering machine to react. As before, Virginia ignored it, stepping back from the canvas, studying it.

"Can't understand why you haven't gotten back to me, Virginia," a woman's voice said. "I'm sorry but I'll have to give that job to someone else." The woman hung up.

"You're not going to have a business, Ginny," Jack said, still holding back his anger.

"I'm chucking it, Jack. Giving it up."

As she spoke the words, he noted that the woman turned her head. Again their eyes exchanged knowing glances. Jack felt isolated, frozen out of their intimacy.

"Are you saying that you're giving up freelance work?"

She nodded.

"I'm not criticizing," he said, increasingly uncomfortable with a stranger being privy to this discussion. "It's your decision. It just seems . . . so . . . abrupt."

"It's not abrupt. It's been simmering for years. I'm an artist, Jack, I can't be postponing my artistic life forever."

She sounded rebellious, as if she were ascribing blame to him. For a moment, he actually felt a pang of guilt.

"Really, Ginny, I'm all for it. . . ." He wanted to say more, but held back, out of both confusion and caution. Above all, he did not want to be accused of keeping her from practicing her art. It had always been on her agenda for the future. And hadn't he always been supportive?

"Madeline was the catalyst," Virginia said. Once again the women looked toward each other and held their gaze.

"Was she?" he said with a burst of sarcasm. More than anything he disliked being in the dark about matters affecting his family. Who in the name of hell was this woman? "Of course it's your choice, but don't you think you might have discussed it with me?"

"I guess I should have," Virginia conceded, "even if it's a highly individual decision."

Was it jealousy he was feeling? Or ego? Was it a question of his traditional role of husband being usurped? Wasn't he at least entitled to a consultation, if not a vote?

"If our places were reversed, I think you could have expected some communication from me," he said.

He was guilting her, pure and simple, a strategy he detested.

"I was going to," Virginia shrugged, her earlier arrogance dissipating, "I really was Jack.

It's not as if we need the money, really need it ... and well ... I just feel that my time has come."

"Has it?" Again he was being sarcastic. He was having great difficulty keeping his feelings masked.

The woman's presence at an intimate exchange between husband and wife was beginning to irritate him considerably.

Virginia must have sensed his simmering anger. She put down her brushes and faced him. "I have talent, Jack, and a future as an artist."

"I have no quarrel with that," Jack said. He felt foolish. He did not want it to appear as if he were a man who needed his wife's money to survive. Not that the money hadn't come in handy. The fact was, in his heart of hearts, he would have preferred her to keep at her freelancing for another year or more.

"Madeline says that my future is assured, but only if I start now."

He looked toward the woman. Her intense gaze met his directly.

"I see what I see, Jack. There are great things in store for Virginia as an artist."

Was this woman some important art critic? Perhaps he was judging her too harshly.

"You've seen her work?"

"I don't have to."

"You don't have to see her work?"

The woman shook her head, offering a cool, thin smile.

"Listen, Jack," Virginia said. Was there a note of pleading in her voice? "I'm not taking this action lightly. It's what I believe as well." She looked toward Madeline and nodded.

"It's perfectly natural," the woman said to Virginia, as if he weren't in the room.

"What the hell is she talking about?" His testiness was beginning to spill over.

"A true Capricorn," Madeline said calmly.

He turned to Virginia. "You're not serious?" he said hoarsely. It had finally dawned on him. *Oh, my God*, he thought, caught on the razor's edge between laughter and shock. A gauntlet had been thrown down and he was very much aware of his inability to react.

Muttering a perfunctory good-bye, he left the room. It was either that or exhibit his frustration and impotence.

·5·

Virginia had followed Madeline's scenario to the letter.

"Above all, I don't want Jack to feel as if I've betrayed him," Virginia had said. She and Madeline had been sitting, Indian style, on a blanket on the wide serene beach of Marina del Rey, watching the rolling surf sparkling in the sunlight. At that time of the morning the beach was deserted.

By then, Virginia had stepped into the complicated nether world of confession and intimacy. Since that first lunch at La Scala, she had either met or talked with Madeline on the phone every day.

At first, Madeline would come up to the house and they would have long talks. Sometimes they drove out to Marina del Rey and walked along the beach, then lunched on the Venice Strand and watched the procession of eccentrics as they paraded by.

Virginia would come away from her meetings with Madeline exhilarated, happy. Virginia worried that time was being taken away from her free-lance work and there was a lingering anxiety about the twins. Fortunately, soccer practice was keeping them away from the house most of the day and she was always home by midafternoon.

Considering Jack's initial reaction to Madeline's psychic gifts, Virginia felt it better to keep her new friendship secret. Once the bonds with Madeline were stronger, she would tell him. In the time and place of her choice.

But keeping secrets from Jack required strenuous effort. Jack was her man, her husband, her protector, the father of her children. Her life and psyche were irrevocably bound up with him. She agonized over this breach of faith.

Madeline had opened Virginia's eyes from the very beginning to the possibility of Virginia devoting herself to her art instead of selling her talent in the commercial marketplace. More important, she had predicted her success.

"But how can you be so sure?" Virginia had pressed.

Madeline had shrugged and smiled enigmatically. "You must trust me," she had said. "I'm absolutely certain."

Naturally, it was what Virginia wanted to believe and it did not take much prodding to make the decision. She had never wanted to paint as a "hobbyist." She wanted to be taken seriously as an artist. And, as Jack had always pointed out to her, "taking risks" was essential if one wanted to be successful in anything.

Why the trepidation on her part? In the first place, she was not consulting him. Indeed, she was making this momentous decision in her life without him. Even though she expected his consent, she would be presenting it to him as a fait accompli. She was chucking her business and no longer contributing financially to the running of the household.

Worse, from his point of view, there was someone beside himself helping her make that decision. And that someone was a professional psychic, which would not sit well with him.

She had no illusions about his reaction. It would hurt him, surely hurt his pride. He was bound to be jealous. And yet, she could not keep up the charade forever. Nor could she simply announce her decision to him without revealing her relationship with Madeline.

She grappled over it for days. Even Jack noted that her mind was elsewhere.

"What is it, Ginny?" he had asked. "You have a funny faraway look these days."

"Your imagination," she had protested.

"Maybe," he had replied with a shrug of skepticism.

That day at Marina del Rey, she knew she was on the verge of a decision.

"In the end, Jack will welcome the change," Madeline had assured her.

"In the end? I don't want him to have a bad time about it now," she had complained.

"He'll accept it, I assure you," Madeline said. "Although he won't admit it, he would rather you continued with your advertising. You see, he's still insecure about the expense of your lifestyle. What he doesn't know is that you and he will someday, sooner than you both think, be a very, very rich couple."

"Really?"

"Not too long from now, you'll find yourselves in an even larger, more expensive house. Jack is going to start his own investment bank-

ing business. He'll have power and prestige."
She played with the sand, letting it fall through
her fingers, looking toward the ocean as if she
were studying it deeply, extracting its essence
and truth.

"Oh, Madeline," Virginia cried, "it's so comforting to hear that."

"And you, my dear, will be the toast of the art
world."

"I . . . I don't know what to say." Virginia's
eyes had become filmy with tears.

"Nothing to say." Madeline smiled and
stroked Virginia's cheek. "I don't make things
up. It's what I see."

Virginia took Madeline's hand from her cheek
and kissed it. "It's wonderful having a true
friend," she said.

Madeline's response was equally warm. "You
can't imagine how much this relationship
means to me."

"I need your strength, Madeline."

"You have that. You know you do."

They were silent for a long time, watching the
water together. Finally, after a long silence,
Madeline spoke. "There's no escaping telling
Jack about our friendship."

"There you go," Virginia said, "reading my
mind again."

"He won't be very happy."

"But you'll feel better about it."

"Yes, I will."

And she did.

Alone in their bedroom that night after she
had informed Jack of her decision, she tried to
soften the blow. Dinner had been strained, although as usual the twins prattled on about

their day's adventures, with particular emphasis on their soccer practice.

"The coach says we'd be celebrities anywhere but in the United States," Bobbie said.

"It's the most popular sport all over the world. But not in the United States," Billie added.

"He says we're the most natural athletes he's ever seen. Imagine that," Bobbie said.

"Imagine that," Billie echoed.

"He says that if we work hard and develop well, we probably could get a contract with some important team overseas."

"In Europe, maybe. Or Australia," Billie said.

"I still think it's too rough a game for girls," Jack said.

"Oh, Daddy," Bobbie whined.

Billie nodded her approval of Bobbie's remark. If they expected a confrontation, none came. Jack just smiled at them and ate the rest of his meal in silence.

"I thought you'd be very happy to hear that," Bobbie said. She knew better, of course, but she was determined to get her parents' attention.

"We are happy," Virginia said, hardly listening, glancing at Jack. It was obvious that this was not going to be the time and place to discuss the twins' future in foreign athletics. The twins, obviously sensing something seriously amiss, pouted through the rest of the meal.

When dinner was over, Jack solemnly excused himself and went off to the bedroom.

After the twins had gone to their room to do their homework, Virginia followed Jack. He was lying fully dressed on the bed, staring into space. Virginia sat on the bed next to him.

"Hey," she said softly, tapping his leg, "the

world is not coming to an end. You always knew that one day I would opt for painting. It's what I always wanted . . . and needed."

He turned gloomy eyes toward her, his anger unmistakable. "It's not the painting," he said, "and you know it."

"Do I?" she asked.

"Hell, money is rolling in." He cleared his throat and she resisted discussing the various bank loans of which she was aware. "It's strictly the meddling with your head that I'm against."

Madeline had advised Virginia to tread lightly, to let Jack articulate the problem as he saw it. Also, she knew he could not keep things bottled up. He had done so all evening and, she sensed, had reached the end of his endurance. As if in response to her thoughts, he swung his legs to the floor and began to pace the room.

"How could you fall for that shit?" he hissed through clenched teeth.

"Fall for what?"

"For her . . . her nonsense." He paused and turned to face Virginia.

"It's my decision," she said, "a long time in coming."

"I'm not doubting that. I'm only complaining about your falling for her line."

"You think I'm such a weak ninny?"

"Not weak. Captured. Brainwashed. The woman has you in her power, for Christ's sake. Can't you see that?"

"What I can't see is why you object to my having a friend, Jack," she said calmly. "We've gotten to be rather close—to use a prehistoric term—girlfriends."

"Girlfriends!" Jack exclaimed with sarcasm.

"It's not as if I've hired a psychic, Jack. That's her business. She's my friend and she has been very helpful to me, especially in arriving at this decision. I would think that if you loved me, you'd be happy for me."

Inevitably, Madeline had assured her, a couple in a long marriage develops a certain strategy in confronting each other. They learn how to take unfair advantage of each other's vulnerabilities. Virginia knew Jack's Achilles' heel. It was to be accused of not living up to his "responsibilities," which meant, above all, to be a loving and supportive husband and father.

"Your art is not the issue here." His face grew flushed. "It's that goddamned phony fortune-teller"—he began to pace again—"she's taken my naive wife and wound her around her little finger." He stopped again and looked at Virginia with burning eyes. "How the hell did she do it? What the hell did she tell you?"

"She said"—Virginia paused, swallowed, cleared her throat—"that one day . . ." Again she paused. "If you're such a skeptic, why ask?"

"Don't stop now," he sneered, "the suspense is excruciating."

"Well . . . she said that one day we were going to be filthy rich."

"How intriguing."

"And that I would be an acclaimed artist."

"That all?"

"She also predicted that you would understand."

"Wrong," Jack said. "Never."

"Why can't you at least give her the benefit of the doubt? She certainly was right about Basil.

She's wise and decent and caring and she's my friend. I'm inclined to believe that she does have psychic powers. Actually, I want to believe it."

"You do believe it," Jack said.

The fact was that Jack was right. They seemed to have arrived at a stalemate. It was impossible, Madeline had told her, to make another person believe. The belief had to come from inside of him.

Jack started to pace the bedroom again, while she remained seated on the bed.

"I admit I do like what she said about our careers," Virginia said softly.

"How can you not?" Jack replied. Then he abruptly stopped and grew thoughtful.

"And how exactly did she say we're going to become filthy rich?" he asked with droll sarcasm.

"She said you would go into your own investment banking business."

"And where, pray tell, will I get the risk capital?"

"She didn't say."

"*Abrakazam*. And the money will materialize. You know what it takes to fund a first-class investment banking business?"

She shrugged.

"This is crazy. Crazy," he cried. "I'm actually talking as if it's a possibility."

"It is," she said.

She noted he was calming down, showing interest.

"I can see what makes her so seductive," he said. "She tells you what you want to hear."

"That's not her way."

"Has she ever told you something you didn't want to hear?" Jack asked.

He had, she noted, become more analytical now, more cerebral. "In a way," Virginia replied as her mind searched for an example. Of course, she had, Virginia decided, but in different ways, not as predictions.

"So all the votes aren't in," he said smugly. Perhaps it was the victory he needed for him to feel some reassertion of his role.

"I told you. My relationship with Madeline is not based on her special gifts. More important, she wants to be a friend to both of us, Jack," Virginia said.

"I don't know if I'm ready for that," Jack sighed.

"She's warm and giving, Jack. I need a friend like that." She got off the bed and came toward him. She brought her face close to his. "And a man like you."

He seemed less unyielding, but as their eyes met, she could see his were still hard. It will take time, she decided.

She kissed him deeply on the lips, happy when he responded.

"I don't approve and I'm not convinced," Jack whispered.

"All I ask is that you keep an open mind."

"I'm frightened of that woman, Ginny," he admitted. "I don't feel any kinship with the supernatural."

"Silly," she said, "who said anything about the supernatural?"

"Clairvoyance, precognition, telepathy, astrology. God knows what else. She's got you on the hook."

"Nobody has me on the hook," she said, pausing, kissing him again, urgent, seductive. She pressed close to him, feeling his arousal, then bit his earlobe and whispered, "I'd rather fuck than fight."

Her swift change in mood surprised her. Him as well. It triggered an erotic response in both of them. It crossed her mind that maybe their marriage needed to be shaken up. Maybe a certain staleness and predictability had set in. Maybe they needed the stimulant of sexual eruption.

She worked at his belt, opened his zipper, then rolled down his jockey shorts, admiring his gorged penis.

"Now there's a sight," she whispered, drawing him to the bed, canting up her dress. "Here. Now." With legs hanging over the edge and Jack still standing and angled over her, she pushed aside her panties and inserted him.

Almost immediately, she gasped with pleasure as a wave of orgasms rolled over her. She felt released, liberated, as she grasped his buttocks and pressed him forward, deeper. When he came, she felt his spasms, heard his own gasps of pleasure and sighs of appreciation.

"Wonderful," she whispered as they cooled, still connected.

"Spontaneous combustion," he said, kissing her eyes.

"Like the old days," she said. But it seemed more than that. Perhaps her friendship with Madeline had, in some strange way, given them both a sense of renewal. Perhaps?

After a while, they disengaged and got ready for sleep.

"I don't want anything or anybody to hurt this family," he said as he got into bed.

"Trust me," she said.

He cradled her in his arms. For the first time since she had arrived in California she was completely happy.

·6·

"**S**he asked me to keep an open mind," Jack said, watching for Jane's reaction as they sat on the couch in her office sipping iced coffee. He had just finished telling her about Virginia and her new friend.

Jane was silent for a long time, staring into the tan liquid in her glass. When she concentrated, she narrowed her eyes and bit her lower lip, raising the corners as if she were smiling. In that configuration, her face seemed to mimic pain.

"And will you?"

"That will be difficult."

"No money changing hands?" Jane asked, running her fingers through her hair.

"Not that I know of. I'll have to wait until our bank statements come in. No"—he checked himself and shook his head—"this is supposed to be friendship, a sisterhood kind of thing."

"And you believe that?" Jane asked, raising one eyebrow.

"Yes, I believe that," he protested. He looked at Jane. As always when she sat on the couch, her dress was hiked up to midthigh. One arm rested on the couch's armrest, stretching her blouse over her large breasts. He supposed that the pose was contrived for maximum seductive power. At that moment, he was surprisingly unmoved, his thoughts drifting instead to sexual images of Virginia and the events of the previous night.

"In the end these things boil down to money," Jane said. "You say the lady is in business. Then business, it is. And business can only be defined in terms of money."

"What about belief?"

"You mean faith?" Jane challenged.

"Okay, faith."

"Why do you think the Catholic Church is so rich, pal?" Jane said, upending her glass, coaxing an ice cube into her mouth, then sucking on it. After a while she spit it back into the glass. "Faith is what gets the money."

"Congratulations. You're even more cynical than I am."

"Life teaches, baby." She sighed. "My first husband, the actor, put his faith in astrology. He was always having someone do his chart. Then he would react to it. If the chart said stay home on such and such a day, he stayed home. Fact is, none of it ever came true, but he lived by it as if it were the gospel." She laughed suddenly. "The month that I left him, the chart predicted that his life would change radically for the better on a certain day. That was the day I left him."

"Maybe that's what the chart meant."

"Bullshit. He didn't have a pot to pee in. For him, my leaving was a financial disaster. He's still up shit's creek without a paddle. I occasionally slip him a hundred for old times' sake."

Jack sipped his coffee and stretched his legs. He told Jane about Madeline's predictions for their future.

"Only natural," Jane said. "The lady claims she can look into your head, read your thoughts, predict your future. That's heavy duty." She turned toward him. "Tell me what I want to hear and I'll follow you anywhere." She winked and moved in such a way to emphasize her breasts further. It was, Jack knew, a thinly veiled proposal. He ignored it.

"If only I knew more about these things," Jack said. "I'm at a disadvantage. I have no arguments that can dispute her. All I can say is: 'I don't believe this bullshit.' Her counter will be: 'If you don't believe then you can't know.' " He paused and stared into space. "There are lots of things we don't understand, I suppose. How do you argue against that?"

"Well, then . . . your wife is right when she tells you to keep an open mind."

"Easy to say." He put his cup down. "But I'm not sure I know what it means. Do I fold my hands and lift my chin and challenge her to a prediction?"

"Not bad for starters."

"And if her prediction comes true?"

"Then you're in trouble."

He detected an element of ridicule in Jane's response. From her point of view, this must have seemed trivial, perhaps laughable, although she maintained a studied air of concern.

"And if it doesn't come true?"

"Try again. Psychics work on the law of averages."

He seemed to be traveling in ever-decreasing concentric circles. "I'm not even sure I know what a psychic does . . . or how or why."

She shrugged. The phone rang and moments later she was into a complicated stock transaction. Before he left, she covered the phone and blew him a kiss.

"When all is lost, remember Jane," she said, waving good-bye.

That Friday night Madeline came to dinner. With her usual thoroughness, Virginia had fussed over the menu, put out the good china and lit the candelabra.

"Big stuff," Jack said, seeing the silver candelabra, polished and candled and enhanced by a centerpiece of flowers. Virginia had a penchant for purple and her artist's eye had created a table that could have been a painting itself.

He had deliberately avoided any further confrontations over Madeline. Time to harness his resources, he decided. Meanwhile, he scrupulously observed his wife. He had to admit she was radiant and loving, glowing with confidence and happiness.

She had, with obvious trepidation, let him see the finished painting of Madeline. He had studied it carefully. On canvas, Madeline looked less of a danger than he had imagined. She looked almost benign, except for her eyes which seemed magnetic and, although he hesitated to use the word, haunting.

Done in a realistic style, although not photographic, Virginia had taken a great deal of care with it. Had she romanticized Madeline? Jack wasn't certain.

"I think the smile is too enigmatic," Virginia
had said.

"You mean mysterious?" he had asked.

"I may have it wrong," she sighed.

"I think it's terrific," he said with sincerity.
He had always been in awe of Virginia's ability
to re-create objects and figures in her paintings
and drawings.

"Did I really capture her?" she had mused
aloud. She had always been a harsh critic of her
own work. "Maybe I'm a little rusty, but Madeline does make a good subject."

"Yes," he agreed, "that she does."

A peculiarity of Virginia's method came to
Jack's mind. He had learned when they were in
college that she would not leave a subject until
she had totally exhausted it to her satisfaction.
He could recall at least twenty portraits and
nudes of himself that she had put in storage in
Connecticut, although they had brought with
them only one portrait, a small one, that hung
now in an unobtrusive corner of the living
room, a kind of nostalgic momento of their
youth. He hoped her method had changed.

Aside from the painting, the subject of Madeline was studiously avoided until Virginia's intention to invite her to dinner was announced.
Acknowledging his own curiosity about the
woman, he voiced no objection.

"Who is Madeline?" Bobbie had asked.

"Mrs. Boswell," Virginia had replied.

"Mommy's best friend," Jack had said, not
without a tinge of sarcasm, which prompted
him to add, "A very nice lady."

"I didn't know Mommy had a best friend in
California," Billie said. Although not as aggressive as Bobbie, she seemed, beyond her role as

echo to her more loquacious sister, deeper, more reflective and observant.

"Well, now you know," Virginia had offered cheerily, "and I'm sure you'll love her."

"A real best friend?" Bobbie asked. Her compulsiveness was tempered by her skepticism, Jack knew. He had often observed bits and pieces of himself and Virginia in the twins. Bobbie, for example, was already showing signs of artistic talent and Billie occasionally revealed flashes of his own sense of discipline and planning.

"Very real best friend," Jack had replied. "If Mommy doesn't object, you can even call her Aunt Madeline." He stole a quick glance at Virginia, who returned it with a frown.

"Sounds so kiddish," Bobbie had said.

"Why call her aunt if she's not our real relative?" Billie had challenged. Their response, Jack thought, was interesting, as if they too sensed that this woman was an intruder.

"It's an honorary title," Jack had said with a chuckle.

"I don't think Aunt Kate would like that," Bobbie said, looking at her mother for approval. Kate was Virginia's only sister.

"We don't have to tell her," Billie said with a giggle.

"Now just stop teasing," Virginia said good-naturedly. "Call her anything you like. Anyway, you'll have a chance to meet her Friday night and I expect you all to be on your best behavior." Virginia had said this with finality and with a knowing glance at Jack, for whom the command was obviously meant. At that point the subject drifted away.

Madeline arrived on Friday evening wearing a purple scarf and purple eyeliner, offering a

compelling accompaniment to the purple flowers.

"She always tries to adapt her colors to the
environment," Virginia said, after a studied inspection and kisses on both her cheeks.

"Like a leopard," Jack said.

"Yes, I like that," Madeline said sweetly,
turning and directing her attention and both
barrels of her considerable charm on the twins.

Much to Jack's dismay, they were captivated
from the beginning. By the time Maria served
the medallions of veal, they were actually calling her Aunt Madeline and vying for her attention.

Madeline listened patiently to their soccer
talk and to their excited expectations for the
championship with a rival school.

"We'll crush," Bobbie said.

"Kill," Billie echoed.

"Now it's the girls' turn to be taught violence
on the playing field," Virginia said.

"Good clean fun," Jack muttered.

"Mommy says that only because she thinks
we'll get hurt," Bobbie said.

"I got a scraped knee and Bobbie got a kick
in the butt," Billie said. "We're quicker and
smarter and the boys are slower."

"Bigger and muscular," Virginia countered.

"Clumsier," Bobbie muttered.

After ice cream the twins said affectionate
good-byes to Aunt Madeline and went off to
their rooms. The three adults went out on the
patio for coffee and after-dinner drinks. Below
them stretched the glistening carpet of Los Angeles. The air was light and sweet, perfumed by
night flowers.

From his vantage and in the flickering light

of two candles that Virginia had lit, Jack could
see Madeline in profile, her angular face half-
hidden in shadows. When she turned, the can-
dlelight was reflected in her eyes. Two thin
beams emanated from her pupils, flowing outward like powerful floodlights.

Was it a deliberate contrivance, he wondered,
or some special force within her that gave the
impression that she was surreal, otherworldly?
He shivered, although the evening was comfortably warm, and tried to rationalize the eerie
feeling as merely the power of suggestion. But
whose?

"It's our million-dollar view," he said, determined to find the lightest touch.

"And well worth it," Madeline agreed.

"You've always lived here in Southern California?" Jack asked.

"Yes," Madeline said.

Jack was silent, expecting more explanation,
but none came. After a while, he spoke again.
"Born here?"

"Yes."

Virginia, who until then seemed lost in reflection as she contemplated the view, now said,
"Will there be an earthquake do you think?"
adding a peculiarly ominous note.

"Within five years," Madeline said without
hesitation.

"You're certain?" Jack probed.

"I am," Madeline said, turning the beams of
her eyes toward him.

"Have you predicted other natural calami-
ties?"

"Some."

"Anything specific?"

She smiled pleasantly and sipped from a glass

of Benedictine and Brandy. In the silence that
followed, it was clear that she was not going to
answer his question. Instead she said, "The
point is that when the earthquake arrives, you
and Virginia won't be living here. Not in this
house."

"You think it's too dangerous?" Jack asked
with a brief stab of fear.

"It will be obliterated," Madeline said. She
held a long silence, then smiled. "You'll be long
gone."

"To where?" he asked, allowing himself to be
sucked in. Strictly investigative, he assured
himself.

"A bigger house in Belair. It will withstand
the jolt."

"Earthquake-proof. How thoughtful. I suppose it will be a large, gated place, with a guest-
house and a tennis court?" he asked facetiously.

"Actually, two guesthouses," Madeline said,
"one for each girl and their families when they
come to visit."

He felt a pang of sadness over the thought of
the loss of his little girls to other men. *God, am
I believing this?* He said, "And I don't even play
tennis."

"You will."

He was working hard to restrain a growing
hostility. As if for support, he looked toward
Virginia, but she seemed to be paying little attention, studying the view. Her lack of reaction
suggested that she was accepting Madeline's
words as gospel, not to be questioned.

"You know I don't believe any of that mumbo
jumbo," he said. He was drinking cognac and
he poured himself another.

"No, you wouldn't," Madeline said, laughing.

"A true Capricorn, I suppose."

"That, too."

"I don't believe in that nonsense either," Jack said.

"I know."

"Doesn't it bother you to know that people don't believe you have, what is it they call it, psychic power?"

"Not at all. I see what I see." She turned suddenly to Virginia. "And I see great things ahead for her. For both of you," she added turning toward him again.

"Who would want to dispute that?" he said. He had, he supposed, been trying to bait her, but she seemed more than skilled at parrying his thrusts.

"What about the bad things?" he asked. "Do you tell people those?"

"Sometimes."

"But not all?"

"If it's beyond their control, why cause them unhappiness?" Madeline said.

"You've got all the answers," Jack replied.

"Many," Madeline said. Then in a commanding tone: "Show me your palm."

"You're kidding," Jack said.

"No big deal, just show me."

He hesitated, looked over to Virginia. "Ginny," he called, "she wants to see my palm."

Virginia turned toward him.

"Then show her."

"Why should I?" Jack said. Despite his recalcitrance, he was genuinely fearful and it disturbed him. Unfortunately, he saw no way of retreating. The sweat glands under his armpits opened like gushers. He felt the cold perspiration rolling down his sides.

Madeline saw his discomfort. "If you don't
believe the mumbo jumbo, why should it bother
you?"

"Is this some high-priced Gypsy storefront?"
he said, offering a nervous chuckle that even he
knew wouldn't pass for a laugh.

"Really Jack . . ." Virginia rebuked.

"It's all right," Madeline said addressing Virginia, "he doesn't have to let me read his palm."
It was a blatant dare. He felt cornered.

"Maybe we should get off this subject," Virginia said, standing up.

"This is 'the' subject, Ginny," he said, upending his drink. He was disgusted with the way
he was handling the situation. He felt thor-
oughly intimidated by Madeline's coolness and
his cowardice.

"You either accept it or you don't," Virginia
said. "Either way it doesn't matter. Not here.
Madeline is my friend."

"I respect that," Jack said apologetically,
"and I'm trying to keep an open mind. Unfortunately, I'm the kind of guy that needs something more tangible to make him a believer.
Hell, the media is full of UFOs, scanners, telepathy, reincarnation, ghosts, the whole smorgas-
bord of the occult. There wouldn't be a horror
genre in the movies without that stuff. It's the
stock-in-trade of those supermarket tabloids.
I've always thought of psychics as being weirdos. . . . I'm sorry about that Madeline, but I feel
I owe you my absolute honesty. Show me one
shred of evidence that demonstrates your psychic ability, old Basil notwithstanding, and I'll
react to it. I promise you that."

The words had tumbled out of him, along with
his perspiration. After they were said, he felt dis-

tinctly better, as if he had retrieved the initiative. Madeline had listened calmly. Throughout the speech, he noted that Virginia had remained immobile, although in the flickering light he could not adequately read her expression.

"He's asking for a parlor trick," Virginia said, which indicated that she was hardly pleased by his speech, no less his attitude.

"I understand," Madeline said.

"How else to know?" Jack said.

"It's like asking for someone to perform miracles."

"Exactly. I'm looking for Madeline's miracles."

"I really think you're being rude, Jack."

"I don't mean to be," Jack responded. "I just want to be out in the open about it."

"And I appreciate that," Madeline said.

Grudgingly, he admired the way she accepted his attack, as if she was accustomed to it and knew exactly how to defend her position. She did not argue or protest, nor did she promise anything.

At that moment, he decided that he had to know more about her. Who was she really? Why had she come here? It was also clear that she would volunteer little about herself and her background. But he would find out, he vowed.

Madeline left a little after midnight, but not before she and Virginia had a long tête-à-tête at the front door. Jack felt that he was being dismissed in his own house. With a handshake, a forced smile and a bellyful of anger, he strode off to their bedroom.

By the time Virginia joined him, he had worked up a good head of paranoia. What were they doing out there for such a long time? Discussing him, he was certain. His attitude. His skepticism.

"That was the longest good-bye on record," he sneered as Virginia began to undress.

"Girl talk," Virginia said.

"More brainwashing," he hissed. Anger and emotion were bubbling to the surface. "In her hands you're a piece of goddamned clay."

Silently, she slipped into her nightgown, then started to brush her hair. But after a few strokes, she turned to him and brandished the brush in her hand, pointing it at him. "You're jealous."

He sat bolt upright. "Jealous?" he sputtered. "I wonder what's behind that implication."

"Now that is truly disgusting. This woman is my friend."

"She's a fraud."

"I won't have that, Jack. Besides, you don't have to believe her."

"I don't."

"Then why were you so afraid to show her your palm?"

"I wouldn't give her the satisfaction."

"Not true. You were afraid she might see something that you wouldn't like."

"Bullshit," he snapped. But he knew that he was on the wrong tack if he wanted to win her over. The idea tamed his anger. He needed to find a different strategy. She continued to brush her hair, then got into bed beside him, lying on her back looking at the ceiling.

"I'm only saying that you just can't accept everything she says blindly."

"I believe in her," she said firmly.

"No doubts at all?"

"None."

He sighed. He had the urge to grab her by the shoulders and shake some reason into her.

"You don't know a damn thing about her," he muttered.

"That's not true."

"Where does she live?"

"She has an apartment in Santa Monica," Virginia countered.

"You've been there?"

"Well, no," she replied tentatively.

"Never had you up?"

"I told you. No."

"Ever speak to any of her other 'clients'?"

"Of course not. And I'm not a client, I'm a friend."

"No money passed between you?"

"Now that is offensive, Jack."

"That's not an answer."

"No," she said begrudgingly.

"Does she ever talk about her past, her parents, her upbringing . . . anything personal?"

"Of course she does," she replied with hesitation.

"Like what? Tell me about it."

"It's private," she snapped.

"From me? Hell, Ginny, do we have secrets between us?"

"This is different. I have no right."

"That knife cuts both ways," he said.

He waited through a long pause, knowing she was troubled by his guilt-inducing interrogation.

"She told me she has never been happy, that her gift had made it impossible for her to lead a normal life."

"That's a generalization. I mean specifics. Genuine information. Like us. An open book."

"You sound like a detective."

"Maybe I should be," he shot back.

In a movement bristling with indignation, she turned on her side, showing him her back.

"Nobody can make you believe in her gift," she said.

"I told you before. Let her show me her stuff. I'm a reasonable, open-minded fellow."

Aping her motion of indignation, he turned on his side at the farthest edge of the bed.

He heard her quiet breathing. He supposed the conversation was over. Then, after a long silence, he heard her voice.

"She'll give you the proof, I promise you."

·7·

Even before she answered the phone, Virginia knew it was Madeline. She had been locked into one of those preawakening deep, dreamless morning sleeps. Shocked into consciousness, she had barely time to register a sense of time and place. The digital clock read six-fifteen. Jack had already left for the office.

"Madeline," Virginia said before the voice at the other end had identified itself.

"You're stealing my thunder," Madeline replied with a soft chuckle.

"Is everything all right?" Virginia asked. Madeline rarely called this early.

"It is now," Madeline said.

Her response was puzzling and her voice reflected a hint of nervousness.

"I don't understand."

"Do you trust me?" Madeline asked.

"You know I do."

There was a long silence on the line during which Virginia could hear Madeline's measured breathing.

"What is it, Madeline?"

"I don't want you to drive today," Madeline said.

"What?" Something jumped inside her. Immediately, she felt menaced.

"You mustn't drive," Madeline repeated. Her tone was commanding and authoritative. "Not today or tomorrow."

At once, a protest rose inside of Virginia. Not drive for two days? Her mind had flooded with the day's planned events. She was, despite everything, still responsible for running a household.

"Today is marketing day," she said. It was a catchall phrase for all the chores she had reserved for Thursday. Prosaic, but necessary. There was the cleaning to be picked up. Jack's suits. The twins' outfits. Food was running low. The night before she had made up a large shopping list. Then she remembered Friday. Her dentist's appointment and the standing appointment at Mel's.

"Give up Mel's and the dentist?"

"Believe me, this is no joke."

"In L.A. a car is like oxygen."

Her own phrase jarred her. Oxygen was life-sustaining. Madeline's implication was exactly the opposite. Her resistance buckled. *I can't dismiss this,* she thought.

"What have you seen?" she asked. It seemed a child's question.

"I need your trust, Virginia, now more than ever."

"It's just . . ." A feeble protest flickered, then disappeared. "I guess I'll just have to hire a taxi," she sighed.

"Not even that," Madeline said.

"Madeline, you're scaring the shit out of me."

"I hope so."

"You think I'll have some kind of an accident?" Virginia asked. Her voice was shaky, tremulous.

"I know it," Madeline said.

A chill went through her. "Are you certain?" Virginia asked.

"Yes."

"What am I supposed to do?"

"Stay inside," Madeline said.

"But I've got things to do, responsibilities."

"I know. I'll do whatever has to be done."

"Take my dentist's appointment?" Virginia said with slight sarcasm.

"I would if I could."

"I suppose I *can* skip a week, but I am sorry about Mel's."

"He'll understand. I'll explain."

"That will be interesting."

"I'll think of something. And I'll take care of the shopping," Madeline said. "What are friends for?"

"Jack will never understand."

"We'll just have to think up some damage control," Madeline said.

Damage seemed too harsh a term for what was happening between Virginia and Jack. Wasn't it perfectly appropriate for her and Jack to have a difference of opinion? And if he chose to pout and mope about it, wasn't that his problem? In fact, he had no right to tell her what and what not to believe. Nor had she any intention of changing anything in her relationship with Madeline.

"It will all come right in the end," Madeline assured her.

"He keeps asking for proof."

"They all do," Madeline replied knowingly.

"Well, then, give him some. That ought to end it."

"Timing, Virginia," Madeline cautioned. "I will know exactly when."

Instead of tearing her and Madeline apart, Jack's aggressive attitude was bringing them closer together. Indeed, Virginia's studio was already beginning to fill with paintings of Madeline in various poses. She had deliberately and defiantly displayed them on the walls of her studio and there were more to come.

The important thing was that she was painting again. Sometime in a month or two, Madeline had suggested, she should begin to approach art galleries with her work. Madeline had promised to tell her when the exact time came.

"We need maximum power," Madeline had pointed out, once again telling Virginia that she would one day be considered an important artist.

Of course, Virginia trusted Madeline. Of course, she would not drive or be driven for two days. Yet before she hung up she again asked Madeline to provide her with the specifics of the vision.

"You wouldn't want to hear it," Madeline replied. "The point is that this is one tragedy that can be avoided."

True to her word, Madeline followed up on the household chores, filled Virginia's list, got Jack's suits and the twins' outfits from the cleaners and bought tubes of paint.

"It seems odd, you doing these things for me," Virginia said.

"Someday it will all make sense," Madeline replied.

That night at dinner, Jack was in a sour non-communicative mood, short with the twins, moody and reflective. Virginia knew his moods well.

When beleaguered he underwent large attitude changes, swinging between attack and withdrawal. He tried valiantly to keep himself on an even keel when addressing the twins, but even this was awkward and clumsy.

The twins did not puzzle over this. The big game was coming up in a few weeks and their own level of tension and absorption was focused on that event.

When the girls had gone up to their room, Virginia noted a change in his attitude. It gave her hope that he might be more accepting when she told him about Madeline's admonition and her consent.

"All right," he said suddenly. "I don't buy Madeline's premise. At the same time, I can't make you reject it. Which leaves me on the horns of a dilemma."

"Where you will remain until shown the truth."

"Where I will remain forever."

"Never say forever."

She knew that he was merely changing his tactics. Something about getting more done with honey than poison sprang to mind. She welcomed the change. She was missing a bit of honey in her life. Oh, she was happy to be painting, happy having a friend and mentor in Madeline, but Jack, too, had an important role in her life. She did not want him to be perpetually hostile.

It must have taken some doing on his part to break through his own wall of pride. Normally it was she who had assumed the role of peace-maker. At those times, when a domestic tiff had disrupted their relationship, it was always she who had made the first move to right the ship. Her mother's admonition resonated in her mind.

"A woman is the glue of marriage," she had told Virginia on Virginia's wedding night. Even then the reference struck Virginia as offensive. It smacked of manipulation and control. Her mother defined it as devotion and strength.

"Only if the glue holds together equal parts," Virginia had parried. Although she loved her father deeply, his passive role had always disturbed her. He would have characterized himself as loving and thoughtful.

"Forget about that equal stuff," her mother had countered. "A woman is more than equal in a marriage."

"Believe me, Jack," she said, "I don't want my friendship with Madeline to come between us. Nor what I believe about her"—she hesitated, groping for the right word—"her powers."

"The less said," Jack replied.

She looked at him and he turned his eyes away. They were still sitting at the dining room table. She stood up and moved behind him, her arms enveloping him as she bent over and kissed his cheek.

"It's still you and me, kiddo," she whispered.

His response was tepid. But when she kissed his ear, he seemed to move his head toward her.

"You're my guy," she whispered.

"Sometimes I wonder," Jack said. She sensed his thawing.

"Jack, I'm happy, I'm painting, the kids and you are doing well. What's to fret?"

Being close to him was arousing. She kissed his neck and leaning over rubbed her breasts against his shoulders. He shrugged, turned and kissed her, long and hard.

"I could do without all this," he whispered.

"Without this?" she said coquettishly.

"You know what I mean."

"It's all for the best. Trust me."

Again, he kissed her and, moving her gently away from the back of the chair, he stood up and they embraced against the dining room wall.

"I missed you, babe."

"And me, you."

Again they kissed. She felt his hands clasp her buttocks.

"Maybe I'm too possessive," he said, "and I don't want anyone else to possess you."

"Silly. Madeline's a friend."

It suddenly struck her that he might have suspected something else. She began to laugh.

"Did I say something comical?" he asked.

She had better tread lightly, she told herself, not break the mood. He was still emotionally bruised.

"You mean everything to me, Jack," she whispered. "I don't want anything to come between us. Ever. Never." Inexplicably, she began to cry lightly.

"A woman's tears will melt the coldest heart," he whispered. He pulled her closer. He was aggressively aroused now. "Fourteen years and it still feels good."

"The best."

"That implies a basis for comparison."

"The only and only best, then."

"God, I love you, Ginny."

They heard the light tread of one of the twins coming down the stairs from their room and quickly separated.

"They're world class in disrupting seductions," he said, his voice low. He sat down again in the dining room chair, largely to hide his erection.

"*Guinness Book of World Records* material," Virginia said as Billie bounded into the room. She was dressed in pink flannel pajamas.

"That's what I want," she said gleefully, "me and Bobbie to make the *Guinness Book of World Records.*"

"You already have," Jack smirked, smiling slyly and winking at Virginia. For some reason, one or both of the twins kept showing up at the wrong moment.

After Billie had made her pass at the refrigerator and had gone back upstairs, Jack stood up again and embraced his wife.

"Better get upstairs to our own room," she said.

"I was hoping for something novel," he winked.

"Like on the dining room table," she teased.

"Or hanging from the chandelier."

Arms around each other's waists they started toward their room. They made an outside detour and came out on the patio overlooking the lights of the city. For a long moment, they watched the sight.

"Forgot to tell you, Ginny, we have a cocktail

party tomorrow night. At the Singers'. It completely slipped my mind."

She started to respond, then, remembering Madeline's admonition, she froze. The change in her mood was not subtle.

"What is it?"

"A chill," she whispered.

He gathered her in his arms and pressed her close. Arousal slipped away. Inertly, she leaned against his body. His hand roamed over her buttocks again. She felt nothing, but tried to fake it. He felt the resistance and loosened his grip. She turned and looked out across the city.

"Something I said?"

She didn't respond, knowing he was reviewing in his mind what might have turned her off.

"Maybe I'm tired," she said, moving away. She could hear his footsteps following behind her toward the bedroom.

"I know what you mean," he said. He sat on the bed and began to remove his shoes. "Emotional upheaval is draining."

"Tell me," she said. *Why tomorrow?* Her mind groped through a grab bag of excuses. Feeling ill at the last moment seemed her only option. But why the dishonesty? She was annoyed at her timidity.

Jack undressed and went into the bathroom, closing the door. From behind it came the sounds of the bathtub tap. She paced the room, debating the issue. All religions had peculiar observances. Orthodox Jews did not ride on Saturday. Catholics did Hail Marys. In Mexico, they walked to the Church of Quadalupe on their knees as penance. Moslems fasted and beat themselves with chains. Hindus worshiped cows, rubbed dung on their bodies. Rituals that seemed silly to others, but were designed to protect their believers against something: evil, tragedy, death.

No shame in that, she decided. As her mind rationalized, her belligerence increased. *This is my belief*, she shouted inside of herself. He must respect that. Her wait for him to come out of the bathroom seemed endless, but by the time he came back into the room her resolution was firm.

"I can't go," she said.

He shook his head, not understanding. "Go where?"

"To the Singers' tomorrow."

He looked at her in confusion. "There's something more important?" he asked with a touch of sarcasm. Singer was, she knew, Jack's largest client. In that respect, she knew her role, just as he knew his role in dealing socially with her clients when she invited them over. It was part of the game. Besides, she liked the Singers, although she would not have chosen either of them as a bosom pal. They were simply bottom-line business friends.

"It's not that," she said. For a moment her courage faltered. *Dissimulation or truth?* she wondered, teetering briefly on the razor's edge. She opted for truth.

"To avert a tragedy, I'm not to go out on the roads until Saturday." He started to interrupt, but she waved her hand and he aborted his response.

"Please let me finish. You won't like this, but you have to know. Let's not make a big thing out of it. Please, Jack, try to understand. Madeline has warned me not to drive or be driven. She indicated to me . . ."

"Must I listen?" he snapped.

"I was just trying to explain . . ."

He raised his hand like a traffic cop stopping traffic. "We have a serious problem here, Ginny." Jack sighed, looking at her as if she were ill. At least she could be thankful that he wasn't erupting.

"Would you rather I took the chance?" she said softly. Was she being cruel? She watched his face, a kaleidoscope of doubt and uncertainty. *Fair game*, she thought.

"Are you setting me up for a guilt trip?" he asked calmly.

"It's a question of belief." She paused, watched him, wished in her heart that, like her, he believed in Madeline.

"Not now it isn't. Tell a person they might have an accident, there's always the possibility of a self-fulfilling prophecy." He shook his head in frustration, then turned away from her and got into bed, putting out the light next to his side of the bed.

She stood for a long while watching him. He must have sensed this. When he spoke his voice sounded far away.

"I'll go myself, then," he said.

"Why can't you believe?" she whispered.

She waited for an answer. None came.

·8·

From his rented Oldsmobile, Jack had a clear view of Madeline's apartment house. Waiting, slumped low in the front seat, he made a leisurely assessment. Typical Santa Monica, three-story walk-up, nondescript, respectable, rent-controlled, six hundred a month tops, postage-stamp pool.

Admittedly, he had expected more. More what? Elegance, perhaps. Madeline certainly had an elegant look about her. Always well-groomed, icy fresh, in the latest styles. Not very L.A., more like San Francisco.

A middle-aged woman was standing near the front door. As Jack watched, Madeline parked her Toyota in an open space beside the building and greeted the woman with a handshake. They chatted briefly while Madeline found her key and unlocked the front door, holding it open for the other woman.

He waited until they disappeared inside of the building, then walked to the front door. The directory was one of those buzzer jobs with a speaker. There was her name. Madeline C. Bos-

well, Apartment 312. He wondered about its location within the building, but there was no way
of knowing.

Back in the car rented specifically for this
task, Jack watched the apartment house. In the
quickening dusk, three windows were already
lit. He couldn't know which one was hers. But
he prepared to wait. He wasn't sure for what.

He had been trying to discover where Madeline lived for ten days. First, he had looked in
the phone book, the obvious place, but her telephone number was unlisted. Virginia, he supposed, had her address somewhere.

One day, when he knew that Virginia was out
having lunch with Madeline, he came back to
the house and went looking for the address. He
assumed it would be on the Rolodex in Virginia's studio. He hadn't been in it since the day
when he came upon her doing a portrait of
Madeline.

From the look of things, it was obviously the
first of many. Paintings of Madeline were everywhere, covering the walls and leaning against
every upright bit of available space. There were
faces, half nudes, nudes, Madeline smiling,
Madeline pensive, Madeline moody. Evidence of
a massive obsession. It was overwhelming. He
was surrounded. Worse, he felt a sensation of
entrapment, as if he were a fly hopelessly entangled in a spiderweb.

There was a physical reaction as well. A bolt
of fear, like a lightning strike, shot through him.
His heartbeat accelerated, his breath quick-
ened. He began to perspire. Virginia's obsession had apparently gone further than he had
suspected.

He wanted to run, but he forced himself to

rifle through her Rolodex. No listing. He started to look among Virginia's papers, once carefully organized for her free-lance work. Now her files were awry. Nothing seemed in the right place.

Discouraged and frustrated, his mind drifted and he began to study the pictures. The nudes were lush, depicting full upturned breasts with large pink aureoles and pouting nipples, small waist, tight stomach, gently rounding, faintly dimpled buttocks. His reaction was distinctly erotic.

For a moment he felt naked himself, fantasizing. A tumescence, hard as ivory, grew in his pants. He felt suddenly ashamed. Then the eyes, Madeline's eyes, God knew how many, seemed to mock him. He felt embarrassed by their imagined ridicule. "Bitch," he cried aloud, pluralizing it as he ran from the studio. "Bitches." He felt conspired against, mortified.

Not finding Madeline's address only exacerbated his uneasiness. He felt disoriented in his own home. A "force," he decided, had invaded it, determined to dispossess him. He ridiculed the thought, rebuked himself for his gullibility. As he fled the house, he accused himself of self-induced mental gymnastics.

Back at his office, amid the familiarity of his working world, he had found some solace. To reinstate himself into an atmosphere of reality, he had picked up a sheaf of messages, shuffled them into priorities and planned his return calls. But he could not find the motivation to begin. The telephone rang persistently, but he did not pick it up. Messages were taken at the switchboard. More calls came. After a while he could barely hear them.

The point was, he told himself, something had

to be done about this. Virginia, his wife, the
mother of his children, was disappearing as an
individual-thinking entity. She was being manipulated into becoming a mental basket-case,
manacled by fear and superstition. She was
slipping away from him and the impending loss
panicked him. She was being dragged into the
darkness, torn from her home and environment, transformed, brainwashed.

How could this have happened? He retreated
into himself, exploring his own motives and
mental state. Perhaps his single-minded pursuit
of net worth and materialism had driven her
away from him, left her open and vulnerable to
exploitation, sparking a search for something
"more meaningful." What, he argued, was more
meaningful than home, family, security? And
yes, loving, sharing. His eyes misted. What the
hell was this woman trying to do? More important, what was he going to do to stop it?

"What's with you, Jack?"

Jane's voice startled him. He tried to make a
show of activity by leafing through his messages. Then he threw them down on his desk
and leaned back in his chair.

"No use," he said.

She sat down on a leather chair beside the
desk. As usual her dress hiked up to her thighs.
He was curiously unmoved. Certainly far less
than the portraits of Madeline had moved him.

"She's blowing up my life," he said, feeling a
surge of outrage.

"That bad?"

"Worse."

He told her about the paintings, describing
them but editing his reaction to them.

"Maybe she's just practicing," she said, with

wise-guy flippancy. He let it pass. One's outrage, he knew, was difficult to convey to another.

"More to it, I'm afraid."

Jane grew thoughtful for a moment.

"It's not what you're thinking," he said.

"Whatever turns you on," she replied with a
shrug. He ignored the comment, but not the
possibility. It had been running through his
mind for days. The idea added its weight to his
need to take some decisive action.

"I can't just let it happen," he said, the words
reverberating in his mind like the plaintive cry
of a trapped animal. The "it" was taking on lay-
ers of meaning that had never occurred to him
before. However she was doing it, Madeline had
invaded his life and was in the process of stealing his wife's mind, perhaps her body as well.

"Maybe it will burn itself out," Jane suggested.

"I don't want to take that chance. I've got kids
to worry about."

"And business," she volunteered, looking at
the pile of messages on his desk. "And soon,
irate clients."

"I can't concentrate on anything." He looked
up at her. "I'll be in and out of here. I've got to
know more than I know."

"You may find more than you want to find."

"That's a chance I'll have to take."

"Worry not, Sherlock, I'll cover."

"I appreciate this, Jane."

"Just as long as you know how to show it."

As always, her implication was clear. Odd, he
thought, how quickly his desire for her had disappeared. It was a subject he chose not to dwell
on.

It surprised him how easily he fell into the mind-set of a detective. Caution first, he urged himself. Above all, he must avoid inviting suspicion, especially from Virginia. Feigning acceptance would be the hardest part. His heart sank at every mention of Madeline.

Even the sight of her was galling. Virginia and she were inseparable. Although Madeline was always gone when he came home from the office, she had obviously extended her influence beyond Virginia to the twins, which only increased his inner turmoil.

"We've been watching them practice," Virginia had announced one day.

"Madeline's our good-luck charm," Bobbie chirped.

"Has she made the big prediction yet?" he asked. The school soccer team was moving inexorably toward the championship game in its class.

The twins looked at each other and giggled.

"She says that would spoil the fun," Billie said.

"She said we wouldn't practice as hard if we knew we were going to win," Bobbie pointed out.

"And if we were going to lose, we would think it was all useless," Billie said.

"Very clever of her," Jack said with a brief glance at Virginia.

"She would never abuse her power," Virginia said.

"She has a keen sense of ethics," Jack said.

"Yes, she has," Virginia agreed. Any hint of sarcasm had sailed over her head.

He did his best to avoid confrontations. Nor could he surrender so completely as to give the impression that he totally accepted Madeline's growing role in their lives.

Madeline and Virginia's strategy was transparent. When the cat was away the mice played.

On two occasions he followed them in a rented car. They drove to the beach at Marina del Rey, then had lunch on the strand in Venice. Another time he followed them to a restaurant, waited, then followed them on a shopping tour. Nothing much was purchased and they were back at the house in two hours.

Very innocent outings, he decided. He noted that they laughed a great deal, held hands, occasionally embraced in a purely innocent way. Afternoons, they repaired to Virginia's studio, presumably to continue Virginia's painting. He could discover nothing more than two women friends, happy in each other's company. At times, his dark suspicions seemed absurd.

Yet when he and Virginia were alone she rarely alluded to these activities, except when, as in the case of watching soccer practice, it was unavoidable.

Madeline was a part of her life lived independently of him, compartmentalized. Apparently Virginia wished to avoid confrontations as well. Nor did Virginia ever again suggest that Madeline stay for dinner. Indeed, her efforts at keeping him and Madeline separated were hardly subtle.

Virginia seemed to be straining to illustrate the normality of the situation. Business as usual in the household. For Jack it was far from it. A great deal had changed.

A stakeout, the police called it. He continued to sit slumped in the front seat of the car watch-

ing the building. He wanted to know more about
her. Knowledge was power and he needed
knowledge to counter her invasion into the
mind of his family.

Mostly, he needed information to discredit
her, bring her down. If she was so clairvoyant,
how come she did not know he had followed
her. Once again he had rented a car. Throughout the trip back to her apartment, she had
shown no sign that she knew he had followed
her and was, at this very moment, staking out
her home like some secret agent.

Suddenly, the middle-aged woman who had
gone into the building with Madeline appeared.
He looked at his watch. She had stayed inside
a little more than an hour. She started to walk
away from the building. He watched her for a
moment, then slipped out of his car. No time to
debate the matter. It was necessary to know.
Know what? He darted across the street, then
slowed, realizing that approaching her from the
rear might frighten her.

Then she veered slightly, stepped in front of
a yellow Cadillac to the driver's side and began
to fish for keys in her pocketbook. He followed
her.

"Excuse me," he said with cloying politeness.

The woman turned to him and frowned. She
was heavily made up, very overdone, her lips
smeared too thickly with cherry red lipstick.
Beneath the patina of foundation and powder,
the wrinkles were still very much in evidence.

"I'm looking for an address," he said, noting
that his voice spurred the woman to hug her
pocketbook to her bosom.

"I don't live here," the woman said sourly.

She had a mean, belligerent look. She fished out her keys and turned toward the car.

"I'm looking for a woman named Madeline Curran Boswell."

The woman turned pale myopic eyes toward him, studying him carefully, assessing him.

"You know her?" he asked.

"Hear tell," the woman said. There was an edge of interest in her tone. He knew he had engaged her curiosity. But it wasn't enough to stop her from putting her key into the car door lock.

"My first time," he said hoarsely, not quite knowing how to proceed. "Lady is a psychic."

"So she says," the woman said.

"Oh, you do know her."

She looked him up and down. He noted that she was bathed in perfume, the kind people used to cover other body odors. Despite her expensive clothes and Cadillac, she seemed unclean.

"You like horses?" she asked.

"What does that mean?" he asked, offering a smile to mask his impatience.

"The ponies. Bangtails," she explained.

"I'm not much for playing the horses," he said, feeling foolish.

"Baseball?"

"I like to watch it sometimes," he muttered, not knowing where the conversation was going.

"You don't bet?"

"No."

She shook her head then flung it back in a throaty laugh.

"I made a joke?" he asked, incredulous.

"What the hell you want with a psychic if you don't bet?" she chuckled.

"She picks horses?" Jack asked.

"She's damned good at it," the woman said. "Does it by the numbers."

He tried to hide his surprise. Once again reality had intruded on his expectations.

"One consults a psychic for other reasons," he said pompously. Then a thought intruded. "What do you mean by the numbers?"

"Fifty-five, fifth race, fifth position. Twenty-three, second race, third position. Big day for fifty-fives tomorrow at Santa Anita. . . ." She shrugged.

"How's her average?"

The woman shrugged again. " 'Bout fifty-fifty."

"That supposed to be good?"

"Better than any tout sheet I ever looked at," the woman said. "Best I ever got was one-third."

"You been going to her a long time?"

"Three months. And I'm ahead for that period. That's what counts."

"You believe in it, of course."

The woman looked at him with exaggerated pity. "You're going," she said. "What reasons do you have? Got a lady friend you're not sure about? Don't know Boswell's average on that stuff." She started to turn again to the car. He touched her on the shoulder. She turned quickly.

"That address you were looking for." She pointed to Madeline's apartment house. "That building there."

"Can I ask you something else?"

"You're a regular question box."

"What kind of a place has she got up there?" He was hoping he was using just the right approach, the correct idiom to keep the woman going.

"No big deal," the woman shrugged.

"She live with anyone?"

She looked at him and shook her head.

"Got something in mind?" she asked with a salacious wink.

"Just curious. You know, first-time jitters."

"Not that I'd blame you. She's a looker. Classy, too. I like that."

"But she only picks winners on a fifty-fifty basis."

"Not bad in life either," the woman said. "I've been widowed twice. Married twice. Widowed twice. That's a two hundred percent loss. I'd have settled for fifty-fifty."

"Where did you hear of her?"

"A girlfriend at Santa Anita."

"How was her record?"

"About the same as mine."

"So you believe her?"

"Listen, sonny, I believe as long as those bangtails sail home. She goes out of the money for too long, I say bye-bye. This is my fourth psychic in two years. When it comes to horses, a lady needs all the help she can get."

That said, she turned the key in the lock, slid into the seat and slammed the door behind her. He stood for a moment watching her, slightly disoriented by her odd revelations. *Cool, beautiful Madeline*, he thought, *little more than a racetrack tout.* His wife Virginia at the mercy of such an obvious fraud. It disgusted him.

He had the urge to go up to Madeline's apartment and have it out with her. But he resisted it. He had no leverage, not as long as Virginia remained committed to her. He wished he had somehow recorded that woman's conversation. If this was the level of Madeline's so-called clients, then she had good reason to keep her life secret.

With a bellyful of self-righteous indignation, he drove the rented car to the Hertz agency, turned it in, picked up his Jag and headed home. Had he won a victory or merely a small skirmish? He wasn't certain.

It did not occur to him until he got inside the front door that he had not called Virginia to say he'd be late for dinner. It was after eight. For a moment, he experienced a stab of anxiety. He always kept in touch. Only on the rarest of occasions had he not called to say he'd be late and in those situations Virginia had been forewarned.

It was a policy within the family to limit unnecessary worry. They had all been conditioned to check in at "central headquarters."

"Daddy, is that you?" Bobbie called from her room.

"Daddy," Billie echoed.

They rushed at him and gave him a big hug and he held them even tighter than usual.

"We were worried," Bobbie said.

"Business meeting," he muttered. "Where's Mommy?"

He knew, of course. She would be in her studio. Except for her outings with Madeline, she was always in her studio.

After the twins went back to their room, he went into the dining room. His place had been set. On a dinner plate was a note. "Food in the oven." He brought it out: broiled chicken breasts and vegetables. He started to eat. Sitting at the empty table, he felt lost, alone. He could not remember the last time he had been alone at dinner.

Pushing the plate away, he looked around the dining room. Virginia had taken great care to strike a balance between the formal and informal.

"Dinner is a ritual," she had said. "It celebrates the heart and soul of a family."

He remembered being enormously moved by that remark. He was moved now. Tears sprang to his eyes. How had he come to this? He tried valiantly to keep the beast of self-pity at bay. Take stock coolly, he urged himself. Virginia has temporarily lost her way, is all. As for the kids . . .

His vow of patience ended suddenly and he attempted to force himself to overcome his reluctance to enter her studio. A half-dozen times he started to get up, then held back. All that evidence of Virginia's worship of Madeline would sicken him, especially in the light of what he now knew. She was nothing more than a sleazy little fortune-teller.

With that thought firmly embedded in his mind, he did finally enter the studio. Once again, he felt Madeline's stultifying presence. *Thou shalt not make graven images*, he intoned in his mind. It was something he wanted to say aloud, but dared not. The onslaught of Madeline's images made his courage waver.

Virginia was standing near an easel wearing a paint-stained smock, dabbing at yet another portrait of Madeline. She was posed on a beach. Behind her was a turbulent sea. She wore a large sun hat, her features in shadow against a bright morning sun.

"Jesus," he muttered. Virginia did not turn

around, continuing to work her brush, deftly
putting whitecaps on the rolling ocean. When
she didn't respond, he cleared his throat and
said, "Sorry, Ginny, a business meeting."

In the ensuing silence, he watched her brush
as it dabbed away at the whitecaps. Despite the
subject matter, he admired her skill. He looked
around the studio. Her output of "Madelines"
was awesome.

"One would think you had exhausted the subject," he said. She turned to him, eyes narrowed, lips trembling with anger. It shocked
him. He had not been prepared for such a reaction.

"You spied on her. It's disgusting."

He was too dumbfounded to answer. He had
been scrupulously careful. Perhaps the woman
he had spoken to on the street had told.

"Clumsy, I guess," he whispered. He felt like
a teenager caught in the act of masturbation.
Despite his own justification, he felt shame.

"How could you be so"—she sputtered—"so
crude."

"I needed to know," he said, trying to find
some solid ground to stand on.

"It's humiliating," she said. "My husband
spying on my best friend."

Pointedly, he gazed like a panning camera
around her studio.

"Best friend I can understand, but not this."

"Wyeth did it—the Helga collection. Painters
do it all the time."

He must treat her differently, he warned himself, deeply conscious of his waning power to
influence her. He felt totally powerless, on the
verge of a profound defeat.

"All of these canvases are just a symptom of

the real problem," he said cautiously, watching her expression. He knew he could not push her too hard. His principal fear now was that she would do something irrational and disastrous. He dared not speculate what it could be.

"It won't work, Jack," she said. "I'm committed to Madeline, and proud of it."

It was the kind of litany he could not bear.

"How did you find out?"

"Madeline knows everything, Jack. Why can't you get that through your head? There are no secrets anymore."

"You want to hear what I found out?"

"Absolutely not." Her voice was uncommonly shrill. It frightened him.

"She's not what you think," he said gently. He wanted to lash out, call Madeline names like "two-bit hustler." He knew it would not move Virginia.

"She's a miracle," Virginia said flatly.

"How sad," he whispered, shaking his head. If reason wouldn't work, he would try something else.

"Sad?" She laughed, a throaty laugh, not unlike Madeline's. So she was now taking on Madeline's personality quirks. "Jack, I've never been more alive."

"Born again?"

"Yes, as a matter of fact. Madeline has given me a new way to look at things, at life. I was trapped, traumatized. Why can't you just be happy for me and let it go at that?"

"Because it's not real," he argued, knowing it was futile.

"It's more real than the obvious reality. Jack, there are things out there . . ." Her voice trailed off.

It was an argument he could not win. Nor did he want to set off another confrontation. He had been careless. Madeline had seen him in the street. There was no other explanation.

Madeline doesn't know everything, he assured himself, not everything. There was no point in belaboring the issue. Without another word, he let himself out of Virginia's studio. In his mind it was little more than a shrine to Madeline.

·9·

They had been sitting in the stands watching the twins at practice for more than an hour. A late afternoon sun cast a golden glow over the field and the glorious young figures glided with graceful energy from one goalpost to the other, moving the ball with the effortless poise of ballet dancers.

Bobbie and Billie played the flanks against the opposing practice team, passing the ball between them in a pas de deux that looked choreographed. Virginia felt a clutch of pride as her children dazzled their opponents with their footwork and speed and kicked goal after goal.

Virginia was delighted by their strong, agile young bodies. They had been born through natural childbirth, after study and effort, with Jack watching, tears of shared agony and joy running down his cheeks.

That moment when she watched them in the mirror emerging from her body would always be her own baseline of joy.

Later, in private glory, she had held the two pink babies, counting twenty toes and fingers, her lips caressing their sweet smooth skin. "We made a miracle," she had whispered to Jack who had bent over the bed, pressing his beard-roughened face against hers.

"Doubles," he had said. "Ours."

She had unwrapped the two bundles for him to inspect as well. "I already counted them," she had giggled. Then he kissed them on their tiny heads as if it were necessary to seal some mysterious pact between the father and his progeny.

And now they were twelve years old. "Aren't they beautiful?" she said to Madeline.

"Wonderful," Madeline agreed. She seemed pensive, a mood that Virginia had learned to respect. After all, important messages were being constantly received. It was pointless, she decided, to fret about Jack. Someday he would come to his senses. Madeline would find a way to make him understand. All in due time.

Meanwhile, she was deliriously happy. Her work, subject matter aside, was beginning to flow evenly, consistent with her vision. Madeline had inspired her. One day she would assemble these paintings in a book. She stole a glance at Madeline, amazed at her infinite variety of angles and planes and moods and expressions. Jack had described Virginia's choice of subject as an obsession. How could he possibly understand the sensibility of an artist? Picasso, too, painted a single subject in a thousand ways, seeing it differently each time.

After Madeline was fully explored, she would choose another subject. Another human being. This was her forte, she assured herself, discovering character in form and color, capturing nuance and moment in a single living subject.

How could she have abandoned this calling for so many years?

The very idea of her work excited her. She was stimulated from the minute she awoke to the minute she closed her eyes. She was thinking like an artist, seeing as an artist. It was as if her eyes had suddenly opened to the light after years of being in darkness.

Of course, she could not blame Jack. That temptation was a cop-out. Life, too, had different rhythms, like the seasons, a time to plant, a time to harvest. For her this was harvesttime. Madeline had helped her understand this, had given her the hope and will. Jack would have to adjust, accept. If not?

The question had intruded many times of late. Perhaps he did not have sensibility enough to understand. The thought frightened her. She could not project herself into imagining a life without Jack. Not that the concept of love had the same meaning as when it had first blossomed between them. No longer did it have the energy of a perfect blue flame. It generated a more diffused heat. It warmed comfortably. Certainly, she did not want to eliminate the goodness of such a warmth.

Her needs and wishes, her demands—and that included her friendship and belief in Madeline—had to be accepted. To be forced to choose between them and Jack would be the ultimate trauma of her life. The idea frightened her. If she rejected Madeline, dismissed her from her life, would it sour Madeline's vision of their future? That was one dilemma she could do without.

A sudden shout from downfield interrupted

her thoughts. Bobbie had scored yet another goal.

"They are something," Virginia said, suddenly wishing that Jack were here with them. Despite their differences, she knew that Jack, too, was looking forward to the championship game next week. Indeed, for Virginia the game had taken on a special mystique of its own. It would mark a new chapter in their lives. Triumph would be a family event. All enmity and suspicion would vanish. They would come together in celebration. All of them, including Madeline.

The practice session was breaking up. The coach was standing in a semicircle giving the players his last word of advice for the day. That over, the players stood up, grasped each other around the shoulders and sent up a cheer. Then they ran off to the locker room.

The coach came over to the stands and greeted them.

"What are our chances, Coach?" Virginia asked.

He was a rotund man with skin burned leathery brown from the outdoors. He had a slight tinge of an accent. The twins had said he was born in Czechoslovakia. "No question," he smiled, squinting into the late afternoon sun. "With your girls in top form, no question."

"The other team is a bigger bunch. No girl players."

"Clumsier," the coach said, echoing Bobbie's assessment. He bowed with a European flourish and went off.

When he left, Virginia and Madeline stood up and started down the path to Virginia's car.

"God, I hope he's right," Virginia said.

Madeline was unresponsive, lost in thought.

It had been Madeline's idea to watch the twins practice and the two women had been coming to the field twice a week for a month. "Shows them that you take an interest," Madeline had reasoned. "Spurs them on to greater heights." But at the last few sessions, Madeline's interest seemed to flag. Vaguely, Virginia wondered what it meant.

In the car on the way back to Virginia's house, Madeline was still silent, looking straight ahead. Was it more than simple reflection?

When they had spent the morning together in Virginia's studio, Madeline had been ebullient. They both enjoyed the modeling sessions. Also, it was a good time for them to talk.

"You're a captive audience," Virginia had told her.

"Depends on which side of the stage you perceive yourself," Madeline had countered. It seemed to Virginia to be a remark laden with mystery and wisdom. Who, indeed, was the performer?

She had turned that idea over in her mind, then left it unchallenged. It was, after all, Virginia who provided the revelations, the details of her life, the raw materials for a clairvoyant response. Madeline withheld personal information. Between them, Virginia concluded, it was she, Virginia, who seemed on the stage. With Madeline as audience.

But why this change of mood? "Is there something bothering you, Madeline?" Virginia asked.

When Madeline continued to be uncommunicative, Virginia said, "Really, Madeline, what is a friend for?"

"Sometimes there are moments beyond help," Madeline sighed.

"What is it, Madeline? Please tell me."

"I'll try," Madeline said. She turned toward Virginia and looked at her with enormous intensity. Virginia felt her pulse thump heavily in her throat.

"I've been hoping it was a false message," Madeline said. "I've not slept in days worrying about it." She moved closer to Virginia and patted her arm. "I'm afraid there is no way out."

"For crying out loud, Madeline, you're scaring the hell out of me."

Madeline squeezed her arm. "I know, but please try to understand." Her lips began to quiver and her eyes misted.

Virginia felt a draining sensation and it took all her willpower to keep her eyes on the road. Peripherally, she could see Madeline struggling to speak. She felt as if some cold hand had gripped her insides and was squeezing with full force.

"You mustn't let the twins play on Saturday," Madeline said, her voice just below the level of a whisper.

More as a reflex and not because she had not heard, Virginia asked, "What?" Her throat had tightened and she could barely get out that one word.

"The twins," Madeline said, clearing her throat, her voice firming and louder, "you mustn't let them play on Saturday."

Virginia's breath came in quick shallow gasps. She could barely see the road in front of her. They were passing through a quiet street, shaded on both sides by jacaranda trees. She pulled up to the curb. When the car had come to a dead stop, she reclined her head against the backrest.

"I can't do that," she whispered.

"I know how difficult this is," Madeline said. Her voice was pleading, tremulous.

"Why?" Virginia asked. She felt tears stream down her cheeks. A brief spasm of hysteria gripped her and she began to shake. Madeline moved closer to her and embraced her.

"I see danger. Injury. Maybe worse."

"Oh, my God," Virginia heard herself wail, the kind of keening sound made by women mourning the dead.

"You must not endanger those lovely girls," Madeline pleaded.

"Are you certain, Madeline?" Virginia asked when the hysteria had subsided. With a tissue, she wiped her eyes and nose.

"You know I am."

"But how . . . ?" Virginia's mind wandered for a moment. She saw the faces of the twins, stunned and confused, tearstained. "How can I tell them?"

"You mean what can you tell them?" Madeline said.

"Well, then, what?"

"The truth," Madeline said.

The girls were comfortable with "Aunt Madeline," who had never made any attempt to hide what she did from them. In fact, she had actually predicted that Bobbie would not fail her math test when the girl was certain that she had. It had been causing Bobbie great anxiety.

"How could you know?" Bobbie had asked. She had come running into the studio flashing her exam paper. For Bobbie, passing was essential. No pass. No soccer.

"You see," Virginia had said, "Aunt Madeline knows."

Remembering the incident eased her pain somewhat. "I'm not sure I have the courage to do it, Madeline," Virginia said. "This is the most important thing in their lives."

"Would you rather expose them to danger?" Madeline asked softly. "Knowing what I know, I couldn't bear it."

"Are you sure?"

Madeline nodded. "There is no way out," she said. "I'm so sorry."

There was no point in postponing the inevitable. Virginia wanted to tell them before Jack came home. In the last few weeks, he had changed the pattern of his life. He continued to go to bed early, but instead of coming home in midafternoon, he was now never home before five.

She assumed that he did so to avoid confronting Madeline. Perhaps he was still "investigating" her, although Virginia doubted it.

Relations between Virginia and Jack were cool and, of course, there was no sexual contact, which she missed a great deal. It was a waiting game and both she and Jack knew it. She knew exactly what she was waiting for.

Patience and fortitude, Madeline had counseled. Above all, neither of them wished to upset the twins, although she was certain that they sensed that something was not quite right between their parents. The trick at the moment was to avoid any skirmishes from which neither of them could retreat.

She dreaded injecting this new issue. But remembering his fear of having his palm read by

Madeline, she suspected that beyond being ini-
tially hostile, he would finally accept the caution. This did not, however, cancel out the dread
of confronting him.

The twins came home, flushed with exuber-
ance and appetite. But before they could get to
their room, she waylaid them and asked them
to come out to the patio. For some reason, she
felt the view of the city would be soothing and
somehow cushion the pain. By then Madeline
had already left.

The twins sensed that something was going
on, something unpleasant. They looked at her,
anxious and curious.

"Something bad, Mommy?" Bobbie asked.

"Is Daddy okay?" Billie asked.

"Nothing like that," Virginia said. "Daddy's
fine." It was difficult finding the right words.

"Do you believe in Aunt Madeline?" she
asked.

The twins looked at each other, puzzled and
uncertain.

When they did not answer, Virginia slogged
ahead. "Aunt Madeline is a most unusual human being," she began, getting a slight nod from
Bobbie. That encouraged her. Bobbie might lead
Billie, who occasionally needed prodding to fall
into line. Bobbie could be a "pointer," sparking
Billie to less internal reflection and more action.

"It's no secret . . ." Virginia adapted a more
adult stance. They would resent obvious manipulation. ". . . that Madeline has special gifts, talents, to see the future. Clairvoyance is the
term." The girls seemed to be concentrating
fully on her remarks. "She gets messages. Like
she did when Bobbie took that test. Remember?

And she's changed my life totally since I met her. I believe in her absolutely. She knows. She can see things that other human beings can't. It's not meant to be scary. She"—Virginia hesitated—"has the ability, well, to see danger ahead. Warnings that must be heeded."

Virginia's voice weakened and she cleared her throat. "Now you know that your daddy and I love you both more than anything in the world. You're our most precious possessions."

"And we love you, Mommy," Bobbie said, tears springing to her eyes. Both girls, obviously sensing Virginia's anguish, fell into her arms. Virginia kissed them on their heads, holding them tightly.

"I love you and Daddy so much," Billie said, kissing her mother's hands.

Gently, Virginia eased them away. They were both red-eyed and sniffling. "That's why if anything happened to either of you, our lives would be ruined."

"Nothing is going to happen to us, Mommy," Bobbie said. She exchanged troubled glances with her sister.

"Not if I and your Aunt Madeline can help it."

She knew the mystery had deepened for them, yet she continued to withhold the denouement.

"Now you both know that the team you will be playing for the championship is made up of very big and muscular boys."

"Pussies," Bobbie said.

"We're going to beat the pants off them," Billie cried, smiling.

"Aunt Madeline has seen something very troubling about that game," Virginia said gently. "I can't argue with that vision. Aunt Madeline does not make mistakes. When she says that trouble is coming, we must believe her. We must heed her words."

She watched the twins through a long silence, barely able to breathe.

"I know this is going to sound awful. I know you will not be happy and any unhappiness for you is unhappiness for me. You understand that?" It was meant to be rhetorical, but both twins nodded. They were showing signs of getting the message, but neither seemed willing to broach the question.

Virginia plowed ahead. "It's even more awful for me," she admitted. And it was. "But I can't go against Aunt Madeline's vision." Then the words rushed out of her. "She says you must not play in the game, that one of you will be seriously hurt"—her voice broke—"perhaps worse." The view of the twins' faces, aghast with disappointment and fear, faded in a puddle of tears. "Now I know this is the most important thing in your lives at this moment. I know that. My heart breaks for you both. But how can we resist such a vision? How can we possibly take a chance?"

The twins were understandably stunned, looking for answers in each other's eyes.

"Please, my sweet darlings, my two wonderful beautiful children. You must understand. You cannot play. Your daddy and I can't risk it."

"Not play?" Bobbie said, her lips trembling. "Mommy we can't not play. The team depends on us. The school, too. Our coach will die."

"We have to play, Mommy."

"We can't not play," Bobbie repeated.

"Aunt Madeline is never wrong," Virginia

said. A firmness crept back into her tone. "I'm not going to risk any danger to my children."

"Well, what did Aunt Madeline say?" Bobbie asked. "Which one of us will be hurt?"

"She didn't say which one. Maybe both."

"We never get hurt, Mommy," Billie said. "Not once. A scraped knee is not hurt."

"Would you want to take that chance?" Virginia asked. "If you were the mother and I were the daughter?"

The example seemed painful to both of them.

"What can we tell them?" Bobbie asked.

Virginia hoped it was the first sign of surrender. "I know it won't be easy," Virginia sighed.

"We'll never be able to go back to school. How will we be able to face anybody?" Bobbie said.

"They're depending on us, Mommy," Billie pleaded.

"Oh, God this is the hardest thing I've ever done. It hurts me so much. You think I don't know what it means? I also know Aunt Madeline is right, absolutely right."

"How do you know, Mommy?" Billie asked, underlining the question. "How?"

"She can see things that we cannot. I know this is true. I've seen it happen. Bobbie has seen it happen. Haven't you, Bobbie?"

"I . . ." Bobbie hesitated, then nodded and shrugged her shoulders.

"Would you like to see something terrible happen to you and your sister? An injury that could ruin your lives? All of our lives? I can't possibly take such a chance. I can't. You cannot play."

Her insides twisted with agony. Nothing could be worse than this, she told herself. But

she could not, would not, under any circumstances, allow them to play.

"Now both of you go up to your room and
think this over." It was an order. Yet she could
not let them go without embracing them again.

"This will pass," she whispered, kissing them
before she let them go. "Trust me."

Without another word, they ran up to their
room.

It hurts, she thought, *but it hurts good.*

·10·

It was in the air, like a pervasive layer of black smog, thick, unbreathable. Worse than ever, he told himself. Coming home was like walking into eternal night.

His working hours, too, were less than joyful. There was something perverse about working for the cause of home and hearth now that that bitch had descended on his family, a predator, poisoning everything that he held dear, everything important.

"You look like hell," Jane had remarked to him that day. Her comment held a touch of alarm and he had glanced into the mirror to confirm her observation. His face was gaunt. He could put two finger widths into his collar. Dark bags had begun to develop below his eyes.

"Why don't you just throw the turd out on the street?" Jane pressed. He was certain she thought him too passive, not manly enough.

"I've got to play out the string, Jane."

Not that her opinion mattered. He didn't need to justify himself to her. He was, he decided, surrounded by man-eating women. Even the twins with their cloying affection toward "Aunt Madeline" seemed to be turning on him.

How the hell had he let this happen? Madeline had captured his wife's mind. Soon the twins, too, would be fully committed. In the face of that woman's power, he felt helpless. She seemed to have anticipated all his objections, turned them around to suit her ends. Was it clairvoyance? His mind rejected that thought. Surely, she was merely a master of deception. One day he'd expose her scam. How could anyone believe her bullshit?

And yet, he cautioned himself, there was a large body of belief out there, countless books and media events that celebrated the occult. Whole categories and subcategories were devoted to it in libraries. He had recently scanned many of them, but they were too painful to read, as if the words themselves were the enemy.

He had racked his mind to summon up clever scenarios that might induce Virginia to end this nightmare. He seemed checkmated at every turn. Madeline had wormed her way into his family and was turning them all against him.

He was not even free from this paranoia when he slept. He dreamt, oddly remembering his dreams which he had never done before. In the cool light of morning, he tried to interpret them. He was forever falling into dark holes, drowning in mud or black water, unable to extricate himself. He also heard croaking laughter, the kind that filled the sound tracks of horror movies.

Sometimes he would awaken and study his wife's sleeping face, watching her shallow breathing and the rhythmic rise and fall of her chest. Her peacefulness, her serenity in the face

of his own agony, galled him. Still he wanted to
reach out to her, kiss her awake. Always, he resisted. Sleeping, she was still his Ginny, his girl,
the mother of his children, his one true love, his
devoted, talented, wonderful wife. Awake, she
was another person, transformed, her focus
elsewhere, programmed for the ultimate destruction of their marriage.

He was remarkably sensitive to the calibra-
tion of his reactions. He tried desperately to
enter the world beyond his own rational powers of observation. Only then, he told himself,
would he fully understand. Try as he might it
was impossible. His mind, perhaps, was too
practical to visualize, no less enter, the nether
world.

Still, he avoided any confrontation that could
result in the complete rupture of his family. It
took every ounce of discipline and caution.

But coming into the house that evening, he
knew something even more foul than before had
taken possession of the house. Maybe everyone
has a natural instinct for clairvoyance, he
thought. It was an idea that made him uncomfortable.

The door to the twins' room was closed, which
was unusual at that hour. Before he could reach
his and Virginia's bedroom, she waylaid him as
he crossed the space which separated the room
from that of the twins.

She was standing by the door to the bedroom
terrace wearing a dressing gown, the blue silk
one that he had bought her on a business trip
and which she knew was a favorite of his. She
also appeared to have taken great care in her
grooming; her makeup was fresh, not a hair was
out of place. A few months ago, this would have

been a harbinger of a romantic evening. Now it
was suspiciously ominous.

"Got a mo?" she said with a flirtatious sweet-
ness that had been sadly absent of late.

Of course, he wished for a miracle. *This* was
the woman he loved and craved, but he refused
to allow false hope to intrude.

Their dinners, once a precious time for family exchanges were hollow rituals now with
both of them going through familiar and mostly
transparent motions for the benefit of the twins.
Thankfully, the girls were so excited by the impending championship game that they either
did not notice the tense atmosphere between
their parents or did not choose to notice.

He followed Virginia out to the terrace, re-
moving his jacket and tie as he went. She had
set up a tray of shrimp, and a bottle of white
wine was open in an ice bucket. The scene, he
noted, had been part of an earlier fantasy. When
they had first moved in, late afternoon cocktails
had been another of their rituals. When the
twins were out, this ritual had always been a
prelude to making love. *Beware*, he warned
himself.

He took a glass of wine. It was cold and re-
freshing, rejuvenating. The air, too, was clear,
and each building in the vast patchwork view
of Los Angeles seemed carefully engraved into
the cityscape.

When she moved toward the terrace wall
where she stood to pass him the shrimp plate,
he was aware of her nakedness beneath the silk
gown.

"To the mysteries of the beyond," he said
raising his glass when she came closer. She ig-

nored his sarcasm. She raised her wine and they tapped glasses.

"Be nice," she whispered.

"Then let us drink to dear Madeline," he said. His sarcasm was inescapable.

"Don't spoil it," she said.

"Is there something still left to spoil?"

"I wish you wouldn't, Jack," she said, frowning.

Any vestige of hope he may have harbored disappeared. "I thought, perhaps, we were celebrating Madeline's exit," he sighed, upending his glass, taking a long swallow.

"I was trying to make peace," she pouted.

"I thought maybe you were trying to get laid," he said bitterly.

"I wish." She drew in a deep breath. "We sleep together but we're separated by half a world."

"A whole world."

"I'm sure there's common ground for us, Jack," she said. "All I ask is that you respect my beliefs and friendships."

It had been days since they had discussed the "issue." Mostly, they had chosen politeness to get through their moments together.

He moved to the wine bucket and poured himself another glass.

"Why don't we just drop the subject," he said. "No point in kicking a dead horse. I've said all I have to say. So have you." He studied her for a moment, knowing there was no miracle that might return her to him. *Show her no heartbreak,* he told himself.

But she could not hide what he knew was anguish and it disturbed him. *What's coming?* he wondered. *Is this it?* He felt an overwhelming fear.

"I've forbidden the children to play on Saturday," she said.

He heard the words, but they seemed disjointed, the meaning unclear.

"What?"

He was asking for repetition, but in an instant his mind grasped what her words portended. He watched her face, determined, lips pursed, eyes narrowed, nose slightly raised. Years of being together had taught him her stubborn indomitable look, a sure sign of rock-hard intent.

"No fucking way," he said, barely able to open his lips. The message was clearly telescoped and he wanted no explanation. Even the mention of Madeline's name, especially at this moment, would seem a pollutant.

"I've explained it to them," she said.

"And they agree?"

"They understand."

He turned away from her and looked out over the city, barely able to get himself under control. While his back was to her, she spoke.

"She said that there will be an accident. I won't take that chance. And I don't think you will. It's their lives."

God, he thought, how awful it had become. For a moment, he felt himself waver. Suppose, just suppose . . . No, he caught himself. But suppose . . . He deliberately would not show her his face.

"Please, Jack, give me my way on this. Even if you don't believe her, even if you think it's all nonsense, don't fight me on this. I'd rather we err on the side of caution."

She came up close to him, sliding her arms around him, resting her head against his back.

"They're our kids, Jack," she pleaded. "Whether we agree or disagree, they're still our kids. I need your support. We have to show a common front. Give me a break. All I ask is the benefit of the doubt."

And if he did give her that? he asked himself. Did that mean assent, even approval of Madeline's influence? And what would be the effect on the girls? They, too, would be stampeded into believing. He felt their pain and disappointment.

"How can you do that to them?" he asked. Inside of him, the fear had turned to anger.

"It hurts, believe me," she said. "Jack, I'm so frightened."

He felt her sense of helplessness. And his own.

"You've got to resist her, Ginny," he said kindly.

She disengaged, moved away. Only then did he turn.

"You can't resist the truth," she said.

"Nonsense. Fraud. That's all it is. It's just her way of getting more and more control. Can't you see that?"

"The issue is beyond that," she said, with a superior air as if, despite his reaction, he had little choice in the matter. "We are talking here of the well-being of our children."

His heart pounded. He was losing her. He felt her eyes explore his face.

"They'll adjust to the idea," she said softly. "It's only a soccer game."

Had she seen weakness in his face? "How can I possibly accept this?" he asked.

"How can you risk their lives?"

"Dammit, Ginny, why couldn't you have left the kids out of it?"

"You're twisting it around, Jack. They are in it. You are in it. Why can't you understand that?"

"Because it's all hocus-pocus baloney."

"You wouldn't say that if one of our children died in that game."

Of all the phrases she had uttered, this was the most offensive, a jagged-edged knife twisted in his gut. There was no arguing with blind faith, he told himself.

Without another word, he left the terrace. But in passing the closed door of the twins' room, he paused, took issue with himself, answering the question he had posed to Virginia. How can I accept this? The answer gurgled in his throat, a croaking sound. "I can't."

Opening the door to their room, he found them huddled together on one bed, embracing as they might have done as embryos. Lost in their grief, they did not acknowledge his presence.

Seeing his children in this state was unbearable. Their pain was his pain. Their agony his agony. My sweet, beautiful, wonderful girls, he cried in his heart. How could anyone destroy their innocent hopes? He wanted to lie down beside them and cry with them.

Only a soccer game? He mocked her in memory. Not to them. It was a golden moment snatched away by unreasoning foolishness, deliberate distortion and blatant manipulation. Anger bubbled up behind the pity.

He sat down on the bed beside them and gently patted their hair, whispering, "Poor sweet babies." Tears misted his eyes.

His voice and touch must have soothed them. After a while, they settled and turned toward him. He enveloped them, kissed their faces. There was a way in which they cuddled, Bobbie on the right, Billie on the left, a kind of preordained shape of loving. His hands roamed the length of them and their hands also soothed him. There was, despite the pain, great joy in this demonstration of need.

Ever since they were babies he had held them in this way. To them he was, indeed, "Daddy," protector, a benign and loving progenitor, and, perhaps in some secret fatherly way, a lover of sorts. Yet, he felt no guilt in such a comparison. Mystical though it was, fatherhood was not without sensory stimulation, erotic perceptions and a type of passion.

Often the four of them, mother included, would caress each other in a similar way. Another configuration was called for then, four bodies had to be accommodated, the memory of which caused a sob to erupt in his chest. The sense of loss left him feeling hollow and empty.

"I don't understand it, Daddy," Billie, the first to calm herself, said. As he might have predicted, Billie, although she was the follower, was the more questioning of the two.

"I'm not sure I do either," he admitted. "But if anything happened to either of you, your mother and I would never forgive ourselves." It was, he knew, a cliché. To the twins, parents could only be perceived, despite their differences, of being in joint charge. Under no circumstances, despite the temptation, did he wish to remove that perception.

"But Aunt Madeline can't be right *all* the time," Billie said.

"Your mother believes she is."

"Well, I don't," Billie said firmly.

Bobbie was surprisingly quiet. He nudged her shoulder.

"I'm all confused, Daddy," Bobbie said. "The team needs us. How can we tell them?"

"How can we not play?" Billie said. "We'll be letting everybody down." Her lower lip trembled, but she held herself in control. "It's just not fair."

"Bobbie," Jack asked, "do you believe that Madeline can see into the future?"

He waited through the long pause.

"Mommy says she does," Bobbie said.

"But what do you believe?"

Her first reaction was a shrug and to push her head deeper into her father's chest. Then, suddenly, she lifted her head and looked into his face.

"What do you believe, Daddy?"

Billie, too, lifted her head and looked at her father.

"I . . . I'm not sure," he said. The lie was hateful. Rebuking himself, he muttered, "I think she's full of bull."

"But the things she said. . . ." Bobbie's eyes had widened. "About the test. That came true. And Basil." At the sound of his name, the dog poked his head out from under the bed and looked around, oblivious to the chaos going on around him. As quickly as he had revealed himself, he hid himself again.

"Can't blame you mutt," Jack said. "The human condition is much too complicated."

"Really, Daddy, they came true," Bobbie said.

"Just coincidences and lucky guesses," Jack

replied. His courage, which had faltered, was returning.

"Mommy says that Aunt Madeline can tell about anything, that she has special powers," Billie pressed.

"Mommy does believe it."

"Well, I don't," Billie said, pouting.

"But Aunt Madeline said it. Why would she do that . . . if it was some kind of lie?" Bobbie said.

"Not a lie," he responded quickly. "More like a different way of looking at things."

He wondered why he could not bring himself to give them what they craved, permission to play. There was cowardice in his reluctance and he castigated himself for it.

"I want to play," Billie said.

"Mommy won't let us," Bobbie reminded her.

"What about you, Daddy?" Billie asked.

"I've never gone against Mommy," Jack said. He hoped they could feel his anguish.

Again, he was nudging the truth. Going against Mommy wasn't exactly accurate. He would be going against Madeline and all her mumbo-jumbo certainty about future events. The very idea that he was in such a quandary triggered his anger once again.

"Would you play if I gave you permission?" he blurted.

There was a brief moment of hesitation as the twins looked at each other.

"I would," Billie said flatly, but the hesitation had revealed an element of internal struggle.

"What about you, sweetheart?" he asked Bobbie.

"She would, too," Billie said, more assertive

than he had ever seen her. Her words buttressed his own fragile resolve.

"Would you?"

Bobbie shrugged, nodded, then cuddled closer to her father.

"Nothing to be frightened of," he said, forcing his cheerfulness. It was as if he had knifed his way through a jungle and emerged into a clearing. He was relieved.

"What about Mommy?" Bobbie asked.

"We just won't tell her," he said, offering a smile, hoping that he had willed a twinkle in his eye. "It will be a little joke between us that doesn't include Mommy."

"Gee, Daddy," Bobbie asked, "won't she be angry?"

"At first," he said, continuing his ruse of cheerfulness, "but you guys will be so great she'll wind up being pleased as punch."

"What about if . . ." Bobbie swallowed the rest of the sentence. But he pressed her.

"About what?"

"She means if we get hurt," Billie said.

"You won't get hurt. No way my little girls will be hurt. Just forget about what Aunt Madeline told your mother. Aunt Madeline is only a human being like the rest of us. She doesn't know any more than we do." He kissed each girl on the head and poked them playfully in their belly buttons. "And that, as the Valley Girls say, is fer sher."

They kissed him then, and he felt that he had dispelled most of their earlier dejection. Of course, there would still be some residual uncertainty in all of them, but that would pass.

"Question is: How do we go about this without Mommy knowing?"

It was traitorous. No question about that. He felt as if he had crossed his Rubicon. Like being unfaithful, an act that was decidedly against the principle of their marriage and their concept of parenting.

"I hope you ladies can keep a secret," Jack said, watching them. They both giggled and he truly felt that he had chased away their fear. It was his own that gave him pause.

·11·

Virginia, in the end, welcomed Jack's acquiescence, even though her elaborate seduction scene had turned out to be a big disappointment. She knew how much of a struggle it must have been for him. Indeed, she could imagine the pain of it, the lost pride, the surrender to something he did not believe in and, worst of all, the hurt it had inflicted on the twins. At least she had the comfort of knowing that she was protecting her children from harm.

But Madeline had predicted all along that Jack would eventually buckle, that sooner or later he would yield to "higher authority." According to Madeline, this was the first major step in that long climb to knowledge, a signal that the true message was beginning to invade his skepticism.

Nevertheless, although relieved by his capitulation, Virginia felt peculiar, uneasy. Jack's earlier arguments had not gone unnoticed. They did linger in her mind.

It was true that Madeline did not reveal much about her background nor had she ever invited

Virginia to her apartment. No, she had not met any of Madeline's other friends or clients. No, Madeline rarely volunteered any but the most rudimentary details of her life, her history, her dreams and goals. But one did not need details to enjoy intimacy. Virginia did not need to know. It was enough that Madeline shared her time and her love and understanding.

If Madeline was not forthcoming about her life, it did not mean, as Jack had implied, that she was hiding some deep, dark damaging secrets. Actually, this lack of revelation added an intriguing element of mystery to their relationship. It embellished the idea of Madeline as seer, a kind of druid who had emerged full grown out of the vapors and who had chosen them on whom to bestow her gifts and to guide to safety as they picked their way across the mine fields of life.

It had not come easy. She had slept fitfully, awakening with sweat-coated skin and unremembered dreams. He had been sitting on the edge of the bed, his back to her, elbows on his knees, head nodding as if the great weight of this decision was bearing down on him. He might have said something earlier, but she had not heard.

"I'm against it," he muttered, "but what choice have I got?"

It was as if he were talking words to himself that he wanted her to hear. "I think it stinks, but we're stuck with it. Madeline decrees. We obey. We'll just have to wait it out. Someday you'll throw the bitch out."

Hearing that, she could not resist a response. "That's a cruel and ignorant remark," she said, regretting it instantly. No confrontations, Madeline had warned. Use the honey approach.

"I mean every bit of it. The woman is an intruder here. She has"—he hesitated, but still he did not turn around—"fucked us up."

She knew exactly how he felt. A rite of passage was how Madeline had explained it. He'd be recalcitrant, downright nasty. A skeptic cannot be pulled bodily into a belief. It is a solo journey, coaxed by an inner pull, aided and abetted by careful nurturing. "He'll come to us," Madeline had assured her. What more could she ask?

"Are the kids still upset?" she asked Jack's bare back, speaking softly. She had heard their quiet whisperings after he had left her last night. Now she wanted him to turn and touch her. Surely, he also missed making love. She wanted to scream at him: "Aren't you horny, Jack?" But she didn't. He would think she had some ulterior motive, like last night.

"Devastated," he replied, shaking his head.

"I looked in on them before I went to sleep. They were very tranquil. Sleeping together in one bed."

Jack stood up. He was naked and she watched him move in the half-light before dawn. She knew every line, every angle of his tall body. He was still lithe, his stomach flat, his muscles tight, his olive skin smooth. A well-made man, she sighed longingly, noting the perfectly proportioned bulge of his genitals, feeling a sensual stir deep within herself.

To her he had always been sexually moving. Even his face, which was even more attractive when he was serious, turned her on. Deep-set blue eyes, a sloping aquiline nose and square

chin gave him an air of decisiveness that she
knew was sometimes deceiving. He could never
hide his vulnerability from her. How she loved
that exquisite moment when she drew him into
her, savoring the sacred time that was the second act of their lovemaking. Damn. She hated
this estrangement.

He stopped at the bureau, pulled open a
drawer and stepped into white jockey shorts.

"I appreciate your cooperation on this," she
said, dismissing her desire. "It would be upsetting to the girls if there was a tug-of-war
between us. They'll recover. They're young.
Besides, they must know that we're doing this
out of love."

"Fear," he snapped.

"I *know* that if they play something terrible
will happen. I know that for a fact."

"Because Madeline said it, plucked it from the
air. One of her great revelations. Fuck."

He turned away and went into the bathroom.
When he emerged later, he was shaved and
combed, the scent of his after-shave titillating
her nostrils. Often, they had made love after he
had shaved and she had enjoyed the sweet-
smelling smoothness of his face as it roamed
her flesh. The memory exacerbated her yearnings.

"I'm taking them to Disneyland Saturday," he
said as he slipped into his shirt, looking in the
mirror as he buttoned. "Take their mind off
things." He stopped buttoning for a moment,
then scowled at his image. "I told them to say
nothing at school. Not until I notify the coach.
I'll figure out some cock-and-bull story. He'll be
pissed, naturally. They all will." He started to
button again. "I'll take the shit detail."

"I really hadn't expected . . ." she began. She had mentally conditioned herself to assume the "cheering-up" burden.

"I want the full taste of it," he said with a touch of malevolence. She pretended that she had not noted his tone.

"I appreciate that," she said with mock sincerity.

"You realize what you're putting them through?"

"I didn't think it would be easy. Not for us. Not for them."

Fully dressed now, he came back to the bed and looked down at her. His expression was one of half pity, half arrogance. "No chance of changing your mind? Of going against her?"

"Absolutely not," she countered swiftly. "No way. Madeline knows and I believe her."

He left without kissing her. That, too, she missed.

She felt self-pity quickly dissolve into anger. There is such a thing as acceptance, she told herself. He doesn't have to believe. Only accept.

She lay in bed a long time, seized by an overwhelming sense of ennui. The twins stirred. She heard them quietly move through the house. Her diligence as a mother had also suffered lately. These days she often lingered in bed until they trooped in to give her a farewell kiss. Then she would call Madeline. Plug herself in. Only then did she feel fully awake, alive. Hearing Madeline's voice was a renewal. Energy and inspiration began. Everything else became secondary, inconsequential.

Although she knew that it would be important on this day to get up and make them breakfast, her courage failed her at the last moment.

She couldn't go over the same painful ground that they had traversed the night before.

When the twins came in, she was propped up on her pillows lost in contemplation. They were, as she had expected, subdued. Dressed in identical green plaid skirts and white blouses, they kissed her in turn. Always Bobbie first. Billie second. She returned the kisses and an embrace for each.

"I love you, my darlings," she whispered as she kissed them. "You must trust me."

They barely nodded as they left the room. Of course, things would be different today, she told herself. How did she expect them to act? Suddenly, a great wave of despair passed over her. In its backwash she felt deeply depressed. As soon as they were gone, she called Madeline.

"It was not easy," she said.

"I'm so sorry, Virginia," Madeline said, "it had to be done."

"No chance . . ." Virginia began, the plea transparent.

"I wish there were," Madeline said, her voice tremulous.

Tears sprang to Virginia's eyes. "If only . . ." She held back a sob.

"I promise you, Virginia, nothing ever happens in a straight line. There are peaks, valleys, detours. I'll lead you through them. I'm committed to that."

"Oh, Madeline, I am so grateful," Virginia cried.

"You mustn't. It's my joy."

Virginia was overcome. Words choked in her throat.

"I'll be right over," Madeline said.

For the past three months, some part of every

day had been devoted to posing. For Virginia, Madeline was a subject without end. She would be content painting Madeline forever. Uncomplaining and patient, Madeline submitted to everyone of Virginia's ideas. Finished canvases were everywhere in the studio.

Neither of them broached the subject of ending the series, although Virginia knew that there had to be some practical reckoning. Perhaps in a month's time, Virginia told herself, she would begin to present the series to various galleries. Madeline had predicted success but there was no pressure to pursue it.

Besides, as long as the series continued, Virginia reasoned, she could be assured of Madeline's attention and concentration. It had worked out wonderfully.

"This is the most joyous undertaking I've ever been involved in," Virginia told her friend.

"For me as well," Madeline had replied.

It had become a repetitive litany. Often, after a few hours' work, the women would sit together on the couch in Virginia's study, looking out on the panorama of Los Angeles, enjoying a loving wordless communion.

But Jack's opposition presented a lingering downside.

"I can't bear the idea that he's not with us," Virginia told Madeline often.

"He will be."

"When? I need my man."

"Soon."

By the time Madeline arrived, Virginia's courage had returned. Once again, Madeline had filled her with hope and energy.

"I'd say we're making progress," Virginia said. They were in the midst of a new pose, this

time a full nude set against a red silk backdrop
which gave a tint of lushness to Madeline's
flesh. The canvas was large, more than six feet
tall, yet just short of life-size.

Madeline's body was a far cry from Ruben's
pink dimpled ladies. Her breasts were high with
small aereoles, more like those of a budding adolescent, her stomach flat, the pubic triangle
dainty and small, thighs smooth, like well-
turned ivory. She was tilted slightly sideways,
revealing a beauty mark about the size of a dime
just above her left hip.

In this pose, Madeline's long body had the
grace of a lily in full bloom. It was the kind of
form that modern women craved and men fea-
tured in their fantasies.

"Your body is beautiful, Madeline," Virginia
told her. "What man wouldn't revel in it?"

"My mother's legacy," Madeline said. Virginia waited for more. None came.

"Nothing from your dad?" Virginia asked.
Deliberately, it was a soft question, a throwa-
way as she dabbed a bit of highlight in one of
the eyes of the portrait.

"Thank God," Madeline murmured.

"When people see these paintings, you might
be swamped with offers," Virginia said.

Madeline shrugged, offering no comment. Nor
did her expression reveal any further information. It was all the probing Virginia would dare.

If Virginia had been a man, she could see herself salivating for a taste of Madeline's body.
Indeed, even she felt a tinge of the erotic in herself, a condition that happened occasionally to
the artist, but that usually passed quickly. It
did not disturb her much, since she'd read that

to some degree all people had such transient episodes of fantasy.

Posing, despite the hard work for both the artist and the model, had given Virginia a great deal of time to dwell on her innermost thoughts. By now, Madeline knew Virginia's needs, impulses, insecurities, aspirations. For Virginia it had been an unburdening.

Today, she gave Madeline all the details of Jack's and the twins' reactions.

"He's taking them to Disneyland Saturday," she explained. "He says it will take their mind off things."

Madeline moved slightly. Her eyes grew thoughtful.

"I suppose it's a good idea," she said after a long pause. But there was something tentative about her response.

"You seem concerned," Virginia said.

"They're obeying," Madeline said, as if she had to convince herself of something, "that's what counts."

"Yes, I thought so, too." Obeying, however, seemed too harsh a word to Virginia.

"You think it might be better if the four of you went?" Madeline asked. The suggestion did not have the authority of a pronouncement. Brief frown lines wiggled across Madeline's forehead.

"I wasn't invited," Virginia said, remembering Jack's tone. She dabbed in a silvery glow to Madeline's hair. "Perhaps they need this time together." She glanced over to Madeline. The frown lines had disappeared. "And it would be too painful . . . knowing that I was the instrument of their disappointment."

"Now, now," Madeline said, "the messenger

always gets a bad rap. You did what had to be done."

"If only they could see . . ."

"They will."

"If the children turn against me . . ."

"They won't."

"And Jack. He won't come near me."

"He will."

"Dammit, I'm not a celibate woman. But it's not just the sex that I miss, it's the whole idea of being touched, emotionally as well as physically."

"Think about his self-imposed deprivation," Madeline said coolly.

"The fact is I'm panting for him," Virginia admitted.

Madeline moved her head to look out of the window. "Families are such an oasis," she said suddenly. "How lucky you are."

"Lucky?" The question was involuntary. She looked up from the canvas at the naked Madeline, studying her face. She was struck by a quality of vulnerability that had briefly emerged. Madeline's eyes, so charismatic and magnetic, appeared dulled, not quite glassy, but unquestionably fearful. Or had it been there all the time? Madeline vulnerable? With that gift of clairvoyance? Such an idea seemed traitorous.

Virginia glanced briefly around the studio at the other canvas studies. She had portrayed Madeline as heroic, invulnerable. It troubled her now, but only briefly, for when she looked back at Madeline the vulnerability had disappeared.

Something, Virginia realized, was hidden behind the placid facade. She had caught a brief

glimpse of it before it had disappeared. At that
moment, perhaps out of her own fear, she hid
herself behind the canvas.

"Are you troubled?" Madeline asked.

"Troubled?"

Madeline was reading her thoughts. There
was no hiding from Madeline's gifts. Did she
know that Virginia wanted to learn more about
her? Of course she did.

Without words, Virginia beckoned Madeline
to discontinue the pose, waving her forward to
view the canvas. Madeline came, studying her
likeness.

"Have I missed something?" Virginia asked.

Madeline knitted her brow in thoughtful
inspection.

"You've romanticized me," she said.

At this range her skin was fragrant, its lumi-
nosity more pronounced than under the light-
ing Virginia had selected for the picture.

"Yes, I have," Virginia admitted. Not only
were the features heroic, but the body was as
well. "Will these pictures really make me famous?" she asked, feeling like a small child
asking her mother for assurance.

"It will provide a beginning. The road will not
be easy."

"But in the end it will come true?"

Madeline came closer and turned to face Virginia. Virginia could feel Madeline's warm
breath.

"Haven't I promised you?" Madeline said,
concentrating her gaze.

"And Jack and I . . . and the twins . . . we'll all
stay together. Always?"

"Always."

"I'm frightened, Madeline," Virginia confessed. Her legs felt weak; it required an exercise of will for her knees to remain locked.

"What is it, my sweet wonderful friend?" Madeline asked.

"Suppose none of it happens?" She was feeling her emotional underpinnings collapse.

"It will. I've seen it."

"Are you sure?"

"Beyond a shadow of a doubt."

"I need to be told. Again and again," Virginia said. Madeline thrust out her arms. Virginia folded into them, feeling the warm resilience of Madeline's flesh. She lowered her head against Madeline's breast, feeling its soft curve beside her cheek. Madeline caressed her head, whispering.

"It will all come true. Your work. Your family. It will all turn out right. We will love each other. All of us. I promise you. I've seen it. As long as I'm here, you will never be attacked by misfortune. I'll keep you from harm. You are my dearest friend. But you must never waver in your trust. Never."

"Never," Virginia repeated.

Without an awareness of what she was doing, Virginia turned and kissed Madeline's breast, her lips caressing a hard nipple. She felt arousal begin. In her core, a charge, a current pulsed.

It struck Virginia that her lips that sucked on Madeline's breast were like a child's. She half expected Madeline to undress her, powder her body, give her the comfort and pleasure of a mother's love. Perhaps a lover's. She wasn't sure, but she knew that Madeline would decide. Her will was Madeline's. Body and mind she was Madeline's. The thought was sweet. She

would prove to the world that Madeline knew.
Madeline saw. Madeline understood.

Madeline led her to the couch where they held
on to each other, unmoving, peaceful, joyous.
Virginia held her lips to Madeline's breast.
Madeline caressed her head, her fingers playing
with Virginia's hair. From somewhere in the
mud of embryonic memory, Virginia was conscious of another self, unformed, more a spirit
than a human entity, merging now with this
great mother of the earth. Coming home.

Was this the ultimate communion, the spirit
transcending the flesh? Only the changing light
in the studio conveyed the passage of time.

"Never leave us," Virginia whispered. Words
punctured what could only be defined as a
"magical experience."

When no reply came, Virginia stirred, looked
up into Madeline's face.

She was smiling, her expression incongruous.
In a split second it was gone.

"Never," Madeline said. "Never."

·12·

Jack disliked the whole idea of it, being furtive, dissimilating, outright lying. The morning had been an exercise in overt conspiracy requiring an ultimate lapse in their vaunted New England value system. Worse, the twins were a party to it. The entire moral basis of their relationship had gone down the tube.

Even rationalization faltered. Virginia had awakened early and before he or the twins could get downstairs, she had organized a lavish breakfast, the old-fashioned kind: flapjacks and sausages, rolls and jam, fresh squeezed orange juice. Even the coffee smell was powerful with nostalgia.

She looked fresh and perky in pale pink slacks and blouse and had taken pains with her hair and makeup. She seemed as youthful as she had when the first flush of their love was explosively alive. It was unfair. She was taking advantage of his guilt, mocking him.

To get through it, he told himself that this lovely person bustling about, smiling, humming, flipping flapjacks, was only an illusion.

Inside of this shell was another person, Madeline's creation.

The twins took their places at the kitchen table, hiding their excitement under masks of solemnity and depression. Their effort at deception was surprisingly effective, a precursor of what they could become. He had only himself to blame. He had stressed stealth, acting, operating on the theory that this person, wife and mother, was distorted, brainwashed. Even the reluctant Bobbie had finally accepted the theory.

Inside he suffered, forced himself to eat. The doughy flapjacks stuck halfway down, resisting the weight of fluids to push them farther. Nevertheless, he managed a facade of cheerfulness, taking his cue from Virginia who, above all, must be made to believe that they were on the same side.

"They tell me that Disneyland is a whole new thing," Virginia said, sitting down at her usual place, serving family style. She poured out the coffee while the twins continued to offer glum expressions, playing with their food. He hoped that Virginia would not suspect that their lack of appetite might be due to the coach's orders to eat lightly before the game.

"It's gonna be great. Right, kids?" Jack chirped, overdoing the performance. The twins, he knew, must be laughing at his clumsy attempt to appear cheerful and ingratiating.

"How long has it been since we all went?" Virginia asked.

"About nine months," Jack said through a toothy smile. "Too hot a day. We couldn't see much."

"There was a smog alert," Virginia said.

The twins glanced at each other and said nothing.

"Weather is perfect today," Jack said.

"Good old sunny California," Virginia said. The effort to be cheerful was painful for both of them. Evasion was the watchword. After a while, they drifted into silence. Virginia, too, just picked at her food.

"Sure you wouldn't like me to tag along?" Virginia asked. For the last two days, she had dropped elaborate hints. It was a dreaded suggestion. They had hoped she had gotten it out of her system.

"Call it a father thing," Jack said, remembering how he had described it to Jane.

"Got lots of holes in the idea," Jane had commented when he had told her of his plan.

"How so?" he had asked.

"I'd be suspicious."

"You don't know Ginny. She trusts."

"And with good reason," she said with a wink. She had not yet found a way to fan his fires despite his deprivation at home. But good intentions die hard and aggravation was taking its toll on his libido. He yearned to have everything back as it was. Even his relationship with Jane, which had evolved on his part into a variation of an old-shoe relationship. His confessions were blow-by-blow descriptions of the disintegration of his marriage. He had even reported on his cursory investigation of Madeline.

"She dispenses psychofraud," he told her. "That's the only conclusion you can come to. No mystery for me. She's a hustler."

"But how come she's zeroed in on your family?"

All roads led to that question. It baffled him.

He traced and retraced it in his mind. Virginia was totally in the woman's power now, little more than a robot.

"Believe me, I'd kill her if I could."

"Jesus, Jack."

"With pleasure. And in some way that would be slow and painful."

Jane had begun to look at him with pity. No wonder. His confessions were a drumbeat of angst.

When he told her about the Disneyland ploy her first reaction was to consider Madeline's clairvoyance.

"It's a fair test," Jane said. "If she gets the Disney thing in advance, you'd better keep the kids out of the game."

"We've wrestled with that one," he had replied. Indeed, he and the twins had discussed it. "The conclusion was to cross that bridge when we come to it."

"She either sees or she doesn't."

"I won't accept that. Too supernatural. The best I will give her is a lucky guess."

"I still think it's ballsy to do what you're doing," she said.

The odd compliment lingered in his mind. Of course, he was scared, but he could not convey his fright to the twins. He had to show them an exterior of strength and confidence.

The twins deliberately chose not to hurry through breakfast. Virginia scrupulously avoided the subject of the game while continuing to hint that she would gladly go with them to Disneyland.

Finally the twins rose and went to their room, ostensibly to go the bathroom and put the finishing touches on their appearances. They had

been careful to leave no clues. Even their soccer gear remained intact in their room. He had
simply bought them another set of everything
they needed: shoes, socks, uniforms. They had
congratulated themselves on their attention to
detail.

"I really think I should go with you," Virginia
said to Jack after the twins left the kitchen. The
chirpiness had faded by then. It had obviously
been an effort on her part to remain cheerful
throughout breakfast.

"Absolutely not," he said firmly, wondering if
his voice betrayed his panic.

"We need to be together on this, Jack," she
said.

"Another of Madeline's directives?" he said
with unadorned bitterness.

"As a matter of fact, not really," she replied.

"What does that mean?" he asked suspiciously.

She shook her head.

"This can't go on," she sighed.

"I'm of a similar mind," he said, standing up.
It was another discussion leading nowhere.

"You have to take me with you," she said
flatly.

"No way," he replied.

What happened to the great clairvoyant? he
asked himself, looking at his watch. No warning from on high? He felt suddenly unburdened. By late this afternoon, he would prove
Madeline was a fraud. By God, he would
prove it.

"I've saved them from harm. Can't you see
that?" Virginia's litany fell on deaf ears. He had
resisted and he felt liberated.

He left Virginia sitting in the kitchen engulfed in rejection.

The twins were ready and in the car before she had time to act. All three of them sensed that she was on the verge of intruding. The twins did not even perform their farewell ritual.

It took its toll on him. He had encouraged them to lie to their mother. He had lied.

"They're only little white lies," he assured them as they drove to the soccer field. They would be arriving early. There would be time to kill before the game began.

"We're going to win, Daddy," Billie said. "I feel it in my bones."

"Just as long as you don't break any."

The portent of disaster had become a joke between them.

He said good-bye to them at the locker room door. As the only females they had a whole locker room to themselves. In the corridor leading to the field, he met the coach.

"Look good?" he asked.

"No way we can lose. Just as long as your kids are up."

"They're up, I can assure you."

He started to walk away, then turned, came back and faced the coach.

"They say the other team is strong," Jack said.

"We'll go through them like a hot knife through butter."

"Just watch out for my kids."

"I'd say the other team had better watch out for your kids," the coach said. He laughed at his little joke.

It struck Jack that the coach was a bit ner-

vous, an idea that he pushed out of his mind.
He took his place at the top row of the stands,
really just long planks set up in bleacher form.
Virginia and he had come to every one of the
twins' games, a Saturday ritual. Once it had
been a joyous family occasion, an outing. After
the game they would go to Hamburger Hamlet
for lunch.

Virginia had wanted Madeline to come along,
but he had protested, and these Saturday games
had become their one oasis in the desert of their
present relationship.

Soccer rarely attracted much interest, except
among the parents of the children in the games.
The championship game, however, filled more
than half the stands. Many of the faces were
recognizable from past games. He nodded ac-
knowledgment, offered greetings and excuses
for Virginia. "Not feeling well," he told them.
"Pity," they said, "to miss the twins' big moment."

Nervously, he eyed the stands for any sign of
either Virginia or Madeline. Thankfully, they
were not there. Nor did he really expect them.

"Halfway home," a voice said. It was Jane,
scrambling up to where he sat. He felt vaguely
uncomfortable by her presence.

"I never expected . . ."

"I know. An impulsive act on my part."

He looked around him. The teams were just
coming onto the field. Despite the surprise and
brief sense of guilt, he welcomed her presence.

"It's okay." He patted her arm. "First test
passed. Not hide nor hair of the great one."

"One for our side," she said.

If her psychic talents were genuine, Madeline
would have warned Virginia by now, and they

would be trooping up to the field loaded for
bear. Worse, they would probably be rushing
onto the field, dragging the twins bodily from
the game. He would not have dared to stop
them. For the twins the humiliation would be
absolute.

"Now we can enjoy the game?" Jane said.

"You know soccer?" he asked.

"Not a fig's worth."

They laughed. He felt relieved. Jane's presence was calming, reassuring.

He saw the twins running onto the field.
Cheers went up from the partisans. He and Jane
rose to their feet. What they lacked in numbers,
the crowd made up in enthusiasm. The twins'
school was the home team and it was reassuring to Jack to have them playing on the familiar
field.

In their red-and-white shirts, white shorts and
close-cropped blond hair, the twins looked like
younger boys who had wandered by accident
into a big boys' game. Respect came quickly
as their feet worked the ball, passing it between
them, their dancing legs working gracefully as
they crossed the field at full speed.

"They're wonderful," Jane gasped.

Jack, hearing the cheers and Jane's compliment, swelled with pride. But the players on the
opposite team triggered anxiety. They were indeed larger and more muscular than a typical
junior high team.

He imagined that all eyes were on the twins
as they practiced, kicking and feinting through
lines of their own players, sometimes one or the
other smashing a goal with a hard straight kick
that seemed remarkable for players of their
size.

"It has something to do with the laws of physics," Jack told Jane as he watched his two little girls fly across the green field.

"Naturals," Jane said.

Watching them for a while eased his anxiety. His confidence soared. Psychic bullshit, he told himself. At the same time, he wished Virginia were here beside him. A flash of guilt intruded. Then anger at Madeline.

After practice, both spectators and players stood at attention for "The Star-Spangled Banner." When that was over, the twins searched the stands for him and he showed his presence with a wave and a blown kiss. They were smiling and happy. Billie pantomimed a phrase: "Don't worry, Daddy." He pantomimed back, "Go get 'em." Then he showed them a thumbs-up sign.

The full team huddled near the bench, arms around each other, then cheered as the starters headed for the field. The twins' expressions changed abruptly. Smiles disappeared. They were all business, concentrated, focused on their roles in the game.

Beside their opponents, they did, indeed, look frail, even spindly. There were no females on the other starting team, although they did have three on the bench. It was hard to see them as twelve- and thirteen-year-olds. They seemed to swagger, aping a young macho, as they loped into position, waiting for the whistle to blow and the ball to swing into play.

His mind focused more on the twins than on the progress of the game itself. Graceful, agile, their movements creating a trajectory of power far beyond appearances, they brought the spectators to their feet time and time again as they stole the ball from their opponents and crossed the field with remarkable speed until they were within range of the goal. The twins' team built up a quick four-goal lead, with one each for the twins.

Jack felt better. The other team was, indeed, larger, but less agile and skilled. Not that they didn't try. Nor were they averse to using their strength to sneak in some illegal action.

Occasionally, they instigated a spill or stuck a foot where it didn't belong. The hawk-eyed referee was quick to call foul, but Jack felt he was being too lenient. When one of the twins' teammates fell to the ground with the wind knocked out of him, Jack protested loudly.

"Put your glasses on referee," he shouted, triggering other protests from allies. The referee paid little attention. Partisan reaction from the stands was often misleading.

Whenever someone fell to the ground, especially when it occurred at the other end of the field from where they were sitting, and the player was in red and white, Jack's heart lurched to his mouth.

Even on the defensive, the twins were dazzling. With quick legwork, they often stole the ball from their opponents, passing it to other teammates as they positioned themselves for a shot at the goal. Jack could see the rising level of frustration of the opposing players, especially when one of the twins bested a player on the other team.

"They're having a great day," Jane said.

"Especially Billie," Jack said.

"How can you tell the difference?"

"Instinct," Jack laughed.

Indeed, Billie was having a field day. He knew

why. Like him, she was determined to put the lie to Madeline. Bobbie, on the other hand, was far more cautious, which obviously inhibited her from taking any reckless chances. Not that she wasn't also playing an outstanding game. But it was Billie who moved to the outer edges, sometimes putting herself directly in front of her opponents' charge as her legs moved to intercept the ball.

He'd have to talk to her at halftime, he told himself. No need for her to push so hard. He tried to frame the proper approach in his mind. Above all, he did not want to appear worried.

"They must be very happy," Jane said, turning to him suddenly. "And you, too."

"I feel unshackled," he said. "Cleansed."

"To deprive them of this would be sacrilege," Jane said.

"I'm going to fight this thing, Jane," Jack barked, "with all my strength. Just wait until I tell Ginny and that Gypsy fortune-teller."

When they came off the field at halftime, the twins' team was winning by three goals. Jack excused himself and rushed down to intercept them before they went into the locker room.

"You both were great," he said, embracing them. Their skin felt moist and cool.

"They're easy," Billie said.

"Big and clumsy, like we told you," Bobbie said.

"We'll just keep up the pressure," Billie said.

"Don't get overconfident," Jack warned, kissing them both on the head. "And don't take chances." He looked pointedly at Billie.

"Don't worry, Daddy," she said, pecking him on the cheek as they started to run under the stands. Bobbie stopped suddenly and jogged back.

"I sure wish Mommy was here," she said, her face screwed into a little girl's pout.

"Me, too, baby," he said, shrugging.

"You think maybe . . ." She hesitated, looked down, kicked her right foot into the dirt.

"I want to call her," he said, knowing exactly what she meant. "Tell you the truth, I'm afraid she'd do something stupid."

"Maybe if she saw us play, she'd see . . . feel better about it."

"Bobbie," Billie called, hands on hips, "the coach wants to talk with us."

"It'll all be fine, I know it will. Let's just get this under our belt."

Bobbie offered a half smile and loped off. He stood for a while watching after them, feeling sad. Of course he wanted to call Virginia. She needed to be here, needed to savor the joy of seeing the twins in action, heroines of the day. During other games, Virginia would hold his hand so tightly that he would feel acute pain. But he never let on, suffering through the painful squeeze until she eased up.

"Those are our kids out there," she would whisper. "We made them."

Damn, he thought, feeling all the sadness of loss as he climbed up the stands to where Jane waited.

"Go okay?" she asked. The question suggested that he was wearing a hangdog look.

"Bobbie would like to see Virginia here," he sighed.

"And she should be," Jane said. "This is a very perishable commodity."

It seemed a peculiar way to put it, but it made the point.

"But I'm glad you're here, Jane," Jack said. Her response was to tuck her arm under his. Cozying closer, she kissed his cheek.

"That's nice, Jack, real nice."

He had looked around furtively to see who had been watching. Apparently no one. He let her arm stay under his, although it struck him as awkward. *What the hell*, he told himself.

The players came out onto the field. The crowd stood up and cheered for both teams. Again the teams formed a cheering huddle and the first-string players ran out onto the field.

After the opening whistle, the game began again. It seemed to be proceeding faster than the first half. The coaches had given their half-time pep talks, particularly the coach of the losing team. They seemed resurrected, more aggressive, tougher.

Billie's performance, too, seemed different, juiced up. She seemed speedier, feet flying across the grass like a graceful bird as she maneuvered the ball forward on the offense. She was playing harder, more alone, grandstanding, doing less passing. Her legs seemed revved up as she coveted the ball, ignoring her sister's gesturing to pass.

At one point she stole a ball from one of the opponents, then danced it forward toward the goal and, once in position, struck the ball effortlessly. It sailed past the goalie and into the net. The audience rose to give her a standing ovation. This one-person performance, however dazzling, seemed strange. Bobbie obviously had expected to receive passes from her sister, fol-

lowing their usual strategy of cautious advance.

This was different. Billie seemed to be firing
the imagination of both sides and, whenever she
stole a ball, the audience stood up with expectation, watching in awe as she kicked and prodded the ball.

"Now that's talent," Jane said after Billie had
scored her third goal of the second half.

"She's pushing too hard," Jack said.

"You can see she loves it."

"I'd feel better if she slowed down."

At the beginning of the last period, the opposing team took the ball out. Tired but determined, they changed their strategy to contain
Billie. She had to contend with double-teaming,
two players keeping her guarded in an imagi-
nary box. But this left Bobbie loose to be the
aggressive one, her normal stance.

Like a real trooper she rose to the occasion,
stealing the ball and kicking it with the same
aggressive grace as Billie, scoring a goal with a
bullet kick that sailed right past the goalie.

After the hullabaloo occasioned by Bobbie's
goal died down, the opposing team seemed to
change tactics, become fiercer, more determined. Their coach, too, seemed to be goading
them on with inflammatory criticism. This
might have been only junior high school level
competition but it was as cutthroat as the
Super Bowl.

Jack looked over to the side where the parents and partisans of the opponents were sitting, scowling with disappointment. They were
mouthing some incessant cheer designed to encourage the team to greater effort.

Their rooting cheer was accompanied by an

ominous drumbeat of stamping feet. He imagined that the opposing team drew greater energy from the vibration that filled the stadium. They seemed to have acquired a, to him, worrisome sense of determination. As if to counterpoint his growing discomfort, the sun of what had been a glorious day faded, and the mist of an oncoming Pacific fog shaded the field.

He was suddenly fearful, filled with anxious expectation of impending disaster. His heartbeat accelerated. "No," he cried, standing up.

"What's wrong, Jack?" It was Jane's voice, coming from far away. He began to sweat. From the field a whistle screeched and he stood transfixed, unable to speak or move, watching the figures on the field. He saw his daughters, high-kicking does, graceful and confident as they sailed over the field, dark green now in the waning light.

No need for speed, he begged them, urging them in his heart to slow down. Their opponents had the ball, kicking it upfield toward the twins' team, husbanding the ball between them, passing short, moving cautiously. As point men, the twins advanced, two pincers closing on the oncoming players.

He looked nervously at the clock. Five minutes to go. No way for the other team to catch up. The game was nearly over, the championship won. Hold back, he silently urged. They would win on all counts, give the lie to Madeline, prove to Virginia that she had been brainwashed. The sense of imminent victory drowned out his brief bout with panic.

"Ouch." It was Jane, reminding him that her hand, which he was holding, was being heavily squeezed.

"Sorry," he said, relaxing his grip.

He saw his girls in time-stretching slow motion, the fans goading their aggression.

"Don't," he shouted through the bullhorn of his hands. A woman's face glared at him from the row ahead.

The girls advanced in tandem on the oncoming players. One of them shot forward. He couldn't tell which. Then, suddenly, one leg seemed entangled in those of an opponent and she began to pitch over. As he saw it, she seemed propelled forward, floating briefly in the air. At that moment, he saw a foot swing back, stop briefly as it completed the widest possible arcing motion, then move forward at full speed.

The kick caught her as she headed downward, her head meeting the foot at its upward journey. He was certain he heard the sound, a loud hollow thump that seemed to pass through his own body, vibrating inside of him.

He was screaming, but no sound came. It was as if all his vital organs had clogged in his throat. Seeing his daughter on the ground whipped him into movement. People made room for him as he dashed and stumbled down the stands, heading for the field.

Billie knelt over her supine sister, tears running down her cheeks. She fell into his arms as he arrived beside her. Bobbie was on her back unconscious, a trickle of blood running down the side of her head.

Reaching down, he tried lifting her in his arms.

"Please, baby. Please, baby."

"Don't," a voice said. It was vaguely familiar. Looking up he saw the coach. He had opened a first-aid kit, broken an ampoule and was hold-

ing it under Bobbie's nose. There was a brief
shudder, a reflexive attempt to awaken, then she
slipped back into the void.

In the distance, he heard an ambulance's si-
ren. He let Bobbie down gently and the coach
applied a pad to soak up her blood, pooling now
on the grass.

"What have I done?" he heard himself say.
"Please, God, forgive me."

Billie was shivering beside him, locked in the
crook of his arm. He was kneeling, holding his
unconscious daughter's arm as the coach continued to stanch the flow of blood. Time froze.
He was aware of a man in white pants and coat
nudging him away. He struggled to his feet, trying to absorb what was happening.

Overwhelming guilt assailed him. "Take me
instead, God," he whispered.

The man in white knelt over the body of his
child, listening with his stethoscope. Another
man in white joined him and they raised her
gently to a stretcher.

With Billie holding his hand, he followed the
stretcher as the men carried it off the field. As
they proceeded under the stands, Jane fell into
step with them. She touched his arm.

"Is there anything I can do?" she asked. He
shrugged off her arm, not answering, and quick-
ened his step. They proceeded quickly to the
ambulance parked at the curb, opened the rear
door and lifted the stretcher inside.

"Let me go with her," he shouted at the men.

"The father," someone said, making room for
him and Billie as they climbed into the ambulance. Bobbie was lying on the ambulance bed,
strapped in. One of the men in white fastened
an oxygen mask to her face and sat on a stool

beside the bed, motioning them to sit on the bed across from him.

"What is it?" he pleaded.

"A nasty kick. Very nasty."

"Will she be all right?"

"We'll try like hell," the doctor said, patting Jack's thigh. Billie whimpered quietly beside him. He looked down at her. Her eyes seemed glazed, her lips trembled. He heard the slam of the ambulance door.

The ambulance pulled away. He looked out of the rear window. The blood rushed to his head. Was that Madeline out there, watching? He blinked his eyes, trying to focus on the image, wanting confirmation. But the ambulance moved too quickly, sirens blaring.

No room for doubt now, he told himself, wondering what could be done to make it right, to make Bobbie recover.

"I'll do anything," he whispered as the ambulance gained speed. "Help me, Madeline."

·13·

Virginia watched Jack as he huddled across from her in a corner of the hospital waiting room, his face hidden behind his hands, his sobs shaking his body. Only when he removed his hands did she see his face, filled with agony and despair.

Next to Virginia, Billie's head lay on Madeline's lap. Madeline's hand brushed gently and soothingly on her forehead. Billie was sleeping, a troubled slumber. Occasionally she would awaken, open her eyes, shudder and burrow her head into Madeline's lap until she quieted, then slipped back to sleep.

Virginia, stunned and heartsick, groped for control over herself. The shock had been awesome. Madeline had come over and Virginia had been putting the finishing touches on the nude. By then, her depression at not being invited to go with Jack and the girls to Disneyland had been dissipated by Madeline's assurances.

"Look at the bright side, Virginia," Madeline had insisted. "Mickey Mouse won't hurt your children."

She had laughed at that. Once again, Madeline had lifted her spirits.

I just wish things around here would settle down to normal."

"They will," Madeline had assured her.

"When the telephone rang, she had looked at Madeline with some trepidation. Madeline's expression did not mirror her own fear. Nevertheless she had let it ring until its persistence was unbearable. She knew. Even in the dead air before she heard Jack's sob-ridden words, she knew.

"I'm so sorry, Ginny. So sorry," he said in a lurching, cracked voice. Then he could barely get another word out. She must have turned ashen. Certainly her knees had weakened and she had to lean against the wall for support.

"What is it?" Madeline had cried, coming out of her pose, putting on a robe.

Virginia had continued to hold onto the phone, and when the first wave of shock subsided, she put it to her ear again.

"You must forgive me," Jack said, clearing his throat, getting himself under tenuous control. Then he explained in short sputtering phrases what had occurred.

Through the pain of it, she felt a tremor of anger.

"You stupid bastard," she cried. Her voice and words were out of character. She exchanged glances with Madeline who said nothing, her expression offering no revelation of her thoughts. She remembered being puzzled by this neutrality. And frightened.

"I told you. I warned you. I begged you."

"Please, Ginny," Jack pleaded, "not now. Come quickly."

Madeline drove her to Cedars of Lebanon where they had taken Bobbie.

"He betrayed us," Virginia said.

Madeline looked straight ahead, saying nothing, maneuvering the car through the heavy Los Angeles traffic.

"I'll never forgive myself. I should never have believed him."

"You had no choice," Madeline said. "There was no stopping him."

Virginia had wanted to explore the matter further, but a desperate fear had intervened. She did not want to ask Madeline what lay in store for Bobbie, afraid that she would be shattered by the answer. Why didn't she volunteer what she surely knew? It was ominous. Hadn't Madeline promised to lead her through the mine fields?

"You said it would happen," Virginia whispered.

"Please," Madeline said, "not now."

Again Virginia repressed the question.

"Please let my little girl live," she said aloud, but not specifically addressing herself to Madeline. To whom, then?

Jack and Billie were in a small private waiting room just off the Emergency waiting room, their tearstained faces reflecting their pain. Jack had risen at her entrance and Billie had flown into her arms.

Holding Billie, she looked up at Jack. As if her look were a weapon, he collapsed in a heap on the chair.

"They're . . . they're working on her."

She felt little compassion for him. At that moment, he was irrelevant. Jack must have guessed her feelings. Instead he looked toward

Madeline, as if he were asking for compassion to come from that source.

Unable to wait helplessly, Virginia ran through the swinging door into the Emergency ward. Doctors and nurses scurried about. Patients were separated by white-sheeted screens. They paid little attention to her as she darted from one section to another looking for Bobbie.

She found her daughter surrounded by a phalanx of doctors and nurses. A bandage had been placed around her head. An oxygen mask covered her face. An IV had been placed in her arm. She was pale, ashen, a forlorn figure looking vulnerable and alone. Her eyes were closed.

"My baby," Virginia cried, moving between two white-coated doctors. Reaching out, she touched her daughter's hand, grasping it. "Mommy is here," she whispered. Bobbie's hand did not respond.

One of the doctors, a heavyset young man with red eyes, turned to face her.

"She's still unconscious," he said apologetically. "The good news is that the X rays show no fractures, but she took a heavy blow, I'm afraid."

"Will she be all right?" Virginia managed to ask. It was the question she had desperately wished to ask Madeline.

"I wish I could say," the doctor said.

It was not the response she had hoped for.

"She'll be transferred to a bed shortly," the doctor said. "Your husband has contacted your family doctor. A neurological specialist has been called in."

The doctor had spoken in a gentle reassuring tone, but the need for a neurologist had some awful implications. Paralysis, mental impair-

ment, or both. She turned toward Bobbie.
"Please, baby. Please get well."

After a while the doctors and nurses went off
to work on other patients. Alone with Bobbie,
she bent down and kissed her forehead, then
squeezed her hand. Was there a response? She
wasn't certain.

She stood over the child until an orderly came
to wheel her up to her room.

"You can come up in a minute," the orderly
told her. Seeing Bobbie being wheeled away
into the sterile-looking white corridor filled Virginia with dread.

But by the time she returned to the waiting
room, dread had turned to rage. Her husband
looked at her with red imploring eyes. Madeline
was seated across the room, Billie still sleeping
restlessly on her lap.

"She's still unconscious," Virginia said.
Again, she imagined that she was on a stage,
performing for an audience of one, Madeline. It
was as if, to save her child's life, she had to
provide Madeline with even more concrete evidence of her own belief and, equally important,
evidence of Jack's ultimate surrender. Was this
the proof that Madeline had talked about giving
Jack?

Of course Madeline had known all along that
this would happen. Hadn't she said, "You had
no choice. There was no stopping him?"

Why then, hadn't Madeline acted? In her own
wisdom, she must have chosen another path.
Virginia found something reassuring in that
thought. Madeline would not let anything happen to Bobbie. No way. Then why had she al-
lowed her to be hurt? An explanation began to

form in her mind. Bobbie's accident was meant to be Jack's revelation.

"Did they say she would be all right?" Jack asked. He was humbled, penitent.

"They didn't commit themselves."

"Dr. Gordon is coming. He's called in a specialist."

"I know," she said coldly.

He looked up at her from where he sat, nostrils quivering as he sucked in a deep breath.

"I should never have done this," he said, his voice cracking.

"You were warned," Virginia said.

His eyes flitted around the room. He looked toward Madeline, but did not meet her gaze.

"I . . . I couldn't bear their disappointment," he answered, obviously still groping within himself for justification. "How is it possible . . . ?" Again he looked toward Madeline. Still, he did not seem to get any response. He wouldn't, Virginia reasoned. Madeline was waiting for his acceptance of her gift, an acceptance that must be complete and total if Bobbie was to recover. There was the quid pro quo.

Virginia was absolutely certain of her mission now. *Save Bobbie*, she begged him in her heart. She said, "Isn't it clear by now that you cannot interfere with preordained events?"

"Look—" he began. Then he stopped abruptly, reflecting. "It was inconceivable to me . . ." Again he stopped. "There's no logic in it." His voice trailed off.

A tremor of panic vibrated through Virginia. Was it possible he was still not convinced?

"It's as simple as X equals Y," Virginia said. "You were told what would happen if the twins played. You defied that prediction. The result was as predicted."

He looked down at his hands as if some knowledge were sequestered there. He was obviously struggling, working toward a realization.

"You deliberately played with the lives of your children." Her tone was accusatory. She was conscious of her cruelty, of goading him.

"You know I didn't, Ginny. That's a very harsh judgment," he whispered. "Maybe it became an exercise in wish fulfillment. You know. If the idea is planted that something is going to happen, it has a better chance of happening than if the idea had not been planted at all."

"And that's your conclusion?"

Jack puffed out his cheeks as if he were gasping for breath. "I know you think I've betrayed you. And I did from your perspective. But you know I wouldn't deliberately put my children in the path of danger."

"I know that, but you wanted to prove Madeline wrong. That has been your objective from the beginning. To discredit her."

Still, Virginia resisted looking toward Madeline. That, she reasoned, would spoil everything. *Help me, Jack,* she begged. *Save our child.*

"All right," Jack cried, "I admit that was part of the motivation. But you know better than to attribute it all to that. The girls were brokenhearted."

"And you wanted to show them your fatherly concern?"

She knew she sounded like a prosecuting attorney. She was also convinced that this was the way Madeline wanted, needed her to proceed.

"All I know is that Bobbie's injury happened.
I saw the event. The other team was frustrated.
They started playing rough. . . ."

"And that came about logically?" she pressed.

"Well . . . in a way . . . I suppose. They were
being creamed. They were being pushed by the
crowd to do something, to get tough. They
were getting clobbered by our team. The girls
were humiliating them. First Billie . . . then
Bobbie was getting too aggressive for their
taste."

"But you knew in advance what would happen."

"Ginny." Her name was an entreaty. "I . . .
you know . . . I didn't believe it."

"And now?"

Shrugging, he looked at the ground. He was
obviously struggling with his entire value system. She did not pity him.

"I'm not sure," he said after a long pause.

"My God. Our child is lying upstairs half
dead." She felt a choking sensation and paused
to clear her throat. "If you hadn't taken her to
the game, she would not be in that hospital bed,
not be an unconscious lump of clay, not be
fighting for her life. . . ."

"Jesus, Ginny," Jack protested lamely.

"Would you defy Madeline again?"

She could see his eyes look helplessly toward
Madeline. This time, though, he received a
flicker of response.

"Would you?" she pressed.

His face puckered with agony. "No. No. I
wouldn't." He was obviously spent, slumping
farther in his chair.

"Haven't you enough proof by now?" she

asked firmly, feeling her strength forge back into her. She watched him agonize. He glanced again over her shoulder to where Madeline was sitting. As he looked in her direction, his face relaxed.

"Yes," he said, "I have enough proof."

·14·

They sat by Bobbie's bed throughout the night. Dr. Gordon, their family doctor, and the specialist arrived for their assessments and, after seeing the X rays, were cautiously optimistic, although the technical terms they used had little meaning to Jack's fogged brain.

As for Bobbie, she breathed more easily and, according to the nurses who cared for her, showed normal vital signs. Occasionally Virginia would whisper her name and implore her to awaken. For Jack her lack of reaction was wrenching and often he would dissolve in a paroxysm of sobbing and grief. Virginia, however, remained dry-eyed and stiff-backed as she sat in a straight chair on the other side of the bed.

"She'll be fine now," Virginia said, "I know she will."

There was no point in questioning her conviction. He had no desire to show her his doubt. Indeed, he had no illusions about how his admitting belief fitted into the scheme that had evolved between Virginia and Madeline. Somehow they had made his belief the linch-

pin of Bobbie's recovery. Now that he believed,
Virginia had obviously reasoned, Bobbie would
recover. It was simply a matter of time. Provi-
dence was holding back merely to make her recovery acceptable to reality and logic.

"I'm sure she will," he commented, although
he did feel slightly uncomfortable with his
freshly minted belief. It frightened him to know
that he had not been entirely truthful, that he
still harbored doubts.

Could someone, a being or a force, look inside
his mind and see the real truth, it would find
every ion of energy groping toward this resolution. *Believe! Save Bobbie.* Certainly his struggle to believe counted, his willingness to at least
agree to suspend logic and see Madeline as a
true messenger from the timeless void.

Fool, he berated himself. You have your
daughter's life in your hands. Believe, he prodded himself. Accept the evidence as conclusive.
I would gladly trade my life for my sweet, loving, beautiful daughter, he cried inside of himself, hoping that the mysterious, unseen being
or force would hear him. Take me instead, he
shouted in the cavern of himself. Make me suffer. Trade her suffering for mine.

Although he was guilt-stricken and contrite
and had admitted out loud that the mishap had
proved the validity of Madeline's predictions, it
was impossible, regardless of his willingness
and desire, to completely shut off his doubt.
Such a concept was against the grain of prac-
ticality and reason.

"She'll be fine," Virginia repeated, "I know
she will."

"Of course," he echoed.

"Now you see, don't you, Jack?"

"Absolutely," he nodded, denying his uncertainty. But Madeline will know, he told himself. Then he asked himself the question: Can she really? Which threw the concept once again into the pot of confusion. Believe, goddammit, believe, he begged himself. Wholeheartedly. Totally. Explicitly. Without question or doubt.

He remembered an incident in his early life that might be influencing his judgment. His family had been planning to rent a house in Stamford, an old Victorian structure on the edge of town, a step up. His father had had a brief, and short-lived, success.

He could not have been more than seven when he walked through the house for the first time. It had been the home of a widow who had died at the ripe old age of ninety-eight. The house had been owned by her father before her and her grandfather before that.

His mother, whose question-box mind was on occasion a source of exasperation to his father, had wondered aloud why a woman would want to live a life without changes, without the adventure of another environment. There was a bit of a needle in the remark since his father was a man addicted to change.

"Because," his father said with certainty. He was a man who rarely argued. His opinions were rather a series of decrees. "She prefers to live with her familiar ghosts instead of confronting a life with hostile strangers."

Retrieving this from his memory did not strike Jack as strange. He had been reviewing his life ever since his daughter had been injured. Despite his grief and guilt, he understood clearly that something monumental was happening, that he was being drawn into an idea of

the world other than the one to which he was
accustomed. He was, he supposed, searching for
guideposts, way stops, signs that might mark
the strange winding and mysterious path ahead.

His mind cast back again to that day when he
first walked through the old house with his parents. Coming back to him were the sounds and
smells of that experience. Creaks, mustiness,
echoes. His heartbeat rang in his ears. He clung
to his mother's hand as they roamed the dusty
interiors. When a closet was opened, he hung
back, certain that from its black interior one of
the old lady's familiar ghosts would pop out and
shoo them away, shouting curses that would ex-
ile him to everlasting purgatory.

The gut-curdling horror of that day returned.
As it had then, perspiration crawled down his
back. A blind all-enveloping fear had possessed
him. He remembered hanging back, refusing to
ascend the stairs while his mother dragged and
pleaded.

"Now this is silly, Jack," she had cried.

His father, he remembered, was calling them
from two floors up.

"Please, Mama," Jack had begged her. "The
ghosts . . ." He was too frightened to expand on
the theme.

"Ghosts!" his mother had cried. She yelled up
at his father. "Jack thinks there are ghosts upstairs."

"There are," his father shouted. Even now he
heard his father's sharp creaking footsteps as
they descended the stairs, coming toward him.
His face was twisted into an expression of ma-
levolent humor. Roughly, he scooped Jack up
and held him against his chest. Jack clung to
his father's neck and shoulders as he walked up

the stairs to what in his mind was a hostile
ghostly lair.

"Let's chase the damn things," his father had
said, walking through every room, his mother
in tow. Before entering each room, his father
shouted in a booming voice, "Ghosts get out.
We want no ghosts in this house. Scram." He
opened closets, banged on walls, stamped his
feet. "Out, you miserable toads. We will have
no ghosts in here. None. Not as long as we are
in this house. Out. Out."

He remembered looking at his mother, whose
face wore the expression of an amused and con-
spiring ally.

"Listen," his father had said, stopping suddenly.

Jack's ears pricked to attention. Had he heard
something?

"Hear that flapping? They're going, the whole
lot of them. Haunt some other house, fellas,"
his father shouted. "And don't ever come back."

That said, his father put him down. Jack was
greatly relieved and accompanied his parents
on the rest of the tour without any fear. Not
once since then had he ever contemplated the
possibility of an unseen world.

Until now.

At three in the morning, the head night nurse
came in and urged that one of them go home
and get some rest.

"You may be called on to make judgments
that require at least one clear head," she told
them. He had begun to protest.

"You go, Jack. I'll stay until she comes to,"
Virginia said, again with dry-eyed certainty.
Madeline had already taken Billie home to their
house. That had generated a flash of repressed

anger in him but he had held his peace, berating himself for his continued doubts.

"Really," the head nurse said gently. "I've been through this before. It's hard enough to be clearheaded . . ." She looked toward Bobbie, then checked her IV, temperature and blood pressure.

"You must, Jack," Virginia said. Remembering what his last rebellion had wrought, he finally left, first bending over the bed and kissing his daughter, whispering in her ear.

"We're waiting for you, Bobbie. Hurry," he said. His eyes filled with tears and a sob lashed his body.

Home seemed strange, a foreign place. His million-dollar house, he thought bitterly, observing all the furnishings and decorations that had been put into it. At that moment he would gladly have given it all away if it would save his daughter.

He looked into the twins' room. Billie lay in bed, an exact replica of the unconscious Bobbie. Panicked, he rushed to her and shook her. She stirred, but lightly. His heart pounded in fear.

"She's had a sedative."

He turned quickly, startled. Madeline stood in a corner of the room wearing a yellow dressing gown of Virginia's. In the darkened room, she could easily be mistaken for an apparition, ethereal. It crossed his mind that she had contrived this effect.

"Thank you," he said politely, kissing his daughter, then leaving the room.

He roamed through the house. Finally he sat down in the den, staring blankly through the

windows at the pinpoints of light that blinked
in the slumbering city.

"I'm sorry about this." Madeline walked into
the room. He wished she would leave him alone,
but he dared not show his annoyance.

"So am I," he said flatly.

"I wanted to stop you," she said.

He was momentarily confused.

"I knew what you intended," she continued.
Her tone, he noted, had a benign neutrality
about it. She sat down on an upholstered chair
a few feet away from him, her dressing gown
primly gathered around her crossed legs.

He searched his mind for some response. Her
eyes seemed to capture all the beams of the
quickening light. "You probably couldn't have
stopped me," he sighed. "I was determined."

"I know."

"So I'm to blame," he said with resignation.

"I suppose," she said. "But it will come out
all right I promise you."

It was an assurance meant to relieve him, but
it didn't.

"How can you . . ." He paused. In the sparse
light, she looked like a young girl. Grudgingly,
he admitted her beauty, remembering how
sensually moved he had been earlier by one of
Virginia's pictures.

"I'm merely a conduit," she said, as if anticipating his question. "I don't know why or how.
All I know is that it happens." She shook her
head. "I also know that it's very hard for a non-
believer to understand."

Until then he had been fatigued by the trying
events of the day. Now he felt suddenly ener-
gized, as if her remarks had jolted his adrenaline. He stood up and began to pace the room.

"I'll believe anything if my daughter comes out of this all right," he said. He stopped abruptly and turned to her. "Why is it so important that I be a believer?"

"Because not believing is disruptive to the family," she said without delay. "Virginia needs you to believe. The children need that. Virginia and I have forged a bond of friendship, of trust. A family, you see, is a circle." She drew a circle in the air. "To be complete it must be closed. A man, a woman and children must believe together. It's impossible to have a true friendship with only one member of a family. Not a true one."

Her argument confused him. She was implying something he could not quite grasp. But she pressed on.

"Jack, we need you," she said softly.

"We?"

"Don't you see?"

He didn't.

She sighed. Then a brief frown of what he imagined was frustration crossed her brow. It frightened him. Was he upsetting her?

"I'm trying to understand," he said softly.

"For some reason, I have been guided toward all of you. I've learned never to question these magnetic forces that draw me to people. They happen. I feel the pull, obey it. In this field, my gifts sharpen, become clearer. I see things in perfect focus, back and forth in time. It cannot be explained rationally. Something drew me to Virginia, then through her to you and the children. I know your past and your future. I'm a part of all of you now."

He averted his eyes to keep her from seeing his confusion.

"Are you saying you've been sent to us?"

"Yes," she whispered.

He felt a chilling sensation. By whom? he wanted to ask. He held back, fearful. Did he want to know more? He felt very much alone, trapped, vulnerable.

"All of this is not in the realm of my experience," he said apologetically.

"It is now," she said.

A vision flashed in his mind. His child. Bobbie lying somewhere in a dark void, struggling to come home.

Madeline had been sitting across from him. Now she moved and sat down beside him on the couch, with enough distance for propriety.

Despite his mental state, he could not dismiss the magnetism of her sensuality. All his senses seemed heightened by her proximity.

"It's hard to get out there on another plane," he said.

"I've had to contend with that all my life," she replied.

Who was she? he wondered. What was her history? He had, during his abortive investigation, concluded that she was a mere fortune-teller, a glorified racetrack tout, a psychofraud, a phony. He had been wrong, he told himself now, afraid that she might be listening to his thoughts.

"Madeline . . ." he said, pausing. Surely there was some logic, a continuum to all this. Still, he was afraid of appearing cynical. He cleared his throat. "What is your life like?" He was fumbling, clumsy. "Is it unfair to ask about you?"

"I have nothing to hide," she said with a smile.

"I didn't suggest that. But you can understand that I want to know."

"For the record?" She smiled.

"A history is important. You must know all about us."

"Yes, I do."

"But you're . . ." He swallowed hard. "You're psychic. You can . . . fathom."

"I'm also a human being," she said, "with a history."

"You don't have to reveal . . ."

"Not at all," she said pleasantly, turning her eyes to the view from the window. It was growing lighter. He was beginning to feel fatigue, but she seemed fresh, rested, relaxed. It puzzled him. From what mysterious source did she derive such energy? His gaze washed over her. Even in his drained and disordered state, he could not deny a compelling attraction.

"But how important is it?" she asked. He became aware of the dressing gown opening, slipping aside to reveal a well-turned calf.

"I'm not sure," he answered honestly. "Perhaps to give me a frame of reference. Let's face it, Madeline, you've been exposed to this family for how long . . . three months? You've seen your impact on us. Just look what's happened."

"Believe me, Jack, I don't cause events, I only see them before they happen." She was watching him and once again he sensed the intensity and turned away. "I see your lives, your futures. I see the pitfalls ahead. I know how to avoid them."

He thought of poor Bobbie and his heart seemed about to burst.

"Did you know?" he asked.

She nodded. He felt his courage wane.

"Will my little girl really get better?" He felt like a small boy asking his mother for some assurance. Will it rain, Mama? When will it rain? How long will it rain? He forced himself from the couch and walked to the window. A sliver of pink dawn could be seen just above the far mountains.

"Yes, Bobbie will get better," she said.

"Are you sure?"

"Yes," she said again, "I promise you."

"When?"

"Soon."

He came back toward the couch, sat down beside her. Lifting her hand, he took it in both of his.

"Make her well, Madeline. I'll give you my life."

With her other hand, she brushed his forehead.

"You won't owe me anything. I told you. I can't make things happen."

It defied all logic, all reason. It was incomprehensible. But if his little girl awakened, became whole, he promised himself that that would be proof positive. He would never again doubt. He would join Virginia in her belief and the family would become well again.

Madeline gathered him in her arms and patted his head. He felt himself letting go, falling, floating in space.

"I've been sent to help you, Jack. All of you."

Then consciousness disappeared.

When he awoke, he was lying on the couch. Someone had covered him. The sun had risen and he squinted into the brightness.

"Daddy."

It was Billie's voice, speaking softly in his ear,

patting him gently on the chest. It took him some time to become aware of his surroundings. His sleep had been deep and dreamless.

"Bobbie," he cried, sitting up suddenly.

"She's okay, Daddy. Mommy called. Bobbie's not unconscious anymore. I spoke to her. She sounds fine."

"Thank God," he said drawing her to him, kissing her head. "Thank God."

"And Madeline," she whispered, "and Madeline."

He felt a brief stab of anger, then remembering, he puzzled over the idea. "I don't make things happen," she had told him. Over Billie's shoulder, he saw Madeline's silhouette. Her presence loomed large, a huge shadow.

"Now she has all of us," he thought, not certain whether or not he said the words aloud.

15

"**E**verything happens for the best."

They were Virginia's mother's words, recycled now for the benefit of her own daughters. They were in the kitchen preparing for Thanksgiving dinner. The twins were making the stuffing. Virginia was seasoning the turkey and Madeline was spreading the premade shell with pumpkin pie filling. Maria, the maid, was doing the grunt work, peeling potatoes, opening the pea pods, and keeping an eye out for the errant pot or plate that needed cleaning.

Virginia was thinking now of her mother without guilt or remorse. Madeline had made her realize that her mother's death from cancer was inevitable. One should never carry the blame for the inevitable, she had instructed. Heading west had been the most important decision of her life. If they hadn't they would not have met Madeline. That, too, was inevitable, Madeline insisted. They had been drawn together by an unseen hand.

Despite Madeline's denials, Virginia knew that in some mysterious way Madeline had,

through her extraordinary gifts, saved Bobbie's
life. Her trial had been necessary for Jack's
"conversion."

Now, only three weeks later, life had righted
itself. Naturally, it would take a little time for
Jack to get rid of his awkwardness, but Virginia
was doing everything in her power to put him
at ease. Once again, they were making love,
playing their secret little erotic games to
heighten their pleasure and reinforce their
trust.

Remembering last night's episode put a hot
blush on her cheeks. They had made love in the
bathtub, an anatomical convolution more hu-
morous than erotic, but pleasurable in an off-
beat way. This "postconversion" sexual reunion
seemed to have more intensity, more abandon,
than she could remember. She attributed part
of that to their previous deprivation. They were
just catching up.

She recognized, too, that it was not sex alone
that made their relationship so joyous. There
was also a greater sense of "lovingness" between them. In bed, even in repose, they clung
together, two necessary parts of the whole, as
if the first romantic flush of their life together
had bloomed again with even greater force.

Even her relationship with her children
seemed more loving. They embraced more,
touched more, kissed more. The children
seemed to be reaching out for affection, an affection that was eagerly returned.

And, of course, there was Madeline's presence. She was like a visiting sunbeam, a ray of
brightness that warmed everyone. Virginia had
no doubt that it was her proximity, her aura,
that pervaded them and gave them this marvel-

ous sense of joyousness. Madeline was for them,
for all of them, the center of the universe.

Madeline had consented to stay in the guest
room until Bobbie fully recovered.

Among the chorus of gratitude, Jack had been
the loudest. It was the one measure of consent
that Virginia had yearned for most of all. There
was, on her part, a brief trill of concern. She
did not wish to impose on Madeline, nor interfere with her life outside of the Sargent family.

"I just don't want you to feel that we're mo-
nopolizing you," she had said to Madeline.

"Not at all," Madeline responded. "I frankly
thought it might be the other way around."

"Never," Virginia said with great emotion. Indeed, in her heart, she wished that Madeline
would be with them forever.

"Please stay longer," Bobbie had begged Madeline.

"You're better. No need for me to stay on."

"Yes, there is," Bobbie asserted.

"Pleeze," Billie had echoed.

"Well, then," Madeline said after a long
pause, "just until Thanksgiving Day."

"Wonderful," Virginia had cried as they embraced each other. It was only then that Virginia remembered the family's plans for
Thanksgiving.

Al Conway, Jack's boss, had made a special
point nearly six months before of inviting them
for Thanksgiving dinner at his house. His wife
Betsy had mentioned it frequently during various office-sponsored "command performance"
social functions.

"We'll show you a real California Thanksgiving," Conway had said repetitively. Obviously,
an invitation to the Conways' traditional sit-

down dinner for fifty in the grand ballroom of their San Marino estate was a company plum, a sure sign to an employee that he had been cut from the rabble and was destined for "big things."

"And I'll leave just before you go the Conways," Madeline had told her.

"You see," Virginia pointed out to the children, "Madeline knows everything."

What pleased Virginia most, in the time that Madeline stayed with them, was the way in which Madeline fit in with the family. She seemed always there, assisting with the children, sharing domestic chores, participating in their family discussions, taking an interest in Jack's work. Not once during her stay had Jack showed any signs of irritation with the arrangement.

At times, Madeline would leave the house. They assumed she had clients to see or that she was going back to her Santa Monica apartment to replenish her clothes. Always, she was beautifully groomed. Her clothes were impeccable, cut in elegant simplicity and immaculately cared for. More important, clothes just looked good on Madeline.

And why not? Her body deserved beautiful clothes. The memory of their particular closeness on that traumatic day always warmed Virginia. Sometimes the memory would flash in her mind while she was making love to Jack. She had no sense of impropriety about it. They had not, after all, made lesbian love in the traditional sense. It had been an expression of an instinctive need, perhaps something dragged from the mud of her own prehistoric experience. Or simply a manifestation of natural sisterly affection.

Most of all, Jack's acceptance of Madeline seemed total. Seeing it happen was enormously satisfying. He had even taken an interest in her pictures, spending a great deal of time studying them.

"They're wonderful, Ginny," he told her. She could detect heightened emotion in him as he silently contemplated them.

On one occasion while he helped her take Polaroids of the pictures, he suddenly grew amorous. She welcomed these little surprises, the only obstacle being the potential interruption by the twins. In this case his sexual urgency was acute. It quickly triggered her own response.

She had been standing in front of the large nude that had been the last picture in the series, Polaroid camera in hand. He came up behind her and began to fondle her breasts, his penis already hard and ready.

She put down her camera, but did not move from where she stood as he rolled down her slacks and panties and guided her into position. Open, vulnerable and exposed, leaning forward, hands braced against the easel, she eagerly accepted him as he took her standing up behind her. It was deliciously animal, basic, down and dirty.

She had turned her head, wanting to see his face, to show him her pleasure and enthusiasm. His gaze drifted from her face upward to Madeline's nude likeness. Then, as if the portrait provided further stimulation, he had begun a shuddering orgasm. It transfused her with a profound and explosive rippling pleasure that drew more energy into her body than she had ever before experienced.

She, too, had looked up at the painting, grateful beyond measure for the sharing that was implicit in the viewing. Perhaps, through the picture, Madeline had sent them a gift.

There was a special poignancy that underlined preparations for the Thanksgiving dinner. Madeline's two suitcases were open on top of the bed in the guest room. Billie and Bobbie had been especially vocal in their entreaties to Madeline not to leave.

"She has things to do," Virginia admonished, although she stood with the twins in their desire to keep Madeline from leaving. Nor did she wish to extend an invitation without Jack's consent. Poor guy, she thought, remembering another potential confrontation two days before. They had weathered that one with surprising equanimity but it had been a tough pill for him to swallow.

They had been sitting in the den, having white wine before dinner. The conversation had been light and pleasant when suddenly, out of the blue, Madeline announced:

"I don't think you should go to the Conways for Thanksgiving dinner."

She had glanced toward Jack, whose forehead puckered in puzzlement.

"Not go?" he asked, looking at Virginia. "Conway would take it as a personal affront."

"I know," Madeline said.

"I can't not go."

Virginia offered neither solace nor consent. It was for him to decide. For her there could now be no question of attending the Conway dinner.

"Thanksgiving is a special time for a loving family," Madeline had explained, "a time to find the frequency of each other's karma once again. We must never take it for granted. Karma must be nurtured, re-created, tuned in again and again. A Thanksgiving dinner is a ritual of such re-creation. It must not be wasted on vanity or business considerations."

How superbly she explained things, Virginia had thought, suffusing them with an importance that could so easily be overlooked.

"Is that reason enough, Madeline?" Jack asked. "How can I tell the man on two days' notice?"

"We'll think of something," Madeline said, as if it were a fait accompli.

Madeline sat cross-legged, her body tilted in a relaxed, almost languorous posture, on a high-backed chair at the opposite end of the cocktail table. Jack and Virginia sat side by side on the couch.

"Any suggestion you have, Madeline, is welcomed by us," Virginia said, noting Jack's confusion. She took his hand and brought it up to her lips. Displaying affection, especially in Madeline's presence, was another of their recent transformations. It pleased her when Jack was also affectionate with Madeline, cheek-kissing her in greeting and departure, holding hands with both of them on occasion. But then, Madeline was naturally affectionate and her attitude seemed to encourage other people to return the warmth.

"I wish I could comply," Jack said, but his protest was very tentative.

"You must," Madeline pressed. She sipped

her wine. Her gaze became intense, suggesting that her mind was in high concentration.

"His wife Betsy is a Colonial Dame," Jack argued. "The event, they tell me, is designed to call attention to that fact. It's her grand moment and beware any family that's a no-show."

"I know. It's awfully rude, dangerously so, but you cannot go," Madeline said.

Jack shot a quick glance at Virginia who turned away. Above all, she did not want a return to their previous conflict. If Madeline had suggested that they not go, she had, as they had learned, profound and fundamental reasons. Jack quite obviously was still troubled by such commands.

"Listen, Madeline, you know I respect your . . . your visions, but I do have to earn a living," Jack said.

"Do you trust me?"

Jack looked at his wife. "May I at least ask why?" he said, already on the edge of surrender.

"Don't grope for logic, Jack. This is a premonition that directly coincides with your chart. There's something subtle here that could have dire effects on your future."

"Can you explain that further?" Jack had asked. He had glanced again at Virginia, but his look had softened even further. He was obviously upset but had backed off from an argument. How wonderfully obedient he had become to Madeline's caveats. Such a far cry from only a few short weeks ago.

"As you know, I told Virginia some time ago that you would, in the near future, form your own firm. To do that you will have to staff it with some of your present colleagues. I don't want to see you endanger a rapport that you will need in order to persuade them to join you."

"But how . . ."

"Jack," Virginia said, squeezing his hand, "listen to her."

"I am," he said hesitantly.

It was, she thought, so difficult for him to abide by this new acceptance. Old habits die hard.

He shook his head. "I just don't understand how all this will come about."

"But it will," Virginia said. "It's inevitable." She looked toward Madeline.

"As inevitable as the equinox of the moon," Madeline said. "In fact, it's the position of the moon that confirms what I have suspected and what my precognition demands."

She studied Jack for any sign of doubt. His eyes were querulous. He was still not letting himself go completely, but his consent, she was certain, was on its way.

"What can I tell him?" he asked.

"Something credible," Madeline said. "We don't want to give Conway cause for suspicion about your future plans. Time enough for that."

"I wish I knew what was coming down," Jack said.

"You'll know," Madeline said with a smile, then finished her wine.

"So we'll have a real family-only Thanksgiving," Virginia said. She squeezed Jack's hand. "For our one and only man." She looked up at Madeline. "Do you think we're spoiling him?"

"Yes," Madeline agreed.

"You make me sound like a pet rock," Jack said.

At that moment the twins came out of their room where they had been watching television. Bobbie, although slightly thinner from her ordeal, looked fully recovered. The color had come back into her cheeks.

"I'm hungry, you guys," she said, taking Madeline's hand. Billie took the other.

The adults finished their wine and stood up.

"One thing, though," Madeline said. She paused for a moment as she studied each of their faces. "We must wear orange on Thanksgiving Day."

"Orange?" Jack asked.

"The color of validation. We must show it on ourselves. All of us."

Virginia fought off any confusion. One must never question Madeline's wishes, she told herself. Orange she wants. Orange it will be.

16

"**O**range," Jane snickered when he told her about it.

"The color of validation," he explained.

"What the hell does that mean?"

"Validation?"

"No. Orange." She sighed in exasperation. He had been telling her about what he called his "transformation" from its inception, when he had finally and fully accepted Madeline's ability as a clairvoyant.

Naturally, Jane had rejected his surrender as "incomprehensible." After all, she had witnessed his determination to rid Virginia of her obsession with and belief in Madeline Boswell's special powers. Now, as she observed his obsession, she surely believed that he had been "inveigled, hooked or brainwashed" into a cult experience.

"You saw what happened when I defied her," he pointed out. He felt a strong desire to convince her to believe. How else could she possibly understand?

"I saw your child injured, yes."

"You know that Madeline had warned us, had absolutely forbidden us to have the twins play. Is there anything more convincing than that?"

"She . . . she recovered," Jane argued. Like him, she tended to be a pragmatist, trusting nothing but the laws of logic and her five senses.

"She was made to recover," Jack insisted.

"The injury was an accident," Jane said firmly, "and the recovery was a natural phenomenon."

"There are no accidents," he said firmly.

"Freud or Madeline?"

"Both. . . . There is more to the universe than what we see," he said pontifically.

"And maybe a lot more than Madeline sees," she said.

"Jane. Jane. Jane," he sighed. "You know me well enough to realize that I'm not easily taken in. I'm a natural-born skeptic. But in Madeline's case, I've become a believer. It's changed my life. With Virginia, too."

"Got some zip back into the old marriage bed?" Jane sneered.

"In a manner of speaking."

He could see that she was not prepared to agree with him. Nor was she prepared to hear about the improvement in his married life.

"Your rhapsody is making me nauseous," she told him. "So you're ecstatic. Big deal."

Despite her annoyance, he felt compelled to continue. "She's been with us three weeks now and it's been great."

"I can tell."

"I've never been happier. She's rather pleasant to have around," Jack said.

"A regular ménage à trois," Jane responded with bitchiness.

"Purely platonic." Jack was defensive. Having Madeline around provided a charge, a surge of energy. But he also remembered the sexual episode with Virginia in the studio, when he was turned on by the nude pictures of Madeline.

Jane shook her head. "Sounds bananas to me. And this thing with turning down Conway's bash. Around here that's like turning a knife in your own gut."

Jack had entered Conway's office an hour earlier, filled with trepidation. It wasn't a question of being fired. He could always move his most loyal accounts to another firm. But Conway still held the key to the grab bag of perks the company offered for fealty: titles, position and authority. And brownnosing the boss was an accepted process to acquire such rewards. He had always been a good player in the stroking game.

However, once in the door, confronting Conway, who was an unprepossessing son of a bitch who had got his leg up from an uncle who was chairman of the board, Jack lost all desire to scale the corporate heights. It was a revelation and he knew Madeline had something to do with it. He didn't have to brownnose anymore. Madeline had set him free from such demeaning acts. He was going to start his own company, be his own boss, the brownnose-ee, not the brownnose-or.

Until the possibility had been raised by Madeline, he had not been conscious of its real priority in his life. It was a dream that even transcended the acquisition of wealth. The real golden enchilada was power. When he entered Conway's office it had occurred to him that that was his true goal. Madeline knew. Madeline had shown him the way.

"We can't make it tomorrow, Al," he had said. No excuses. No beating around the bush. No made-up stories. He watched Conway fight to mask his dismay. This is a command performance, his expression said. Jack saw the death knell of his future with this company and was happily unmoved.

"We'll miss you and the family, Jack," Conway said. "Betty will be upset."

At that point, Jack offered a sop to politeness. "Maybe next year."

It was, he knew then, a delicious lie. By next year, he might be using the holiday to exhibit his own family pride, perhaps a display of Virginia's soon-to-be famous paintings or some newly acquired skills of his two beautiful girls.

Leaving Conway's office, he had felt wonderful. *Nice to have a psychic around the house*, he thought gratefully.

When he told Jane about his meeting with Conway, she looked at him archly.

"You, my friend, are fucking yourself up. Your brain cells are getting tangled."

He bore the ridicule with patience. No point in arguing. There was no way to convince her. Faith was never easy to inspire in others.

"Madeline believes that I'm on the verge of opening up my own investment firm," he said.

"You're talking big bread, really big bread. Is that going to drop from the sky?"

"Maybe."

"She's playing with your head," Jane said. She paused and stroked her chin. "Or she could be ready to throw you some hot stocks," Jane snickered. "But then, if she knew any, she wouldn't be living on your dole."

"She's not on my dole. She's a guest."

"However you put it," Jane said.

It occurred to Jack that Jane might be right, that the money to set up his firm was to come from one or more spectacular stock transactions. "Hell, there *is* logic in such a possibility."

Jane grew thoughtful. The idea obviously intrigued her. "Unless your wife is about to hit it big," she said. Always, when she spoke about Virginia, a hint of maliciousness crept into her tone.

"Maybe," he said. "Her work lately is awfully good."

"You mean dear old Madeline from all angles. I thought you once thought it was shit."

"I see it differently now."

"You see everything differently." She paused, studied him.

Jack knew she was referring to the change in their relationship. He saw her now only as a good friend, a confidante. In a way, she represented how he had once thought, a mind-set far afield of his present way of looking at life.

Madeline, he admitted joyously, was at the heart of this new life. Virginia, he and the children warmed themselves on her hearth. She was the great earth mother enveloping them in her love, protecting them from the evils of the world, guiding them. With his belief in Madeline had come an enormous sense of peace. Tension had disappeared, had faded. In its place had come courage, security, love.

"Listen," Jane said, patting his thigh. He came out of the haze of his thoughts. "If a fortune-

teller told me how good things were going to
be, I'd follow her anywhere."

"It's not the same as that connotation implies," he said, irritated but not angry. Indeed,
he thought, he hadn't been angry for days. "She
proved it to me."

Jane shrugged in frustration.

"No point in pursuing this," she sighed.

"What would it take to convince you?" he
said.

"Are you trying to convert me, Jack?"

There was some truth to this. He did not like
feeling alone, way out on a limb, reinventing
the wheel in explanation. He hadn't been told
by Madeline to spread the word, yet he wanted
Jane to believe. He saw their friendship fading
away if she didn't. He would be shoved aside.
Jack the eccentric fool. He would be shunned.

"I just want us to stay friends."

"Whatever for?"

He wondered if, despite his capitulation to
Madeline, he still harbored a residue of doubt.
Jane was his link with the old values. If he could
win her over would that prove that his path was
well chosen?

"You may be right," he heard himself say.
"Maybe she is about to give me some hot
stocks."

"That would make a believer out of me," she
said, offering a mock punch to his jaw. "Like
you, I'd follow her anywhere."

17

Madeline wore an orange silk slacks suit. Virginia had taken the twins shopping at Bullock's and found two identical orange dresses for them and, for herself a long flowing orange skirt. She accessorized it with an orange scarf and touches of orange eye shadow. Jack wore an orange tie and matching handkerchief in his jacket pocket.

They sat at the dining room table where, as a centerpiece, Virginia had filled a turkey-shaped ceramic bowl with a mound of mandarin oranges. It rested on a bed of ferns.

Basil, dressed for the occasion—the girls had put an orange ribbon around his neck tied in an elaborate bow—sprawled on the floor next to Jack waiting for his Thanksgiving scraps. Even the two men in the house seemed to be getting along, Virginia thought with a smile.

"Could it be any more perfect?" Virginia said as Maria placed the well-browned aromatic turkey in front of Jack.

Jack rose and brandished the carving tools. "And now for the ritual dismemberment," he said, slipping the knife into the turkey's shoulder blade.

"Don't you just love this part?" Virginia said.

"Everything about it," Madeline agreed. "We've calmed all disruptive forces. We must always keep them at bay."

"I've never felt such peace and fulfillment," Virginia said, happy to see Jack nod his approval as he doled out the turkey portions. Virginia completed the offering by scooping out the stuffing while Maria brought out plates of brussels sprouts and cranberry sauce.

"Now, Mommy?" Bobbie asked.

Virginia nodded.

Bobbie lowered her head and placed her hands in front of her in an attitude of prayer. She closed her eyes.

"We thank thee, O Lord, for the gift of your bounty and especially for bringing us Aunt Madeline who we all love with our hearts and souls. And most of all, O Lord, I thank you for letting Aunt Madeline save my life."

"Isn't that beautiful?" Virginia said.

Madeline's eyes had grown moist. "I think," she said, "that you might be giving me more credit than I deserve." She smiled. "My greatest joy is in knowing how well things are to be for all of you. I knew that you would get well, Bobbie just as I know that your mother's career as an artist will be spectacular as will your father's new business when it comes about. And I know something else. . . ."

She paused and her eyes moved slowly from person to person.

"You, Bobbie will have a set of twins of your own. Two beautiful girls just like you. Imagine that."

"Really, Aunt Madeline? And what about Billie?"

"Billie will not have twins," Madeline said. "She's going to have . . ."

"Not triplets?" Billie giggled.

"Three boys."

"I hate boys," she said, disappointed.

"You won't hate yours," Madeline said. "In just a few months you may get to really like them as a gender."

Billie made a face. "The only boys I like are the ones we beat in soccer," she said.

"Have you noticed something interesting?" Madeline asked. They looked around in puzzlement. Madeline waited, then spoke, a touch of solemnity in her voice. "Five. The number five. We're sitting here as five. You will have five children between you. This is a most important number for this family. I was born with five veils, a true sign of one chosen. It's the ultimate symbol of the gift of seeing. As a matter of fact, at any given moment in time, there are only five of us on earth."

A shiver of pleasure vibrated down Virginia's spine. She felt privileged to have Madeline as a friend, fortunate that her presence made them five. She lifted her glass of white wine.

"*Bravo* to you, Madeline," she said. "We are so grateful."

"I'll drink to that," Jack said lifting his glass. The twins lifted their water glasses.

"I've always wanted this. To be part of a family, a special loving family. You can't imagine how wonderful it is for me. . . ." She stopped abruptly, although Virginia, and surely the others as well, had expected her to continue. When she didn't, Billie asked:

"Were you an orphan, Aunt Madeline?"

She smiled benignly. "An orphan?" She paused again, then said, "You might say that."

It was a small revelation, and to Virginia it bespoke an early unhappiness. Of course, she wanted to learn more, but at the moment it was enough to know that she was filling a void in Madeline's life.

Jack, who a few weeks ago would have pressed Madeline with aggressive curiosity, was happily silent, chewing on a turkey bone and feeding bits to Basil who had now found a place under the table.

Billie started to ask more, but Virginia stopped her with a look of subtle rebuke.

"Isn't this turkey marvelous?" Jack said with a quick glance at Virginia, showing her that he agreed with her tactics.

Virginia decided that it was the right moment for what she had in mind. "Is it so necessary for you to leave today, Madeline?"

Madeline looked up and sighed. "I'm afraid I've overstayed my welcome," she said.

Virginia looked at Jack who nodded. "We'd like you to stay. Both of us."

"Can you, Aunt Madeline?" Bobbie begged.

"Can you?" Billie echoed.

Madeline smiled and put down her fork. "Really . . . I'm overwhelmed," she said.

"Now, that's not a proper answer," Virginia said.

"I . . . I don't know what to say. I don't want to be disruptive."

"You disruptive? Really, Madeline," Virginia said. "We're asking you to be part of our family."

"You can't imagine how that makes me feel."

"I hope good," Jack said.

"Very, very good," Madeline said.

"Then you will?" Virginia pressed.

"I have my own place. I . . . you might want to use your guest room for legitimate guests."

"You're the only legitimate guest we want," Virginia said, flashing Jack a wink.

"You can keep your apartment for meeting with clients. Go to work every day like me if you like," Jack said.

Madeline became pensive. Her eyes glazed over. "I'm not sure," she said with an air of finality. It was a signal to stop pressing her.

Virginia changed the subject, directing it to the twins' upcoming roles in the school Christmas play and Maria served the pumpkin pie.

Throughout all the chattering and chirping as the twins described their roles in what seemed like a highly creative version of Dickens's *A Christmas Carol*, Virginia observed Madeline's expression. The girls were both playing ghosts, Billie, the Ghost of Christmas Past, and Bobbie, the Ghost of Christmas Present.

Suddenly, Madeline, without a word, left the table.

"What is it, Mommy?" Bobbie asked.

"Maybe we pressed her too hard," Jack said.

Billie got up from the table, disappeared, then quickly returned.

"She's on the terrace looking at the sky," Billie reported.

"We must allow Madeline these moments," Virginia said. Madeline often disengaged herself. Sometimes it would happen while she was in the middle of a conversation. She seemed to turn inward, lost to the reality of present time, listening for something deep within herself.

Perhaps it was during these moments that Madeline received her messages. Virginia would never ask. In Madeline such trancelike conduct seemed so natural that an explanation was hardly needed.

But this time, Virginia had noted something awry. Madeline's forehead had puckered and she had grimaced, as if a shaft of anxiety had suddenly penetrated her mind.

"You think something's wrong?" Jack asked.

"Not at all," Virginia said with a smile. "Madeline is needed elsewhere." That seemed the only way to explain the sudden absence.

After dinner, the four of them went into the den, where the fireplace was set with logs and kindling. Jack struck a match and in quick order a crackling fire was dancing in the fireplace.

Through the sliding glass doors, they could see Madeline. She was standing close to the brick protective wall at the edge of the property, looking upward into space. She barely moved. Watching her, Virginia was strangely uncomfortable, although she wore a reassuring smile. But there was, indeed, a changed atmosphere in the house. What was wrong? she wondered. Earlier, everything had been so wonderful. She had felt happy, joyous.

But whatever was happening seemed important, essential. Despite the sense of discomfort and danger, Virginia was sure that something significant was occurring, something that would affect their lives.

"What is she doing?" Bobbie whispered.

No one replied. All eyes were on Madeline. They were waiting for her to shake herself out of this trance and come back into the house.

Madeline seemed frozen in space. Then, as

suddenly as she had left the table, she came into the den. In the soft light, she seemed pale, her eyes dulled, as if she had been drained of energy. They watched her, saying nothing, waiting for her to speak.

She stood for a long time, silent, her back to the fire, her gaze washing over their faces. It had been chilly outside and her lips chattered.

"There is no choice for me, my dear friends. I must stay now."

"Why, that's wonderful," Virginia said.

"That's exactly what we wanted," Jack said.

The twins had jumped off the chairs on which they were sitting and ran to embrace Madeline. She hugged them close to her and kissed them.

"We must be very, very vigilant," Madeline said.

"Vigilant?" Virginia asked, confused.

"There are forces at work here that must be countered. We must not let force interfere with the karma and lengthen the resolution."

Virginia wasn't quite sure what that meant, but she was, as always, grateful for Madeline's presence and, she felt certain, her protection.

"No harm will come to any of you, I promise."

During the weekend, Virginia and Madeline spent a great deal of time together in the studio preparing Virginia's presentation for the various art galleries in the city. She assembled all of the Polaroids of her paintings into a book and showed them to Jack.

"Very professional," he told her. "A sure winner."

It was Madeline who had suggested this approach.

"Even though we're certain of the outcome," Madeline explained, "there cannot be any short-cuts. Everything must run its course. I must warn you, though, you will have to endure some rejection."

"I'm fully prepared for that, Madeline," Virginia said. The prospect of showing her work to the galleries excited her. She had drawn up a list of those most likely to be interested.

"And one will definitely take me?" Virginia had asked.

"Definitely," Madeline said. "But only if we guard against those forces that could thwart a quick resolution. And there is one thing more."

"What's that?"

"This must be a private passage. While it's happening you mustn't report to me or consult me on the specifics of what is occurring on your journey to this resolution. You must be alone, however painful. Always, however, you will be aware of my presence and guiding hand."

"Pain?"

"I know this must sound incomprehensible to you, even ridiculous. But my instructions must be followed to the letter."

"Oh, Madeline," Virginia cried, embracing her, "it's my joy to do just that."

On Saturday, Madeline insisted on going shopping for food.

"We can wait until Monday," Virginia said lightly.

"No, we can't," Madeline replied.

Madeline drove Virginia in her car to a meat shop in West Los Angeles, one of the rare butcher boutiques in town. Inexplicably, Madeline ordered two rabbits.

"Rabbit?" Virginia asked, startled by the purchase. "We've never eaten rabbit."

"We must tomorrow night," she said with an air of finality. "Sunday."

"I'm . . . I'm not sure that the twins will eat it. I used to get them live rabbits every Easter until they were ten years old. They were very attached to their bunnies. We couldn't keep them, so after Easter it was a regular ritual to drive to one of our farmer friends and give the bunnies away."

"They have to eat it, Virginia. You and Jack as well. In fact, all of us."

"But why?"

"Virginia," Madeline said firmly, "you must trust me."

On Sunday night Madeline made rabbit stew for dinner.

"Doesn't taste like turkey," Jack said, spooning up the piquant stew. They had already had two meals of leftover turkey.

"It's not," Madeline said.

Virginia had hoped that Madeline would not tell them what the stew was made of. From a corner of her eye, she noted that the twins had begun to eat theirs with relish.

"Tastes like chicken," Bobbie said.

"Rabbit," Madeline said. She turned toward Virginia. "I'm sorry. They must know that they are partaking of the flesh of one of the most fertile mammals on earth. It's essential."

"Not bad," Jack commented.

But Billie had dropped her spoon into the stew and run off to the bathroom. Virginia ran after her. When she reached her, Billie was on her hands and knees, vomiting convulsively.

"I can't, Mommy," Billie said between heaves. "I just can't."

After Billie's stomach calmed down, Virginia led her back to the table.

"She can't hold it down," Virginia said.

"But she must," Madeline insisted, a tremor of panic in her voice.

"Why is it so important?" Virginia asked, showing her anguish.

"This family has too much at stake," Madeline said, looking at Billie. "I need your cooperation."

"I'll try, Aunt Madeline," Billie said, glancing at her mother and father. She sat down, looked at her plate, made a face, gagged and turned her eyes away.

"It's good," Bobbie said. "Think of it as chicken."

"But it's not chicken," Billie replied.

"Even Basil likes it," Jack said with reassurance. He had spooned some into Basil's bowl. "He lapped it up in two seconds flat."

"I can't, Daddy."

"Is it so important?" Jack asked Madeline.

"Very," Madeline said firmly.

Billie looked at the now cold stew in front of her. Virginia could see that it was hopeless.

"We'll try later," she pleaded. "I'll take it in to her."

"You must," Madeline said. She seemed greatly disturbed.

"I'll try, Aunt Madeline," Billie said, trying to hold back sobs. "I promise."

Later, after the twins had gone to their room

to watch television, Madeline made an effort to explain.

"I know what I'm asking seems crazy, certainly illogical. But believe me, I'm following a necessary course of action. There are ways to ward off the forces bent on changing the inevitable."

"But you assured us . . ." Jack began, then checked himself. He put up his hands. "I'm not questioning, Madeline. I'm sure you have your reasons."

"I do."

"Is it so necessary for Billie?" Virginia asked.

"I am afraid we are all one here. Flesh to flesh."

"But, in the end, it will happen as you've predicted?" Virginia asked, her anxiety rising.

"Nothing can change that."

Then why this? she wanted to ask, but held off.

"We must focus on next week. . . ." Madeline looked first at Virginia then her eyes drifted to Jack. She studied their faces. "There are numerological configurations that must be obeyed. Karma is in perfect focus for both of you. Nothing must interfere with that. Nothing."

Later, Virginia tried again to make Billie eat the rabbit stew. She brought a heated bowl of it into the twins' room. She watched as the poor child gagged and suffered.

"Please try, sweetheart," she begged.

"I am trying, Mommy."

In the end, it led to another fit of vomiting.

"Maybe some of it went down," Virginia said when Billie came back from the bathroom.

"Will something bad happen if it didn't?" Billie asked.

Virginia was not certain how to answer that question. Finally, she ignored it. I'm sure some of it went down, she thought, knowing that Madeline would certainly be tuned in.

·18·

As soon as he said it, he was sorry that he had told Jane.

"She's rattling bones over your head, you asshole," Jane said, her disgust palpable.

"I knew you'd react like that," Jack replied. "I shouldn't have said anything."

He had edited out the incident with Billie. That would have been too painful to relive. All right, it had been confusing, he admitted to himself. Perhaps even cruel as far as Billie was concerned.

"I'd get that woman the fuck out of there," Jane said angrily.

"No point in discussing this with you, Jane," he sighed.

"No point at all."

He was sitting in her office. He got up to leave. She called after him.

"Jack, all I'm trying to do is open a window of reason in your head."

"That's exactly the point. You cannot apply reason to this phenomenon. You either believe it or you don't."

By then, any doubts that surfaced were growing weaker. He felt himself developing true belief. Even this morning, bending over Virginia for his good-bye kiss, he had told her how sure he was that she would get an important gallery to represent her.

"The sooner the better," she had said.

Later, as he thought about her response, he grew worrisome. Madeline had told her that she would have to go through a rejection cycle at the beginning. She had talked about certain forces interfering with the karma. He wondered if they had obeyed all of Madeline's directives. He hoped Virginia's "resolution" would not take too long. His "resolution" as well, although it puzzled him how he might find the funds to finance an investment banking operation. Madeline would provide. That was the foundation of his hope.

During the weekend, he had spent time on his computer working out spreadsheets on what exactly would be needed to begin such an operation. No matter how he calculated and recalculated the numbers, there was no way to achieve a start-up without an opening expenditure of six million dollars.

Six million. Not a penny less. Of course, Madeline was sure to know that figure. But that did not solve the problem of acquiring the cash. He would need a bonanza.

That evening when he got home, he asked Virginia, "How did it go?"

She put a finger to her lips. "Later," she told him.

He, too, had been advised not to discuss any of his "private passage" with Madeline, although the restriction did not apply between him and Virginia.

Madeline had been standing nearby, which explained Virginia's reluctance to report.

"Good day?" Virginia asked, kissing him on his cheek.

"Uneventful," he said.

"Won't be for long," she replied, offering a wink.

After dinner, the twins went to their room, and Madeline, Virginia and Jack sat in the den before the fire. Madeline, who had been quiet through dinner, looked tired.

"It is draining," she told them. They did not inquire what "it" was, suspecting that she was expending a great deal of energy on them. After a while, she excused herself, kissed them and went to bed.

"No bites so far, Jack," Virginia confessed when they were alone.

"It's only the first day," Jack said reassuringly.

"I was very industrious. I showed my work to six galleries. They were all extremely cooperative. They spent time with me and studied my pictures with great care."

"No reactions?"

"Three polite. Three very frank. The polites said they weren't taking on anyone new but offered encouragement. The franks said my work wasn't up to their standards, that I needed more training, that the work was too derivative. Things like that."

"As Madeline warned. I'm sure it's all going according to some mysterious plan, known only to her."

"I certainly hope so."

He caught the tiniest sliver of doubt in Virginia's voice and attributed it to fatigue and discouragement. This was dangerous. Madeline had also said that negativity could unleash the forces of interference.

He got into bed and embraced her. "Rejection builds character," he said. "And Madeline did say there would be pain."

He started to stroke her body, but although she did not reject his advances, sexual excitement eluded her. Obviously, her thoughts were elsewhere.

"One of the men said he thought the woman in the pictures was not mysterious enough." She laughed.

"Who could be more mysterious than Madeline?"

"I'll try again tomorrow," she said yawning, assuming the embryonic position against the length of him. She fell asleep in his arms.

He was up before the alarm rang, as if something had goaded him into rising early. Perhaps he had heard a sound. Virginia was in a deep sleep. For some reason, he had awakened in an aura of expectation. Was today a special day? Madeline had told him that this was going to be an important week. Surely, he told himself, this will be the week that marks the start of Ginny's climb to fame. In the refreshment of the morning he felt certain of that. But it did not quite explain the fullness of his expectation. Something was going to happen *today*. He knew it in his heart.

His morning habit was to go outside and pick up the *Los Angeles Times* that was usually thrown through the bars of the electronic gate. Today it could not be found. It happened from

time to time and it was always an annoyance.
He would have to call the delivery people.

But when he went to the kitchen to make
the phone call, he saw a paper on the kitchen
table. It had been disassembled and was open
to the financial section.

At first he thought it curious, checking the
date to be sure it was today's paper. It was.
He noted a circle of green Magic Marker on the
New York Stock Exchange tables. Instantly, he
knew what was happening. Message received.
Madeline had picked a stock. So this is what he
had been expecting.

He looked at the name of the stock that lay in
the center of the green circle. Conductor Industries. It was selling for fifteen dollars a share of
common.

Excited, he took the paper and went back to
the bedroom. He shook Virginia awake and
pointed to the green circle.

"This is it," he said, waving it in front of her
face. She took it and looked at it.

"Conductor a good stock?"

"Hasn't been, up to now," he said.

"You're sure it's Madeline?"

"Who else?"

She shrugged and kissed him deeply on the
mouth. He was gratified that she had whipped
the mood of last night.

"It's starting to happen, Jack," she said when
they disengaged their lips. She embraced him
snugly and whispered in his ear. "Wanna?"

"Always," he assured her, "but today I've got
other excitements to pursue. Like Conductor
Industries."

"I'll take a rain check," she said.

He tore himself away from another long lingering kiss. "Break a leg," he said as he left.

"You, too," she called after him.

When he arrived at the office, he checked the price of the stock. Still fifteen dollars. Plunge or not? He certainly wished he could discuss it with Madeline. Of course, he cautioned himself, that was the old Jack talking. As if to counterpoint that fact, he walked into Jane's office. She looked up from her computer as he came in.

"Conductor Industries," he said. Then, with a flourish, he threw the paper on her desk. Stretching her neck, she looked at it.

"So?"

"That's her pick. She's circled it in green. Color of money," he said.

"The lady guru. Your permanent boarder."

He ignored the sarcasm.

"I'm buying fifty thousand shares," he said.

"Your fucking funeral," she said. "Leastwise you could do some research."

"I have all the research I need," he said.

She looked at him and shook her head. "Why not test it first before putting in your cojones?"

"She knows something we don't know, Jane."

Meanwhile Jane had punched up the stock, studying its vital statistics. "Dog," she said.

"You can't say I didn't let you in on it. You wanted proof. Now's your chance."

"I'll sit this one out," she said.

He shrugged, waved good-bye and went back to his office.

Jack made his buy and called his bankers. Actually, he had developed relationships with three banks and had spread his business among them, also referring them to his clients. At this level of purchase, he needed to work with two bankers in tandem. The third he kept as an ace in the hole, to be used when needed.

He worked out arrangements with two of the banks to extend him lines of credit totaling three hundred thousand dollars each. He reassured them that he and Virginia would put up their signatures and the purchased stock as collateral.

He'd done this dozens of times but never with these amounts. Besides, neither of the banks knew that he was dealing with the other. Ordinarily it was very risky business. One bad deal could wreck his relationships. So far he had been extraordinarily lucky. With the added security of Madeline behind him, he was certain to extend his luck. Since he already knew the outcome, he felt no hesitancy at taking such risks. None at all.

After confirming the loans, he called Singer. Nothing like plugging in a little demand.

"Conductor Industries," he said, his voice in hype mode. "You've got to make a buy."

"You do the research?" Singer asked.

"Right down to the keel," Jack replied.

"How many fathoms?"

"I'd go for three at least." This meant three hundred thousand dollars worth of stock.

He listened to the long pause. Singer was always nervous about a buy. To prod Singer further, Jack reminded him of how much the fund was ahead and who had been responsible for the rise.

"This one's going to go thirty knots. Shall I make it anchors aweigh?"

He knew his enthusiasm was catching. Singer assented and Jack made a buy for the fund. The stock kicked up half a point. Jack wasn't the least bit nervous about it. By the end of the day it was up one point. Profit, forty thousand dollars.

He was just getting ready to leave when Jane came into his office.

"You got lucky," she said.

"Luck has nothing to do with it," he assured her.

"Are you out of it?"

"Not yet."

"Damned fool."

She swung on her heels and left the office in a funk.

When he got home, he found Virginia alone in the house. She was lying in bed fully clothed, eyes open, looking at the ceiling.

"We're on a roll," he said. "Madeline's right on the money."

"Wish I could say the same," she said. "If rejection builds character then I'm indomitable."

She had gone to six more galleries. Only two would see her. Both thought her work was "workmanlike."

"Workmanlike?"

"Called damning with faint praise."

It puzzled him why she was having such a bad time. Not that he was an art critic, but he thought Virginia's work was wonderful. He wondered if he was being swayed more by the subject of the paintings than by their execution.

"It'll happen, Ginny, I know it will. If Madeline says so, it will definitely happen."

Virginia shrugged.

"Of course it will."

She said she felt drowsy and was soon asleep. He searched the house for Madeline, then discovered that her car was gone. Good thing, he

decided. He would surely have broken the ca-
veat and talked to her about his hot day in the
market.

The next day Conductor Industries was up
three points by noon. He was faced with a dilemma. When was he supposed to sell? He
called Jane.

"What would you do?" he asked.

"Why ask me? Call the guru."

"That's a no-no," he said, trying to put a hu-
morous spin on his response.

"Jesus, Jack, you've got four points on a dog.
I say sell. What are you up?"

"A hundred and sixty thousand."

"Schmuck." She hung up.

By the end of the day, the stock was up another two points. Profit: two hundred and forty
thousand dollars.

Again, he could not share the joy with Virginia.

"I've nearly run out of the string," she said.
She looked exhausted. "The galleries in this
area are finite." She sucked in a deep breath, as
if she were screwing up her courage. "They're
trying to tell me something, Jack. I'm not listening."

"Don't. Listen only to Madeline, I know she's
right. She's certainly proving it to me."

"Maybe it has something to do with the rabbit? Billie's not really getting it down?"

"I thought you said she did." He felt a brief
trill of panic.

"I lied," Virginia said.

Lied to Madeline? Could that be? "Then she
knows you did," Jack said.

"I haven't got the guts to ask her. I'm afraid."

"So am I," Jack said. He studied his wife. She

looked agonized, anxiety-ridden. What was it?
Had she done something wrong, violated which
of Madeline's tenets? Had she provided grist for
those unseen enemies who would interfere with
the resolution? Would it spill over to him? The
twins?

That night Virginia did not join them for dinner. Rehearsals had been called off and the
twins were home. Madeline took Virginia's
place at the table. Again he felt an irresistible
urge to explain what was happening. What he
needed to know most of all was when to sell.
No. That would be a violation of her prohibi-
tions. Surely she would let him know in good
time.

The next morning, the paper was missing
from its usual spot. He rushed into the kitchen
and found it on the table. Once again the financial section was open. This time the green Magic
Marker had circled a stock in the over-the-
counter tables. Centaurian. Gotcha, he told
himself. Sell Conductor Industries. Buy Centaurian. A clear signal.

Before leaving the house, he told Virginia
what had happened.

"Good luck, darling," she said as she kissed
him.

"You, too," he said. "It's happening, Ginny,
and it'll happen for you as well."

"Maybe," she whispered. Her response was
alarming, but he quickly put it out of his mind.

The first thing he did in the office was to sell
out Conductor Industries. It had risen still more
in the first hour of trading and when he sold he
had made four hundred thousand. Counting his
line of credit with the two banks, and adding
his profits, he now had about one million dol-

lars to work with. He called Jane, knowing that there was a drop of malice in the act. He really did want to gloat.

"I made four hundred thousand on Conductor," he announced flatly. "Even Singer's fund picked up a fat bonus."

"I've been snacking on crow all morning," she sighed.

"Still a doubter?"

There was a long pause. "I'm not ready to open my legs, if that's what you mean."

"I'll throw another one on the table. Centaurian on the OC. Going for around ten."

He heard her working her computer. "Dog of dogs," she said.

"I'm going for a million."

"Asshole."

He heard the click at her end.

"This is it," he whispered aloud. He was on his way. He felt it in his bones.

"Madeline, oh, Madeline," he said, "I'll follow you anywhere."

·19·

Virginia was in her studio, dressed to begin her trek for the day, gathering up her portfolio of Polaroids. She was puzzled by the rejections she had received so far. Considering Madeline's assertions, she had expected swifter results. Like the kind Jack was having. Comparing apples and pears, she decided.

She had, she admitted, been afflicted with a creeping negativity. She hesitated to call it doubt. She believed implicitly in Madeline and, to the best of her ability, she had followed her instructions, although the incident with Billie and the rabbit stew was troubling. Perhaps it was that or this tiny ripple of ambivalence that was causing what Madeline characterized as interference.

It certainly had not affected Jack. He was having a spectacular success. All his earlier doubts had disappeared. No, Virginia decided, barring any problem related to Billie, she was not truly holding up her end. This morning she would fix all that. Good-bye negativity. Hello optimism.

Knowing the ends, she would somehow have to cope with the means.

"There's my girl."

It was Madeline's voice. Virginia turned. Madeline was wearing a yellow dressing gown, her hair and makeup done to perfection. She looked lovely and her smile was bright. They kissed.

"Off again?" Madeline asked.

"Yes."

"This morning we must do something highly significant," Madeline said.

"How wonderful," Virginia said. She wished that she could talk about what she was going through. Indeed, she wished that Madeline would join her. In Madeline's presence her confidence soared.

Madeline stood in the center of the studio. The paintings were stacked around the room. Her eyes drifted from one to the other.

"Which is your favorite, Virginia?"

Virginia smiled.

"They're all my favorites," she said.

"I mean your absolute favorite," Madeline said.

Virginia contemplated the paintings for a moment. Because of her rejections, her confidence had wavered. It now came rushing back at her. Her gaze stopped at the large nude of Madeline, the one before which she and Jack had made love.

"That one," she said pointing, "but, of course, you know."

Madeline nodded. "We have to burn it, I'm afraid," she said casually.

Virginia had assumed that she was past the point of being surprised by any of Madeline's pronouncements. They were to be accepted, blindly followed, not questioned. But this came as a stunning shock.

"Burn it?" She was aghast.

"It's throwing up a barrier," Madeline explained, still casual. "It must be eliminated."

"I'm very confused, Madeline," Virginia admitted.

"I know you are, dear." Madeline came closer and embraced her. Virginia felt her enveloping warmth. "But you see, it's been contaminated. Sometimes when a creative object provides too much pride and joy it becomes contaminated by those who want to thwart the inevitable. When that happens we have to take drastic action." Virginia could feel Madeline patting her back.

"Now, now," Madeline said soothingly, "it's throwing off bad vibrations, interfering with the karma. Your reception at the galleries has not exactly been warm, has it?" She held Virginia out at arm's length and looked deeply into her eyes. "No need to comment. You simply must do it."

So that's it, Virginia thought, the spirit of hope rekindled. "Then lets," she said. She lifted the painting.

"They always attack the one that means the most to its creator," Madeline said cryptically as she helped Virginia carry the painting to the den. Virginia had to disassemble the frame to fit it into the fireplace. Rolling up the canvas, she threw it in on top of the wood and lit a match.

The flame ate away at the canvas then burst into hot flower as Virginia watched. Beside her, Madeline lifted her arms skyward and with closed eyes moved her lips in some silent ritual.

Her face became a frozen mask. Her body
seemed to vibrate with energy. Peripherally,
Virginia could see the flames recede as they finished licking at the painting. Then Madeline
lowered her arms and opened her eyes.

"There now," Madeline said after the fire had
burned to ashes, "good riddance." She held out
her arms toward Virginia who folded into them.

"I am so grateful," she said.

They made coffee and took mugs out to the
terrace. Although warm, it was a cloudy day.
The panorama of Los Angeles was cloaked in
gloomy grayness.

"I know all this seems mysterious to you,"
Madeline said, "but don't you already feel a
weight lifted?"

"Yes, I do," Virginia said, "I feel wonderful."
The depression of the last few days had disappeared.

"Remember how God created the universe.
Everything came in bits and pieces. As if God
had tested each of his creations before starting
another, although he knew the outcome of his
commands. Light actually came last. I have
never been betrayed by what I have been sent.
But I do have to validate truth occasionally.
Test intent. It's important to follow the path.
There are no shortcuts." She sighed and turned
to Virginia, her eyes burning with magnetic
zeal. "I tell you, it will all happen exactly the
way I have seen it."

She hadn't been wavering, Virginia told herself firmly. She wanted that message to be perfectly clear in her mind. She had been tried, but
she had resisted doubt. That was the important
part. There was one other nagging thought that
had to be articulated.

"Madeline, I lied about Billie eating the rabbit stew."

"I know," Madeline said gently.

"I hope nothing . . ." She could barely get the words out.

Madeline grew thoughtful. Her eyes drifted toward the city view, still locked in morning mist.

"We'll have to see, won't we?" she said. Then, turning to Virginia, she smiled. "In the end, it will be just as I have seen it."

Virginia went off on her gallery search brimming with confidence. Miraculously, the destruction of the painting seemed to have changed her reception. She chose to visit only five galleries, and one of them, a gallery called Emerging expressed some interest.

"Naturally, you'll have to see Mrs. Horning," a young woman told her after looking over her portfolio. "We'll set up an appointment. Is that all right?"

"All right? That's wonderful."

Her morale skyrocketed. She called Jack from a phone booth on La Cienega.

"Fabulous," he told her. "You see?"

"It was my fault, I know it was."

"We're rocking and rolling here as well," he said, chuckling. "We've got a million in Centaurian. I've rolled over the note and four hundred thou is our profit on Conductor. It's already up a quarter. Against the grain, too. The Dow is down twelve."

"Fantastic."

"Like taking candy from a baby."

"Jack, I'm so happy, so grateful."

That night they all went out to dinner, careful

not to make the occasion seem like a celebration. It was difficult for them to keep the subject matter of the events of their day and, at times, Jack had very nearly slipped.

"How do you view tomorrow?" he asked.

"Weather-wise?" Madeline asked innocently. It was obvious that she was deflecting the question.

"Market dropped twelve points on the Dow," he informed her at one point. She acknowledged with a nod that he had passed the information, but held off further comment. Virginia quickly changed the subject.

The next day Virginia visited five more galleries. Each rejected her politely. Disappointed but not discouraged, she felt certain that Emerging would take her work. Only need one, she thought.

At home she checked her answering machine. No message from Emerging, but Jack had called. She called him back immediately.

"Any luck?" he asked.

"Dry day," she replied, "but I know it will be Emerging, I just know it."

"Of course, it will, " he told her reassuringly. She heard him suck in his breath.

"How's Centaurian?"

"A little shaky today," he said, clearing his throat. "Lost a quarter. But it's holding. No sweat."

"Like me and the galleries, Jack. In the end it comes right."

"What Madeline wants, Madeline gets," he said, laughing.

The next day Virginia visited five more galleries and received five more rejections. She was almost to the bottom of her list of prospects.

And there was still no call from Emerging. No negativity, she begged herself.

That night Madeline told them she would not be home for dinner. With the twins out for rehearsal, Virginia met Jack at the Hamburger Hamlet off Sunset for dinner. He seemed drained and oddly introspective.

"Dropped another quarter," he said after his second martini, a most unusual act in itself.

"Maybe you could mention it to her?" he asked. She sensed his nervousness. "Damn thing's down a half."

"A passing phase," she assured him.

"If only she would say something."

"She will when the time comes."

"These, I suppose, are the times that try men's souls," he said half-joking, upending his martini down to the olive.

"And women's, too . . . if we have souls," she said, laughing. "I wouldn't worry, though. It's all preordained."

"I know that," he said, "but I've never had this much at risk before."

"Old habits die hard," Virginia said, patting Jack's hand.

"I just hope we haven't missed anything. Done something that is . . . well . . . offensive."

"Nothing that I can think of," Virginia said. Still, she could not get Billie out of her mind.

The next morning, he had barely been gone a half hour when he called her from the office.

"Opened still down a half," he said anxiously.

"It will pass. I know it."

"I've got to talk to her."

"Absolutely not."

"I have to," he pleaded. "We've lost fifty grand

so far. But the point is that it has to go up. I'm
going to talk to her, Ginny."

"You can't. Please."

"I'm scared, Ginny."

"I don't want to hear that kind of talk, Jack.
It implies you're losing faith. She'll know."

"I just need her reassurance."

"It will happen, I know it will."

But doubt was resilient. No matter how firmly
she struck it from her thoughts, it came back
to attack her with renewed strength. Jack's fear
mirrored her own. She had not pinned down a
gallery. Her visits on that day had proved fruit-
less and a stock that Madeline had recommended was going down. Madeline had even
burned a picture which, as she put it, "inter-
fered with the karma." Something was going
wrong. Was it something they had done?

Billie's refusal to eat the rabbit stew began to
loom larger in her mind. If Madeline thought it
was so necessary for all of them to ingest it,
then how could Billie's refusal to participate not
have a profound impact on events?

By the end of the day, Virginia's fears had
flourished. Worse, as if fate had timed it perfectly, Billie skipped rehearsals and came home
sick.

"I feel rotten, Mommy," she sighed. She
looked pale and was lethargic and weary and
running a slight fever. Virginia gave her an aspirin and put her to bed.

It was unusual for Billie to be ill. Both girls
were blessed with strong constitutions. They
rarely got sick.

By the time Jack came home, Billie's fever had
risen to 103. Further alarmed and prodded by
Jack, she called the doctor. After she outlined

Billie's symptoms, the doctor told her that a virus was making the rounds and he increased the dosage of aspirin. To add to their consternation, Bobbie told them that Billie, who had always been an excellent student, had flunked their last math test.

"Are you sure she'll be all right?" Virginia pressed Madeline.

"I'm certain she will," Madeline had responded, "but you must let me spend the next three hours with her. Alone."

"Of course," Virginia said, knowing she was speaking for both herself and Jack.

"It's imperative that you don't come into the room during that time." Her expression seemed, for Madeline, unusually stern. Virginia felt a sudden lurch in her chest.

"Is there something . . . ?" Virginia aborted her question, fearful of its answer.

"We'll do exactly as you say, Madeline," Jack said. She watched his nostrils quiver as he sucked in a gulp of air.

It was six P.M. To relieve themselves of the tension of waiting, they took Bobbie out for dinner and sat through a silent meal at the Old World Restaurant on Sunset.

"She'll be all right, I know she will," Bobbie said. She was completely confident and undaunted in her appetite.

"Of course, she will," Jack told her, but he could not hide his depression.

To deflect any ominous thoughts about Billie, Virginia asked him how things were going at the office. Unfortunately, it brought her down a road she did not wish to traverse. Not at the moment.

"The same," he told Virginia.

"But it hasn't gone down further?" she asked, searching for a ray of optimism.

"Not yet," he sighed.

"We're slipping Jack," Virginia warned. The statement did not need an explanation.

Bobbie tried to inject some cheerfulness, but neither Virginia nor Jack seemed able to shrug off the intrusive weight of worry and foreboding.

Virginia would never question Madeline's motives but, in a tiny chink in back of her mind, it now occurred to her to wonder why Madeline had not foreseen that Billie could not eat the rabbit stew. Or had she? Of course, she had. The idea seesawed in her brain.

They had learned that the occult embodied many strange rituals, incantations and ceremonial foods. Everything had its reasons, a sequence, a logic. All actions fit into the grand design. Madeline was their guide through the thicket of the present. Her stated objective was to keep them from harm's way. And she would. Above all, she must not be questioned. Only obeyed. There could be no deviation from the grand design. It made Virginia feel better to work these things out in her mind.

"Leave it to Madeline," Virginia urged, fearing that the slightest doubt of Madeline's powers would have its effect on Billie.

"I'm not questioning that," Jack snapped. Obviously, his thoughts had followed the same direction as had hers.

They returned home at a few minutes to eight and resisted the temptation to burst into Billie's room. Instead, they waited in the den for Madeline to come out. Bobbie put on the television.

"Not now, darling," Jack said.

"Please, Daddy," Bobbie responded. She studied her father for a moment. "Billie will be fine. Really. Aunt Madeline won't let anything happen to Billie."

"Let her, Jack," Virginia said. Jack shrugged and nodded and Bobbie put on the television.

At exactly eight o'clock, Madeline came out of the twins' room. She was smiling as they stood up to meet her.

"No problem. She's sleeping peacefully and her temperature is almost normal." Without another word, she left the room.

"Thank God," Jack said.

"What a relief," Virginia said.

"I told you," Bobbie said without taking her eyes off the television program.

Before going to bed, they visited the twins' room. Billie slept peacefully, hugging Basil, who snored beside her. Virginia bent down and felt Billie's forehead with her lips.

"Cool as a cucumber," she whispered. Jack bent down and kissed her cheek.

"Sleep easy, pumpkin," he said, then bent over Bobbie and kissed her as well.

Before slipping into bed, Virginia felt compelled to say good night to Madeline. It was strange for her to disappear without saying good night.

"We must thank Madeline," Jack said, echoing her thoughts.

They padded in their bare feet to the guest room. The room was dimly illuminated by light from the corridor, but they could see Madeline's face and form. She lay propped high on pillows, her body covered by a blanket. Her eyes were open and seemed iridescent as they watched Virginia and Jack enter.

"Madeline," Virginia whispered. When Madeline did not respond, Virginia called her name again. They moved closer to the bed.

"I'm here," Madeline said, her voice strained.

"Are you all right?" Jack asked.

"Just tired," she said.

"We came to thank you," Virginia said.

"We're very grateful," Jack said.

As they came closer, Madeline lifted her arms. They moved toward her. She drew them down beside her, caressing them, kissing them each in turn.

"My dear sweet wonderful friends," she whispered.

"We are so privileged to have you here," Virginia said. Her heart flooded with emotion. Her eyes misted.

"You are my treasures," Madeline said. "I will protect you with every ounce of my substance." She squeezed them closer. Virginia felt a sudden chill. Her lips trembled. Madeline lifted the covers and they both got in beside her.

Her naked body radiated warmth. Virginia reached over and joined Jack's hand with hers.

"Everything will be exactly as I have seen it," Madeline whispered. "I promise you."

"We don't doubt that for a moment. Do we, Jack?"

"Never," he whispered.

Virginia felt her body suffuse with warmth. The touch of Madeline's flesh both soothed and excited her. Every cell in her body seemed alert to Madeline's presence. She unclasped her hand from Jack's. Both now roamed and caressed Madeline's body, which seemed to swell and ripple, responding to their touch.

What was happening, Virginia assured her-

self, transcended sexuality. Something magical,
ethereal, sacred, was occurring between them,
a melding of pure feeling, a response to a natural need to connect, absorb, fuse. Madeline
kissed them both deeply in turn, sucking energy
from them into herself. Mysterious, explosive,
volcanic forces were being tapped within each
of them, forces never before experienced.

Although it expressed itself in what might be
considered the primitive urges of sexual need,
Virginia knew it was something more, a gift
perhaps, deliberately given as if they were chosen by spirits beyond not only themselves, but
beyond the planet, from some intelligence deep
in the universe.

They arranged themselves as if Madeline's
body were a temple in which they must worship. Jack's blood-engorged penis, projecting an
ivory hardness that she had never experienced
before, seemed to express its own need and Virginia inserted it into Madeline's body. Suddenly
it seemed electrified. Strange inchoate sounds
rumbled in Madeline's throat as her body
bucked and rolled. Virginia held her, caressed
her, urging Jack to greater energies until he,
too, quivered with release.

Later, they lay quietly. Virginia fell into a
dreamless sleep, awakening to shadowy dawn.
Tapping Jack, they disengaged themselves and
quietly left the room.

She lay thinking in their own bed for a long
time, trying to assess what she had just experienced. She searched her mind for any sign of
guilt or jealousy or any other emotion that
might render the experience unclean, aberra-
tional, somehow sinful. No, she decided, she
was proud of having lived through those mo-

ments, proud that Jack had shared his sexuality with Madeline. The pleasure Madeline had surely experienced was, Virginia felt certain, the ultimate gift that one woman might give to another.

She turned and embraced her husband. His eyes were closed and she could feel the steady heartbeat in his chest. She whispered in his ear.

"I am so grateful, my love."

She was not sure he had heard.

·20·

Nothing in Jack's life had prepared him for such an occurrence. Indeed, nothing in his life had prepared him for any of the events that had transpired since Madeline had come into their lives. Certainly not what had happened the night before.

He did not deliberately dismiss it from his mind to protect his inner integrity, as he might have had to do in the pre-Madeline era of his life.

Plumbing his deepest sense of personal and moral integrity, he simply could not find in himself the slightest sense of shame or guilt. Virginia had participated in the act, had aided and abetted it, hadn't she? And, even in retrospect, the act had the feel and quality of ritual, perhaps of duty and necessity. He felt good about it, joyous. It had been a celebration of friendship and sexuality, as profound and committing as the marriage bond itself.

Nowhere in his heart and soul did it mirror the sleazy image of self-gratification and moral taboo that was traditionally associated with a ménage à trois relationship. This was something completely different, more like a sharing, a gift of oneself.

Of course, they had protected the knowledge of it from the twins and had crept back to their own bed at dawn. That was the only thing that gave him any uneasiness because it implied that it was not something that could be observed by the twins without confusing them.

There was also another thought in his mind. Surely Madeline had known that at some point this experience would occur. If she knew everything else, she surely knew this. Thus, what had occurred was preordained and, therefore, unavoidable.

He marveled at the way his thought processes had changed since he had invested his faith in Madeline. How clear everything had become. The old logic had been turned on its head. He had, he was certain, discovered a higher truth, the only truth. And this truth had set him free.

Even the tension of the stock transactions seemed a pale shadow of how he would have felt in pre-Madeline days. Centaurian would go up soon. As day follows night.

It surprised him to see the paper open on the kitchen table. With Centaurian flat, he had not expected another message until an upward movement had occurred. But there it was, circled in green as before. The ink had soaked through the paper, but none had covered the name of the stock, which seemed to stand out as a beacon: Compulaser!

Bingo, he thought. This was the stock he had believed in, had researched, had put in his own and Singer's portfolios as well as those of his other clients. Compulaser, he mused. Of all stocks. Compulaser. This was it. The one. Vectors converging.

Madeline was closing the circle, validating his own hunch, bringing him to the real launching pad of her prediction. From this would come the first real seed money that was to propel him into his own business and, ultimately, to the wealth and position that she foresaw.

"It's happened," he told Virginia waking her from a sound sleep. He showed her the paper. "Compulaser. That's my hunch stock. She's picked it. That has to mean something."

"It does, I'm sure of it," Virginia said, rubbing her eyes and smiling. She lifted her arms and kissed him deeply. "I told you."

"She is so important to our lives, Ginny," Jack whispered. "And you'll see, it will begin to turn soon for you."

"I know," Virginia whispered, kissing him again.

On his way out of the house, he stopped at Madeline's door, listened, then opened it silently. She was sleeping peacefully, her face Madonna-like against the pillow. Bending, he put his lips on her forehead.

"Thank you," he whispered, then he tiptoed out of her room and closed the door silently behind him.

He could not wait to get to his office. The thrill of expectation tingled every nerve ending in his body. His first act was to check the price of Centaurian. Another miracle. It had risen to its original price. His loss was trifling. He put in his sell and buy orders, then went to Jane's office and told her what he had done.

"She's pulling your chain," Jane snickered. "I

took a small position in Centaurian just to say
I told you so."

"She tested me, I'm sure of it. She was probing for weakness. Now she's giving me the big
one. I know it. I feel it. . . . It's Compulaser,
Jane. This is the one we always believed in."

"We're already in it up to our kazoos," she
told him. "Besides, I thought Centaurian would
be the so-called big one."

"I told you. A test. Conductor sucked us in.
Centaurian tested our belief. Now we're ready."

"You certainly are zealous, Jack," she
shrugged. But he could see that she was wavering.

She turned her desk chair toward him and
crossed her legs. As always her dress crept far
up her thigh. It amused him that she continued
to believe that she could seduce him. It was
laughable. He felt nothing. Once not going to
bed with her had been a point of honor. He
chuckled to himself.

"We've been great friends, Jane," he told her.
"I'm sharing this with you only because I know
what this means. You have been wonderful to
me, sympathetic, patient and more. You can do
what you like, but I tell you, this is the moment."

"What in the hell is new on Compulaser?" she
snapped. "We've followed that stock for
months. We're in it already. Have you done any
additional research? Have some flashy new patents been granted? Why now?"

"It will go up," he said emphatically.

"On hard information? Or a prayer?"

"You know where my information comes
from."

"That's where we got Centaurian."

"Not my problem, Jane," he said, turning to leave. Before he could reach the door, she called his name, standing up.

"Sounds like you're ready to take a giant plunge."

"I am."

She shook her head.

"Risk everything on a hunch?"

"It's not a hunch, it's a direction."

"I can't believe this is you," she said, studying him.

"Believe it," he said. He felt his face heat. "I feel it in every corner of my being."

He could tell she was studying him carefully. On her face was an expression of bewilderment.

"You sound . . . well . . . fanatical Jack," Jane said.

"The way I sound is immaterial." He was suddenly angry with himself. Jane was part of his old way of thinking and viewing the world. It struck him that she was not part of his life anymore. She was aeons away from any significance to him. She had become a sounding board, really, an exercise for his own vanity. All that was yesterday.

Without another word, he walked out of her office and back to his own. He punched in the price of Compulaser on his computer. It was selling at five. He could buy two hundred thousand shares. Not enough, he decided. He needed to buy more. Time to call on his ace in the hole, the third bank. With a phone call to the vice president, he arranged for another million, putting up his home and all the stock in his personal portfolio as collateral. This meant he could buy another two hundred thousand shares.

His loan arranged, he spread his buys among various brokers. Compulaser had always been an active trading stock, although recently its fluctuations had been narrow. He knew that such an enormous buy would kick the price up and was pleased to discover that he had averaged his buy at a little over five dollars a share.

Considering the risks he was taking, he was surprisingly calm, his actions deliberate. He sensed Madeline's comforting and approving spirit behind every move he made. When his buys were confirmed, he called Singer.

"I want you to quadruple your position on Compulaser."

"Must be the winds up," Singer said.

"Raise the spinnaker, Captain."

He waited through a long pause. The fund held twenty-five thousand shares of Compulaser.

"You don't think it's too much of a speculation?" Singer asked.

"It's not even remotely a speculation," Jack answered. He listened through a few moments of expressed doubts. His fund had held Compulaser with no movement for months.

"We've got the trade winds on this one," Jack said, his tone as clipped as his words.

"What's it going for?"

"Under six," Jack said, knowing that Singer's buy would cause the stock to rise further.

"We going for the quick in and out or the long haul?"

"Not the long haul. But we want to get out as near to the top as possible."

"How will you know?" Singer asked.

"I'll know."

Singer's agonizing seemed to sweat through

the phone. Jack waited patiently until Singer's pain had subsided.

"Anchors aweigh," Singer said. He hung up quickly. The buy brought the stock up another point.

Not long after, Jane called.

"I hocked the family jewels, you bastard," she said in mock tough guy. "Now all I need to know is when we sell. I want to go up in your balloon."

"I'll let you know."

"Jack?" There was a tone of urgency in her voice.

"Yes."

"I've got everything on the line on this one."

"Good," he said.

"You can't leave me hanging."

"No way," he said.

He watched the stock until closing, checking with brokers throughout the country. By the end of trading the stock had gone up five points.

When he came home, he found Virginia waiting in the den with an iced bottle of champagne. It startled him. He had wanted to surprise her.

"Madeline told you," he said.

"Told me what?" she asked curiously.

"About Compulaser."

It was obvious she didn't know. He told her what had happened.

"Are you surprised?" Virginia asked.

"Not in the least," he answered.

The she told him the cause for this semicelebration. Mrs. Horning of Emerging Gallery had responded. Her assistant had called and Virginia had set up a meeting with Mrs. Horning for tomorrow. Nothing committed on the telephone, but the promise seemed implicit in the request for a meeting.

Jack's first reaction was to caution her optimism. But that was the old Jack, he told himself. Madeline's predictions were simply taking their inexorable course.

"Where's Madeline?" he asked as he struggled to pop the cork carefully.

"Gone back to her place to see a client. She told us not to wait dinner. The twins will have a late rehearsal. They're having dinner at school."

He poured out two glasses. They clinked and drank, looking into each other's eyes.

"I am the happiest woman alive," she said.

"Change the sex and ditto for me."

"And I love what happened last night."

It reminded him of his brief consternation and he felt relieved. Suddenly a shadow crossed her face.

"Did you?" she asked.

With his free arm, he embraced her and kissed her on the lips. "I think it brings us closer together," he said.

"All of us," she said.

They sipped their drinks, but continued their one-armed embrace.

"And Madeline," he asked, "did you both talk about it?"

She moved away coquettishly and laughed. "Maybe."

"Secret women's talk, right?"

He appreciated her playfulness. It was fun to be lighthearted. He was not even in the least worried about the risk he had taken in the market. What risk? In the face of certainty, worry had disappeared.

"What a lucky day that was," he said, moving closer to her, "meeting Madeline."

"The most important day in my life. Our lives." She turned and looked through the glass wall of the den. The city was outlined sharply in the declining afternoon light.

He came up behind her, reacting to a sudden impact of desire. He buried his head in her hair, breathed in the familiar perfume and cupped his hands over her breasts.

She was unexpectedly unresponsive, which puzzled him.

"You say the kids will be late?"

She nodded. He continued to knead her breasts and press his erection against her buttocks. Still he got no reaction.

"God, you turn me on," he whispered kissing her neck, tonguing her ear. It was the kind of foreplay that stimulated her. Releasing a breast, he began to rub her belly.

"Please, Jack, not now," Virginia said, although she remained in his embrace.

"Thought it was as good a time as any," he said. He had spoken in a whine which was not his intention. He could respect reluctance, although in Virginia's case it was a rare occurrence, especially these days.

"I'd love to," she said, patting his cheek, "but not without Madeline."

It took him a moment to absorb what she had said. He wondered if he fully understood it. A stab of fear poked him in the gut. His erection fell.

"You understand, darling, don't you?" she asked, her hand still caressing his cheek.

"Of course," he said, but he wasn't sure.

·21·

A slanting persistent rain beat against the windshield as Virginia inched the car down Melrose. Rain was beautiful and enriching. An image of herself jumped into her mind. She was dancing naked in the middle of the street. Raindrops fell around her as she danced, a translucent apparition shrouded in a heavy mist. The image was audible as well and she heard her voice singing to the world: Have a Happy Day.

She giggled. Today, she was certain, would be the beginning of yet another path on her preordained journey to fulfillment. Every atom in her mind and body knew it. She needed no reassurances.

She had deliberately resisted imagined scenarios. After all, she giggled again, there has to be some suspense in life. She parked the car as close to the gallery as possible and walked the two blocks, unconcerned about the rain's effect on her hair. What did it matter? She did not have to make an impression. Her work had already sent the message to the gallery owner, Mrs. Horning. Emerging Gallery, as its name

implied, had a fine reputation for introducing
new talent, which was exactly what she wanted.

"Mrs. Horning's taste is impeccable," the assistant had told her. It was she who had called
to set up the appointment. Ten A.M.

"Mrs. Horning is anxious to meet you," she
had said, conveying just the right sense of polite urgency. Naturally, she hadn't yet discussed this with Madeline. She was beginning
to understand why. To Madeline, means were
less material than ends. That did not prevent
Virginia from looking forward to announcing
to Madeline that her prediction was taking a
tangible turn toward fulfillment. "She's taking
me on," she would say, and they would embrace.

Surely tonight, stimulated by the good fortune exploding in their lives, the three of them
would need to make love together. She wanted
to put Madeline in a stupor of pleasure. It had
been so lovely to see her in the full splendor of
her enjoyment. Jack had been marvelous, burst-
ing with masculine vigor. It had all seemed so
natural, so universal. Body and mind had
merged with the essence of joy.

The high tide of emotion continued as she entered the gallery. The assistant came out to
greet her. She was a tall woman who spoke with
a foreign accent.

"So good of you to come," she said politely.
"Mrs. Horning will see you in a moment."

Of course she will, Virginia thought, as she
roamed the gallery looking at pictures. The artist dealt with abstract images. Very good. But
not to her taste. She had never been attracted
to abstractions, especially in art.

"You may go in," the assistant said.

Virginia walked confidently into Mrs. Horning's office. The woman sat behind an antique desk. She was gray-haired and smiling with a rosy and crinkled face, like a lady Santa Claus.

"I'm so pleased to meet you," Virginia said.

In front of the woman, on the desk, was Madeline's portfolio of Polaroids.

"I do appreciate your showing me your work, Mrs. Sargent. Have you been painting a long time?"

"I've been raising my family and doing commercial illustration up until a few months ago. The portfolio represents my most recent work," Virginia explained.

"Only one subject," Mrs. Horning mused. Virginia was mildly surprised at her neutrality.

"Like Wyeth's Helga pictures," Virginia said.

"In a way, I suppose," Mrs. Horning said. "An artist must have extraordinary self-confidence."

"Absolutely," Virginia agreed. She watched as Mrs. Horning's hands patted her portfolio.

"Your work shows promise, Mrs. Sargent. I think you are heading in the right direction. But I'm afraid I can't see my way clear to take you on."

Virginia was bemused. Was she absorbing words with opposite meanings?

"I think you must get further away from the representational. There's an advertising quality about the work . . ."

Mrs. Horning continued to speak, but Virginia blocked out the words. She had been so certain of praise and approval. Hadn't she felt it in her bones? She forced herself to sit still until there was a break in Mrs. Horning's lecture. Then she stood up.

"I really must go," Virginia said.

Mrs. Horning handed her the portfolio.

"I try to see all the artists who submit. It's an act of faith. I know how difficult it is. From personal experience. Selling other artists' work has always been a second choice for me. . . ."

Madeline was in the den drinking coffee and reading the *Los Angeles Times* when Virginia returned home. She was wearing a silk dressing gown, and, as always, she was perfectly groomed, makeup carefully applied, not a hair out of place. Madeline looked up as Virginia came into the room, but her smile of greeting quickly faded.

"The gallery owner said my work had an 'advertising quality' about it," Virginia blurted, unable to obey Madeline's prohibition any longer. It had been a long time since she felt this discouraged. She kicked off her shoes and slumped on the couch.

"You should have told me sooner," Madeline said, surprising Virginia.

"But I thought you preferred not knowing the specifics. You said that it might interfere with the karma and lengthen the resolution. I remember you said—"

"You must listen to me now," Madeline said sternly. Then her expression softened. "I have charted trying times ahead. You must take my guidance. We must get through this period. I'm doing this for you, dear friend."

"I'm so sorry, Madeline," Virginia said, her feeling of depression deepening.

Madeline watched her for a long moment, then sat beside her on the couch, taking Virginia in her arms.

"Poor baby," she said stroking her hair.

"I had such high hopes that this would be the one," Virginia whispered.

"It might have been if I had known. There is a self-correcting mechanism in the spirit world. We could have called on the unseen beings to help."

"Unseen beings?"

"They're all around us. Even now, in this room."

"People watching? In this room?"

"Not people, Virginia. Beings. They surround us and can, if they are summoned, effect changes in the living mind."

Had Madeline mentioned "unseen beings" before? Virginia looked around the room. In here? Were they effecting changes in her mind? "Can you summon them?"

"Of course. But not if I don't know what's troubling you."

"Surely—" Virginia began, then stopped abruptly. She had assumed from the beginning that whatever was in her mind was an open book to Madeline.

"You see," Madeline said, "even though we know the inevitable truth, we have enemies out there always plotting to change that outcome. I must always be on the alert to protect you."

Virginia was having trouble absorbing the concept. "There's so much that I don't know," she acknowledged, fighting the emergence of doubt. It was as if a pinprick had pierced her armor. Like poison, it was seeping into her. She wondered if Madeline could detect it. If she could, she showed no outward sign.

"It may be that we'll have to do some channeling, reach someone in the spirit world who will know the strategy to shorten the time of resolution."

Virginia hadn't realized that fulfillment would be fraught with such problems. She had expected at least one of the many galleries she had canvassed to take her on. Indeed, she had been systematic in her approach and had gone through the entire list of serious galleries in the Los Angeles area.

The fruits of all this canvassing had been nothing but rejection. Some had been merely polite. Others apologetic. A few were insulting. Mrs. Horning's comment seemed to synthesize them all.

"Is it possible, Madeline, that what you've foreseen for my future will be . . . well . . ." She felt a sudden fear and could not finish the sentence.

"Thwarted?"

"I'm just trying to understand, Madeline."

"It's not a question of understanding. That implies worldly logic. We're dealing with another dimension here, another plane. It's very complicated and difficult to explain."

"I've always been open to learning," Virginia said.

"I know, dear," Madeline said soothingly, "but there are some things that are naturally beyond your understanding."

There was something in Madeline's tone that Virginia had not detected before, something patronizing and parental. Worse, Virginia did feel inadequate to understanding any of it.

"You must trust me, Virginia," Madeline said sweetly as she picked up the paper again.

"Haven't I always?" Virginia asked with

mounting irritation. After all, hadn't she put her life in Madeline's hands?

Vaguely discontented, she went into her studio and studied the paintings. Too representational. Too much like advertising. She had tried to be truthful, to portray Madeline in all her various moods. Was there something missing from these works, some quality of truth that she could not capture?

Was it in the artist? Or in the subject?

·22·

By the end of the day, the price of Compulaser fell back, although Jack remained in a profit position. By no means was he panicked. A quick rise often shook out the heavy speculators and high rollers. Hadn't he expected that? Now, he was certain, the smart money would follow his lead, bidding the stock up to yet another plateau.

"It's going according to form. Like tacking. Moving with the wind, but always on course."

He explained this to Singer, who had called him at the end of the day, slightly anxious.

"Maybe we should have taken our points and run," Singer said.

"Don't be a nervous Nellie," he said cheerfully. "I'm very sure on this one. Very."

"Hard to argue with a believer," Singer said, not knowing how close he had come to the nub of the issue.

Jane came into his office at the tail end of the conversation. She looked tired.

When he hung up she said, "You're setting

me up for another sleepless night, Jack." She slumped into a chair opposite his desk.

"Not me. I slept like a baby."

"The damned stock slid back in a matter of minutes. I went to the john and lost a fortune."

"Paper profits, Jane. You know better."

"Just chicken, I guess."

"Then get out."

"I suppose I should." She shook her head. "But I won't."

"Up to you. I know it's the big banana, Jane," Jack said.

"From your mouth to God's ears."

"That matter has already been settled," he said cheerfully.

He felt not the slightest consternation. His attitude seemed to calm her. When she left, he turned on his computer and analyzed the spreadsheet that he was creating to project his cash needs for the investment business he would soon be creating. He punched in revised figures and calculated what it would take in personnel and future business to reach the break-even point. After a couple of hours at this he went home.

When he got to the house the twins were alone in the kitchen eating TV dinners, a rare event. He had assumed, too, that they were scheduled to rehearse every evening that week for the school Christmas play.

"Rehearsal called off?" he asked, after kissing each in turn on the head.

"We're not going tonight, Daddy," Billie said, "we're going to do channeling instead."

"Channeling?"

"Madeline is going to consult unseen beings," Bobbie explained.

It came as a surprise, but he didn't show it. Madeline, as always, must have her reasons.

"Where is Madeline?" he asked.

"In her room, getting ready."

He went into the bedroom. The sun had already set and the room was quickly darkening. He started to remove his jacket, when he discovered that Virginia was sitting in a corner of the room. She seemed lost in thought, almost in a trance.

"Virginia?"

He had to call her name twice before she mumbled a response.

"Why are you sitting in the dark?" He went to one of the lamps beside the bed and turned it on. Virginia shielded her eyes from the sudden brightness.

"I hadn't realized," she murmured, offering an anemic smile. She looked wan, pale.

"Don't you feel well?"

"I'm fine," she said.

He moved closer to her, bending slightly to study her face. "I don't understand," he said.

She reached out and caressed his face. "Maybe I've been working too hard," she said.

He detected a weakness in her voice, but he was not alarmed. "I think we all need a vacation. Hell, the Christmas holidays would be a perfect time to cut out. The five of us. We'll go skiing. Doesn't that sound great?"

"That would be fun," she said, making an obvious effort to brighten her expression.

"We'll have a lot to celebrate this year," he said. She nodded.

"It's just a bout of depression," Virginia said, getting up from the chair. "Pay no attention."

She shrugged, as if physically shaking off bad feelings. "I'm being silly."

She seemed to gather up her energy. She went off into the bathroom, while he changed into slacks and sport shirt.

Virginia's presence had sidetracked his thoughts from what the twins had told him. Channeling? He knew it was part of what might be called the occult vocabulary, but he had no idea what channeling entailed.

When Virginia came out she had put on her makeup and seemed refreshed.

"The girls told me what was up," he said, "something about channeling."

"Madeline will explain it," Virginia said. There was a quiver in her voice. She cleared her throat, coughing into her hand. He detected an uncommon disturbance behind the cosmetic repair.

"They mentioned something about 'unseen beings,' " he said. The words alone seemed foreign to him. "I wish I knew what that meant."

Virginia forced a smile. "Something about making contact in the spirit world. Reaching an unseen being who might use its influence to persuade other unseen beings to eliminate bad karma in those who want to stop Madeline's predictions from happening."

She had blurted out the words and he found it difficult to understand their meaning. Perhaps her explanation was faulty.

"You'll have to make it clearer," he pressed.

"Her predictions . . . I really don't know how to put this . . . they're taking longer than she expected. She thinks there's deliberate interference that's lengthening the process."

"Longer?"

He felt a thump in his throat and his thoughts leaped to his purchase of Compulaser. Considering the interest that had to be paid on his notes, time was essential. He could not hang around forever waiting for Compulaser to soar.

"When I told her that Mrs. Horning had turned me down . . ."

"Oh, my God, I completely forgot."

It had, indeed, slipped his mind. He was guilt-stricken, but at least it explained her mood. "Her loss," he snapped.

"For some reason Madeline feels we need help . . . to speed things up." She paused and he detected a note of hesitancy in her tone. "She knows it will happen."

"Of course it will."

"I don't doubt it."

"No way."

"She says that nothing can interfere with the grand plan."

"Of course not," he agreed. But there was no denying to himself that she was fighting off an onslaught of doubt. Above all, he must not help feed such negativity. He took her in his arms and kissed her cheek. "Madeline knows," he whispered.

"I know she does."

Hand in hand they walked out of the bedroom.

"In here," Bobbie called. She waved them into the den. Madeline was sitting cross-legged on the floor, her eyes closed, her hands raised in an attitude of prayer. She was heavily made up and her face resembled that of a porcelain doll, deeply rouged against a stark white face. Bobbie resumed her place beside her sister. They both sat cross-legged facing Madeline. Surrounding them was a circle of flickering and perfumed candles.

"Sit down beside us," Bobbie whispered.

"And hold hands," Billie said.

Madeline opened her eyes and motioned to Jack and Virginia to sit on either side of her. Then she held out her hands and motioned for them to clasp hers and the twins'. They formed a circle now. It was, he decided, eerie, scary, but very exciting.

The twins seemed mesmerized by the event. A protective instinct assailed him. Were they too young for this? Would this harm them in any way? Would it educate or alarm them? Scar them in some psychological way? No, he trusted Madeline. No harm would come to them, he was sure of that.

Madeline's face was calm. Only Virginia seemed wary, unable to put herself into the spirit of the ritual. A nerve palpitated in her jaw, always a sign of tension.

Madeline had closed her eyes again. He watched her, serene and immobile. Her hand in his felt strangely invisible, as if her flesh had adapted exactly to his body temperature. He had no idea what to expect.

The room was deadly quiet and the light from the flickering candles threw odd shadows across their faces.

From far away, he heard a scratchy sound, as if from an old steel needle record player on which the volume had been turned down to its lowest point. He could not tell where it was coming from. It vaguely resembled words and music. As he strained it grew louder. Still he could not make it out.

Bobbie gasped, her eyes widening as she stared at Madeline. Madeline's mouth had opened and the staticy sound seemed to be rumbling deep within her. Madeline began to quake. A long string of strange sounds gargled out of her throat, as if her larynx had turned to sandpaper.

Jack had the sensation that inside Madeline was a trapped animal determined to tunnel its way out. For a moment, he thought the thing inside was choking her. Billie cowered closer to her mother. Bobbie seemed paralyzed with fright, her hand tightening around his.

The strange sounds coming from Madeline continued. The muscles in her throat constricted, then expelled an endless stream of odd noises. Slowly the sounds seemed to evolve into an unrecognizable language, words without meaning, combinations of phonetic configurations, as if she were monitoring the conversations at some Tower of Babel.

Bobbie began to whimper beside him as she burrowed into his side. The evolution of the language continued and he began to catch hints of English. Then sentences. Then meaning. The voice, emanating from Madeline's mouth was not Madeline's. It sounded like that of an older man with the hint of a German accent.

"I haf found you. I haf found you," the man's voice announced. "What is it you vant?"

Suddenly, Madeline's voice spoke. "We need your help."

"I am at your service," the man's voice said.

"The family Sargent," Madeline's voice explained, "do you recall the earlier messages?"

"Of course," the man's voice said. "It is confirmed on this side."

"And the time frame?"

"No change."

"Are you certain?"

"Yes."

"We are getting conflict," Madeline's voice said. "There are things to be smoothed out at your end."

"The interferers are resourceful."

"Are they a threat?"

"Not if we are vigilant."

"Will everything happen the way in which it was told to me? I must spare them every doubt."

"They, in turn, must do the same."

"They will, I promise you."

"If they waver, it will make things difficult."

"They will not waver."

"Then it will be done."

There was a long silence, then the distant rumbling, the cacophony, the scratchy, sandpaper sounds, a reversal of the previous experience. Jack had been concentrating so hard on watching Madeline's expression that he had not looked at the faces of the others. Billie's eyes were shut tight as if by that act she might shut out the sounds. Deep frown lines had broken out on Virginia's forehead. Her lips trembled. Beside him, Bobbie seemed to have turned to cold stone.

The sounds faded until the room became silent again. Then suddenly, from Madeline's mouth, came a bloodcurdling, earsplitting scream. The room seemed to vibrate. Bobbie lurched forward. Tears streamed down Billie's face. Virginia gasped for breath. Madeline's scream had startled Jack. His heart seemed about to burst through his chest.

Then Madeline fell back, releasing her hands. She lay on her back, eyes closed. She was perspiring profusely. Her chest rose and fell as if she were fighting for breath.

"Is she dying?" Virginia asked. It was an odd idea, injecting a further note of terror. Billie threw herself into her mother's arms. She was crying hysterically.

He ran to the kitchen, poured out a glassful of water, then hurried back. Kneeling beside Madeline, he lifted her head and put the water to her mouth. A few drops spilled down her chin, but she managed to take a sip. Coughing, she seemed to shake off her trance. Gently, he lifted her head and cradled it in his arms.

"Are you okay?" he asked.

She nodded.

Billie still whimpered in her mother's arms, but some color had come back into Bobbie's cheeks. Virginia said nothing as she held Billie, kissing her hair and rubbing her back.

Madeline sat up. She took deep breaths, recovering before their eyes.

"I'm so sorry to have put you through this," she said gently.

"What had to be, had to be," Jack said. He was conscious of having suspended all judgment. "Sounds to me like a troubleshooting effort," he said, trying to put a light touch to the event. He got no rise out of either Virginia or the twins.

"In a way," Madeline said. She appeared disturbed by the reaction of the others. "Believe me," she said, addressing Virginia, "we had to make this trip."

"I didn't say you didn't," Virginia said. He was surprised to see her snappish and irritable. "It just scared the children."

"I'm so sorry," Madeline repeated as she reached out and drew Bobbie to her. "No harm will ever come to you as long as Madeline's here. So you see, there is nothing to be frightened of." Bobbie lay her head on Madeline's breast. "Is there sweetheart?" Madeline asked.

Bobbie shook her head.

Virginia's attitude troubled Jack. The voice within Madeline had implored that the believers at Madeline's end must not waver. There was no doubt that the voice was referring to Virginia. Not himself. He had no doubts whatsoever, especially now after what he had just witnessed. It was Virginia who had become the source of worry.

The evidence was indisputable. Hadn't they seen with their own eyes and heard with their own ears what surely was a direct link between Madeline and another world, the spirit world, the source of all her knowledge of the future? He pictured a place where all things were known, where the unseen beings linked to Madeline struggled constantly with the interferers who wished to thwart this link.

"Are you certain that what you have seen will come to be?" Jack asked with some trepidation, but without doubt.

"It always has," Madeline said. She released Bobbie and stood up. Then she gathered up the candles, blowing them each out in turn.

"You said something about time frame," Jack said. He glanced at Virginia who continued to soothe Billie. She did not return his gaze.

"Yes," Madeline replied. She put the candles on a shelf.

"Is it possible to be more specific?" he asked, glancing again at Virginia. The voice of the German man seemed to be saying that there was a time frame and therefore a moment when what was to happen would happen.

"I'm sorry, Jack, it's necessary to withhold that from you. . . ." She paused and looked sympathetically at Virginia. Something in either the glance or Madeline's answer seemed to stir her to action. She rose from the floor and, with the twins in tow, left the room. The action startled Jack. Was it a sign of wavering belief? He dared not speculate further.

"I don't know what's come over her," Jack said apologetically.

"It is puzzling," Madeline said. "I noticed it today."

"The latest rejection has probably put her into an old mode of thinking. I'm sure it will pass." Was he violating some prohibition here? Noting her expression, he assumed he had not.

"We'll watch her, won't we?" Madeline said. She came close and put her hand against Jack's cheek. Reaching out, he took it and kissed it.

"We won't let you down, Madeline. No way."

He left her and hurried off to join Virginia. She wasn't in the kitchen. Nor did he wish to eat. His stomach was too agitated. He found her in the bedroom. The twins lay on either side of her. Billie was still whimpering.

"There's nothing to be frightened of," he said sharply, addressing himself to all of them.

"I'm not frightened," Virginia said, "they are."

Her voice was tinged with anger, which confused him.

"You can't be angry at Madeline," he said.

'Why not?" she answered.

"You heard the voice."

"I heard a voice."

"Mommy." It was Bobbie. "You mustn't."

"Mustn't what?"

"You know," Bobbie said.

She kissed Billie. "This child is petrified," she said.

"There's no reason to be. Nothing has changed. In fact, nothing must change," Jack pleaded. "This is not the time to question. Not at this moment."

"I'm trying not to, trying my best."

"If you're starting to doubt, she'll know. You heard the voice. And you also know from first-hand knowledge. Have you forgotten what happened to Bobbie. To Basil." And what about Compulaser? he added silently.

"I resent my children being frightened. She didn't predict that." Billie whimpered. "All right, baby, Mommy's here." Virginia looked at Jack, her resentment and frustration palpable. "They're staying here tonight." Bobbie said nothing in protest and he sensed her confusion and fear.

"We have to accept these things," Jack said in a placating tone. Virginia was wavering in her belief. Her disappointment with Mrs. Horning had shaken her. "The point is that you can't lose faith. Not now." He sucked in a deep breath. "Especially not now."

When she didn't answer, he went into the

bathroom and took a hot shower. He needed to
reflect, husband his resources, not panic. Virginia's maternal instincts had clouded her vision. Hadn't he, too, been a victim of parental
overreaction? It would pass. She would get over
it. She had to get over it.

He tried to expand his thoughts, validate his
belief in Madeline to himself in such a way that
Madeline, who was surely tuning in to them,
would understand where things were going. He
believed. If Virginia was having a crisis of confidence it would pass. He promised this outcome to Madeline in his mind.

But no amount of internal explanation could
totally chase his fear. He had borrowed far in
excess of his resources. A fuse had been lit. The
slightest drop in the stock could start an avalanche of financial failure. It was an idea he had
managed to hold at bay and once again he
fought it back.

By the time he left the bathroom, he clearly
understood his role. He must recharge Virginia's faith. He would have to be the instrument
to bring her around. I will. I promise, he
shouted in his mind, certain that Madeline
would hear.

They had made room for him in the bed and
he climbed in. The twins were asleep. Bobbie
slept beside him, Billie, who occasionally sighed
deeply, was on the other side of her mother.

"I'm so sorry, Ginny," he whispered.

"I understand," Virginia said. "I just feel . . ."
Her voice drifted off.

"You heard her. The bottom line is: no faith,
nothing will happen."

She was silent for a long time.

"I'm very confused," she admitted.

"I'm not," he said.

Reaching out, he grasped her hand.

"There's too much at stake," he whispered. "We could be wiped out."

She was silent for a long time.

"I'll try," she said. "I'll try my best."

·23·

She did try. Instead of sleeping, she spent the night searching for the old faith. It was slipping away. Despite the threat of disaster, which did chill her, she could not find her way back to that point of absolute belief. Yet she did fear the consequences. Didn't that imply that she still believed? She wasn't sure.

Faith was still alive in her. It had to be. Otherwise she would be wallowing in shame and humiliation. Virginia had violated the vows of her marriage, had passed beyond taboo in the nether world of moral ambiguity. Perhaps this was, indeed, a reaction to that. Perhaps this was shame and guilt manifesting itself in another way.

It felt strange to be applying logic to her relationship and belief in Madeline. She thought about Madeline's earlier predictions, especially about her warning that the twins not play in the championship game. When it came to that, Virginia's doubts about Madeline turned to jelly. And hadn't she wrought a miraculous cure when Billie was sick? Nor could she deny that her stock market predictions had so far been right on the money.

And yet ... she could not shake the feeling that something was missing or not understood or, perhaps, misinterpreted. Yes, she had heard the voice emanate from Madeline's mouth. Voices can be distorted. Mysteries can be manipulated. Effects can be manufactured.

Or perhaps she had listened in a state of non-suspended belief and, therefore, could not fully comprehend it as the other-worldly occurrence it was.

When morning came, she still could not stop thinking about it. She heard Jack bend over her and felt him kiss her cheek.

"You'll see," he whispered. "The doubts will disappear."

She could hear him kiss the twins and whisper words of encouragement to them. Later, she was relieved to see that Billie seemed rested and apparently had come to grips with the events of the night before.

"Maybe I was just a scaredy cat," Billie said.

"I was scared myself," Virginia admitted.

"I hope Aunt Madeline isn't mad at me."

"Of course not, silly."

"If we don't believe, we could be in real trouble," Bobbie said.

"I very much doubt that's what Aunt Madeline meant," Virginia said in a scolding tone, but she knew better.

Determined to show her children cheerful nonconcern, she sent them off to school with smiles and hugs and kisses. She was relieved to see them functioning and, at least on the surface, content.

But she was worried. The trial in her mind

had led her in a complete circle. Reality and logic had invaded her consciousness. Also courage. And cunning.

In the kitchen, she drank coffee and tried to concentrate on the newspaper. She found no meaning in the print. Her mind was on Madeline. There were things she needed to know, desperately needed to know.

Madeline came into the kitchen in her dressing gown, as always carefully groomed. As if the events of last night had not occurred, she kissed Virginia who returned her greeting in kind.

"I didn't want to wake you," Virginia said, searching Madeline's face for any hint of knowledge about Virginia's most secret thoughts.

"I would have welcomed it," Madeline said, pouring a cup of coffee and sitting down beside Virginia.

"I want to apologize for last night," Virginia said. It was, she decided, important not to show any change. "Billie's reaction set me off."

"Perfectly understandable," Madeline said.

"Jack was very upset with me," Virginia continued.

Madeline's gaze met hers. Even the power of her eyes seemed diminished. Nevertheless, Virginia turned away. Above all, she must not let Madeline think that her power over her had weakened. It felt odd to be following these new rules. Also reassuring to find that Madeline did not appear to have the slightest suspicion. Or was she, too, being clever, toying with her? Virginia shrugged off the fear.

Madeline put her hand over Virginia's and squeezed it.

"I know."

"It wasn't doubt, Madeline. Just concern for Billie."

"I know," Madeline said, smiling gently.

"Mrs. Horning's rejection threw me. But I'm over that. I know it will happen and I'll continue to submit my work throughout the country. Maybe Europe as well. There's someone out there who will get the message."

"That's exactly the point, Virginia." Madeline brought Virginia's hand up to her mouth and kissed it.

"I'm so lucky to have found you," Virginia said.

"It was I who found you," Madeline replied, setting off another train of thought in Virginia's mind. Was that fateful meeting really preordained? Such internal questioning increased Virginia's boldness. Or had that meeting in Mel's been manipulated? With use, the fear of thinking such thoughts dissipated. She searched Madeline's face for any untoward reaction. None was visible. Not enough reason in itself to lower her guard. She would have to probe and test constantly.

"Anyway, enough of that, Madeline," Virginia said. "I am happy to report on this lovely morning . . ." The weather was perfect, hardly the kind of pre-Christmas weather one could expect in Connecticut. ". . . that there are no inner clouds on the horizon either. And I'm sure that Jack feels the same general optimism."

She continued to probe Madeline's face. There was neither a physical nor a verbal reaction. Considering Jack's financial commitment based on Madeline's predictions, this was worrisome.

"I'm sure he does," Madeline said, almost offhand.

It was a very frightening reaction. Jack had put their entire financial future on the line. As Virginia thought about it, the matter grew in seriousness. According to Jack, Madeline had never even discussed her choices with him. She had simply circled with a green Magic Marker those stocks that she recommended.

Virginia debated with herself whether to explore the matter further at this moment. No, she decided. Lack of knowledge about Madeline put her at a decided disadvantage. Earlier, Jack had been right; nothing could be taken at face value. Nothing. She had to know more. Besides, she was losing her fear of knowing.

From experience, Virginia realized that questioning Madeline was useless. Madeline was especially clever at deflecting information about herself, which left only one alternative, an aggressive personal investigation.

Taking her leave, Virginia went back to her bedroom and quickly dressed. By then, Madeline had gone out to the terrace where she continued to read the paper. Virginia went out to her, kissed her cheek and said good-bye.

"Back later. This family still has to eat."

"I'll be glad to go," Madeline said. She often accompanied Virginia on trips to the supermarket.

"You rest, Madeline," she said, "you've earned it."

Again she studied Madeline's face. Still no hint of suspicion. Nevertheless, Virginia wondered if Madeline knew what was in her mind. If so, the matter must be tested. If not, it must be challenged.

Virginia was fully aware of the danger in what she was doing, but she was determined to

see it through. It was as if she had ventured out
into the world after months locked away in a
basement dungeon.

Making sure Madeline remained on the terrace, Virginia stole into the guest room. She
knew exactly what she was after, the keys to
Madeline's apartment and information about its
exact location. It was, Virginia reasoned, essential to investigate Madeline's private environment. It was the logical place to start. Jack had
also been right about that.

She looked through Madeline's drawers. She
was neat to a fault and her carefully cared-for
clothes were folded perfectly in their space. The
upper drawers were less organized. In one, she
noted the green Magic Marker that Madeline
must have used to circle her stock picks.

Madeline's pocketbook lay in a bureau
drawer. Virginia looked at it a moment. She was
definitely not comfortable in this situation.
There was the lingering fear that Madeline was
monitoring her actions. She could not completely discard the feeling. But her most overwhelming discomfort was of violating someone
else's privacy.

It took some effort on her part to lay the matter to rest. With trembling fingers, she opened
the pocketbook clasp and poked around inside.
As expected, she found a set of keys. They were
attached to a ring on which there was also a
small electronic "genie" gate opener. She took
the keys, peeked into Madeline's wallet, found
her license, checked her address then closed the
pocketbook.

Her mind was racing with scenarios. Suspicion and fear gave way to ingenuity and
resourcefulness. The keys posed a special prob-

lem. Madeline's car keys were on the same loop
as what appeared to be the apartment keys. Virginia would not dare to separate them. If Madeline decided to go out she would discover that
they were missing. The only solution was to
make copies.

She stole into her car and, working on an inspired guess, opened the electronic gate with
Madeline's "genie." It seemed odd. Virginia had
always assumed that Jack had given Madeline
one of the spare handheld "genies" that they
both used to open and close the gate. Checking
the gate to be certain that Basil was inside, she
started down the hill.

She found a hardware store open on Sunset,
made copies of the keys and was back in the
house in twenty minutes. She wondered if Madeline, who was still sitting on the terrace, had
heard the door open. She was also curious as
to whether Madeline would reveal in her expression any hint of knowing what Virginia was
up to.

Poking her head out the terrace door, she
waved. Madeline was still reading the paper.
Virginia noted that it was open to the financial
section. It reminded her of the risks Jack was
taking based on Madeline's suggestions. She
chased the memory, although she began to feel
an inner tug of panic. Mustn't give in to that,
she protested to herself. She could not deal with
that just yet, not until she was certain. Certain
of what?

"Forgot something. I've got to go back to the
market," she chirped to Madeline, smiling benignly.

Madeline waved and went back to reading the

paper. Quickly, Virginia returned to Madeline's room and replaced the key ring.

Using her own handheld "genie," Virginia opened and closed the gate. In less than a half hour she was at Madeline's address in Santa Monica. It took some fiddling with the keys before she was able to let herself in the front door of the apartment building. Madeline's name and number were clearly marked on the board. Although she was agitated, Virginia was able to function with efficiency and alertness.

She found Madeline's apartment and, taking a deep breath, let herself in.

Virginia's overall impression was of extraordinary neatness. Every object seemed in its place and meant to be there.

The furniture was serviceable but not elegant. In the living room was a couch and two upholstered chairs set in a conversational group, a wall of bookcases filled with books on the occult, astrology, numerology, clairvoyance . . . all the subjects in which Madeline was involved. In a corner of the room was a small desk on which stood a portable typewriter.

After studying the living room, Virginia went into the bedroom. There was a double bed, a bureau, a *Poudreuse* and a single French provincial chair. Nothing untoward or mysterious. In fact, aside from neatness, Virginia's second impression was of banality, an apartment like thousands of others with little character, yet practical and comfortable.

She went into the bathroom, which was decorated in pink, and into a small kitchen equipped for only rudimentary cooking. Absorbing the details of the apartment calmed her agitation. It seemed so pedestrian, so incongru-

ous, considering the monumental effect that its
occupant had had on her life and the lives of
her family. There was no mystery here, no eerie
atmosphere, not the slightest hint of Madeline's
access to the so-called spirit world of unseen
beings.

Calmer now, although sparked by a sense of
urgency, Virginia let her eye wander about the
place searching for details, clues that would
open her mind to some understanding of how
or why this obsession with Madeline had come
about in the first place.

Where does one begin? On the desk in the living room, she found a framed photograph of
two young girls, about the age of Billie and
Bobbie. Their arms were wrapped around each
other.

She picked up the picture and studied it. The
two girls were posed in front of a tree. They
were smiling and seemed genuinely happy as if
the photographer had caught a joyful moment
in their lives. Obviously they were people who
loomed large in Madeline's world, relatives perhaps, or even daughters. Considering how little
she knew of Madeline, any speculation was possible.

But on closer inspection, Virginia saw something in the picture that startled her. They were
obviously identical twins. And both girls had
Madeline's face, a much younger Madeline, but
unquestionably one of them was Madeline.

Virginia knew instantly that she was on the
trail of something profound and it frightened
her. For a moment her courage wavered. Was
it a trick? Were these so-called twins actually
two Madelines, set up deliberately to confuse
and demoralize her? She shrugged off the sud-

den invasion of paranoia. It indicated that she hadn't completely shed the yoke of Madeline's influence.

There was no going back. Stay on the side of logic and rationality, she begged herself. She continued to study the picture. Her artist's eye caught differences in the two faces that were not apparent at first. One thing she knew about was twins. Though technically identical, she could easily separate her daughters by both looks and personality. In a few moments, she was able to pick out Madeline. Virginia's fear receded and she knew that she had found an important link between Madeline and her family.

It fired Virginia's curiosity and she began to rummage in the desk drawers which were remarkably neat and organized. Once again it struck her how ordinary Madeline's possessions were, especially against the backdrop of her awesome power over them. Virginia found pencils, ball-point pens, Magic Markers in all colors, spare check books, coupons for supermarket savings, paper clips, envelopes. She opened a small box and saw that it contained calling cards similar to the one Madeline had handed to her on the first day of their meeting. Madeline Curran Boswell, Psychic.

In one of the drawers she found neatly stacked manila envelopes. Each was labeled with green Magic Marker, similar to the type Madeline had used to circle her stock picks. The envelopes were labeled with such diverse names as "Horses," "Baseball," "Football," "Fights," "Stocks." She went through each of them quickly. The material inside ranged from tout sheets, to other forms of sports and stock data used for betting. She recalled Jack's earlier accusations, smiled and shook her head.

She found another item beside the envelopes. It was a note scrawled on the letterhead of something called "Hendley."

"We regret to inform you," the note read, "that your father, Vincent Boswell, died in his sleep on Wednesday, a peaceful end to a turbulent life. Although your father had been a deeply troubled man earlier in his life, we can be thankful that eventually he did fully regain his grasp of reality and a perspective on past events as his relationship with you will attest. He had become a valued member of this institution and we will miss him. Yours truly, Miles Harper, Director."

Hendley meant nothing to Virginia, but it did suggest that the man, Madeline's father, had been in some kind of an institution, had once lost his grasp of reality, had subsequently regained it and had been reconciled with his daughter. Elementary, she teased herself.

Virginia didn't stop there. She wanted to see if somewhere in the apartment there was more evidence of this relationship. She tried to imagine herself as Madeline, with her passion for neatness and compartmentalization. She opened more drawers, then closets. On the upper closet shelf in the bedroom she found a shoe box labeled, "Daddy." Opening it, she saw another neatly stacked pile of letters held together by rubber bands. Once again, she congratulated herself on her detective work. It was all so easy, so logical. If only she had done this earlier, taken Jack's advice. She shook her head, overtaken by a wave of sadness.

She brought the shoe box into the living room

and sat down at the desk from where, as a precaution, she would have a clear view through the window of the street below. One by one she proceeded to read the letters. They were more than she bargained for. Heartrending and emotional, they were written in a flourishing clear hand, always beginning "My Dearest Daughter."

Intruding on the sanctity of this strange father-and-daughter relationship seemed sinful. Obviously, the father had meant the words for his daughter only. It was against all of Virginia's principles. A matter of life and death, she reasoned as she pressed forward in her reading, mesmerized by what the letters revealed. Mostly, they were pleas for forgiveness. The man had obviously done something that had traumatized his daughter, caused her excruciating mental pain.

I cannot understand what was in my mind at the time, seemed to be the dominant theme. What had he done that required such elaborate soul-searching and mordant pleas for forgiveness?

"The specter will always haunt me," the man wrote. "It is my cross and I hope I shall never be relieved of this burden until my dying day."

Always the letters contained gossip about the institution in which the man was, quite obviously, committed.

"Now that I'm no longer 'criminally insane,'" he wrote, "the punishment finally fits the crime. Such irony. To be normal among the misfits, to know what I have done and why I am here. The punishment is the only thing that keeps me alive. And you, my darling daughter."

The letters gave the picture of a haunted man desperately trying to hold on to his daughter. Often, he wrote how impossible it must be for her ever to love him, rejecting what must have been her written profession of love for him. What struck Virginia as most odd was that not once in the letters was there any mention of the other twin. Nor of Madeline's mother.

She checked the dates of the letters. The first was dated in May 1967, the last less than a year ago. She wished she could see the other half of the correspondence, those revealing Madeline's thoughts and observations.

Having loved her own parents and having lived with the guilty idea that she had abandoned them when they needed her most, Virginia felt a renewed warmth for Madeline, a sympathy that transcended the reasons why she was there and what she was looking for. She wondered if what she had discovered was truly relevant. What had it to do with Madeline's so-called psychic powers? What did it mean?

What she had discovered, pure and simple, were dark and hidden secrets about Madeline's life that seemed perfectly appropriate to have been kept hidden. To resurrect them in confession might have been too painful for Madeline.

Virginia felt ashamed. Her investigation was sleazy and underhanded.

Not liking herself very much, Virginia began to put the letters back in the shoe box. She noticed a yellowed newspaper clipping on the bottom of the box. Carefully unfolding it, she began to read it. Almost from the first word, her heart leaped to her throat.

MAN MURDERS WIFE AND TWIN DAUGHTER, the

headline read. She had difficulty focusing on
what came next, but the gist was clear. For
some mysterious reason Vincent Boswell had
come home from work and taken a hammer and
crushed the skulls of his wife and one of his
twin daughters. The other twin apparently had
seen it coming and jumped through a window
to escape. When found, according to the clipping, she was hysterical and traumatized. Vincent Boswell was found near the bodies,
confused but without remorse. He was a stockbroker and, according to interviews with co-
workers and relatives, had shown no signs of
being capable of such an act.

Virginia could graphically visualize the horror, the crushed heads, the bloody hammer, the
effect on a child about the age of her own children. It was chilling and it nauseated her.

It crossed Virginia's mind that the discovery
of the article was Madeline's planned retribution, punishment for her investigation. For a
brief moment, she felt that she was waffling, returning to her previous state of belief.

It passed quickly and she groped for understanding. Certainly the murder of her mother
and sister had had a profound effect on Madeline. Again Virginia returned to the central
question. But what did it say about Madeline's
psychic powers?

She put the clipping and letters back into the
shoe box, then put the box back on the shelf in
the bedroom. As she did so, the telephone rang.
She froze. Was this Madeline calling to prove
her power? She listened. It continued to ring.
Should she answer it? Admit that she had questioned, sinned? The telephone continued to ring,

but she could not bring herself to confront the possibility. Finally it stopped.

For the moment Virginia would have to live in a world between speculation and reality. But it irritated her to know that her courage had wavered. She hoped that her cunning would not.

·24·

Compulaser remained flat for most of the morning, which gave Jack a chance to attend to other business and also calculate exactly what he had at risk or, as he preferred to characterize it, what he stood to make as the stock rose.

His exposure was more than two million dollars, which represented double his hard net worth. Although it was, as the bankers say, hypothecated, he controlled over four hundred thousand shares of Compulaser, which meant that every point up or down meant a four hundred thousand dollar gain or loss.

He fully expected the stock to double, although he felt assured by Madeline's prediction that the stock, in light of what he needed to start his business, was more likely to do even better than that.

Naturally he was nervous. In terms of believing Madeline, he was one hundred percent pure. What he was worried about was Virginia's commitment, which was ironic since it represented a role reversal from the time when it was he who had been skeptical.

At noon Jane came into his office. She was wearing more makeup than usual, obviously applied in a valiant effort to hide strain and sleepless nights.

"We're fading," she said. Her voice was weak. He knew what she meant and punched in a request for a stock quote.

"Down a half. No big deal."

"It is to me," she said.

"A watched pot doesn't boil," Jack said. He regretted having ever confided in her.

"I just want to know when it's supposed to happen?" she asked.

"I told you," he said in measured tones, "it will happen."

"What I asked is *when*?" she persisted.

"I'm really getting tired of these questions," Jack said. "If you can't stand the heat get out of the kitchen."

"It's your morning for clichés is it?" she said, nonplussed by his rebuke.

"And it's your morning for whining."

"Jesus, Jack, my life is on the line."

"So is mine."

She looked at him with hurt eyes and walked out of the office.

Soon after she left, he got a call from Singer.

"Down a point, Jack," Singer said.

"No way," Jack began, punching in another request for a quotation. It confirmed Singer's information.

"An aberration," Jack said. "I'll call around."

After hanging up, he called various brokers throughout the country, making casual inquiries.

"Compulaser. Funny you should ask. We just dumped a potful," one of the brokers responded. He was based in Dallas. Compulaser was based in Houston. The proximity was enough to cause Jack's stomach to tighten.

"Anything we should know?" Jack asked. "We have some minor positions in the house."

"Haven't heard," the broker volunteered, meaning he was not going to tell if he was still moving stock. There was, however, something ominous in his tone.

"I really think this one has a future," Jack said, trying to elicit a response.

"Depends on how long a time frame you're looking at."

"You don't see it in the short term?"

"Not the way this one's dropping."

Hanging up, Jack punched in for another quote. The stock had dropped another point. As expected Jane rushed into his office.

"It's on the down elevator," she said, her voice sputtering with anger.

"It'll go up."

"Bullshit."

"I told you. Pull out. I'm holding."

Her nostrils quivered as she ran out of the office. When she had left, he called the main office of Compulaser in Houston and asked to talk to the president. A hard-boiled secretary tried to put him off.

"I own a boatload of your stock, four hundred thousand shares to be exact, and I control another hundred thousand shares. Your boss either talks to me or I dump it on the market within the next three minutes." Jack's teeth chattered with fear at the prospect. The man was on the phone in seconds.

"Nothing profound," the president said, explaining that one of the company's patents had been challenged by another company. The president sounded evasive and self-serving as he explained it. ". . . but our core business is not affected in the least and we've got a huge contract pending with IBM."

"And the stock?" Jack asked.

"Might get bashed at first. It'll only be temporary. We're not worried at this end."

Not worried? Jack felt his energy drain. He could barely say good-bye. A spreading deep depression was taking hold of him. Virginia, he thought. He had warned her. Her negativity was causing havoc. She had put the kibosh on it. *Help me Madeline*, he screamed inside himself. *Help me*. He wanted to cry.

The telephone rang, but he could not summon the will to answer it. Instead, he got up from his desk and left his office. He wasn't sure where he was going. When he passed Jane's office, he looked in. She was sitting at her desk staring at the wall.

He continued down the corridor. People greeted him, but he barely responded. Summon reserves, he begged himself. Madeline would protect him. Hadn't she promised? I have faith. I believe. A flicker of optimism bubbled up inside of him. It was temporary, he assured himself. A short-term thing. The president of Compulaser had it right.

Problem was that Jack could only be in it for the very short term. As soon as the bank got wind of it, it would move in, discover that he was badly overextended, force him to sell out, make up the difference. His house would be gone. Nothing would be left. Nothing.

Out in the street, the sun was sparkling, setting a scene totally incongruous to his mood. It

will all go away, he told himself. Madeline was
leading the charge against those unseen beings
trying to thwart them. *Bring Virginia back*, he
told her in his mind. *Call her back to you.*

By rote, he found his car in the garage and
moved out through the parking lot gate. He
headed west on Olympic toward the ocean.
Madeline would win, he was sure of it, but he
could not take the tension of the battle.

Reaching Pacific Highway he felt the revital-
izing effect of the ocean, an endless patch of glorious blue stretching into infinity. Turning
north, he headed up the coast, opening the car
windows to the wind. Had he wavered? If he
had, he offered his apologies to Madeline, certain she would hear them. *Not my fault*, he told
himself, broadcasting the message in his mind.
He was being absurd. Stocks were mercurial.
This was a fluke. Compulaser would weather
the storm and head upward again.

By the time he reached Trancas, he felt suffi-
ciently recovered to brave a call to his office.
Turning off the highway, he found a telephone
booth outside of a gas station.

"Jack Sargent here. I need a quote on Compulaser," he told the woman who answered.

"Two and a half bid. Three asked."

"Are you sure?"

He waited until she verified the quote. "Two
and a half bid. Three asked," the woman repeated.

His pores opened, releasing an avalanche of
perspiration. Couldn't be. He leaned against the
metal wall of the booth for support. More than
half the value of the stock had disappeared.
What he needed now, above all, was reassurance.

With shaking fingers he punched in the number of his home. The telephone had barely rung before it was answered. It was Virginia.

"Ginny?"

"Where were you? I've been worried. I called the office."

"We've got a problem," he said, fighting off a breath-quickening hysteria.

"Yes, we do," she said, her voice conspiratorial, lowering to a whisper. Her response chilled him. "Come home, please, we must talk."

"I need Madeline," he said.

"Madeline?"

"I've got to speak to her."

"Be careful," Virginia whispered. He sensed her skepticism.

"You've ruined us," he said.

"No," she responded. "We need to talk."

"I'm not coming home until I talk to Madeline. Is she there?"

There was a long pause.

"I'll get her."

He listened to the quiet hum of the empty line, his patience strained, the sweat soaking his clothes. *Bitch*, he cried within himself. *You destroyed us.*

"Jack?"

It was Madeline's voice, calm, measured, a far cry from his own fevered state.

"Madeline?"

"Of course it's me," she said smoothly, unruffled.

"Where's Ginny?"

"In her studio, I think. She just called up for me to take the phone." She sighed. "She's been acting strangely all day. Went off for a couple of hours."

"What are we going to do?"

"Do?"

"You know."

"Whatever are you talking about, Jack?" Madeline asked, not the slightest hint of consternation in her voice. He was confused. Should he be relieved?

"Compulaser," he blurted.

"Compulaser?"

"The stock you told me to buy," he said, surprised that she needed to be reminded of something that was in the process of ruining his life.

"Are you all right, Jack?"

Something cold clutched his chest. The perspiration running out of his body froze.

"Compulaser." By now he hated the name. "The stock you gave me to buy."

"I did?"

"Compulaser. For crying out loud, Madeline, you circled it in the paper."

"You mustn't fantasize," she said sternly.

"Madeline," he pleaded, "you did it. I know you did. No one else could have done it."

"Now you're being hysterical," she rebuked. Hysterical? He was panicked. His life was going down the drain. Was it possible he had fantasized it? Was his memory faulty? Had he imagined this?

"Are you saying that you never recommended Compulaser?"

"Recommended? What is it, Jack? What is going on with you?"

It struck him that this was a trick. Someone, an unseen being perhaps, had intercepted his call, had assumed Madeline's voice and identity and was deliberately torturing him.

"Are you Madeline?"

"Of course I am."

He could not think of anything more to say.
He held the phone to his ear, groping for words.
Yet his ear remained alert to sounds at the
other end. He heard faint breathing.

"Virginia?"

A tiny click followed. Virginia had been listening, he was sure of it. This was all Virginia's
doing. Hostile unseen beings had invaded her,
had created mischief in her name.

"We're in trouble, Madeline," he said. "I'm
heading home."

·25·

Above all, she would have to hold herself aloof from any emotion that could prevent her from doing that which she had to do. No wallowing in guilt or self-incrimination. No surrender to fear or hysteria. No panic that might cloud her imagination. She needed to gather every ounce of guile and cunning that she could muster. The enemy was crafty, persuasive and without morals or conscience.

Of that she was convinced. She would leave regrets to the future. The objective now was to salvage their lives, restore logic and rationality and emerge from this black tunnel of manipulation and deceit. Once freed, there would be plenty of time to lick the wounds of humiliation.

It had to be confronted. And defeated. She and Jack had given away their minds and their bodies. The image of the latter filled her with disgust. How had it happened? Why them? How had Madeline moved in on them? Was there something so obviously vulnerable about them that made them an easy target for Madeline's brand of psychic persuasion? How had she known so much about them? Had she guessed? Had she started with any preknown hard facts?

At first, the sheer volume and weight of these questions threatened to overwhelm Virginia. She had to consider each one in turn, carefully, calmly, analytically. Her mind, thankfully, had begun to function again. She needed to take the kind of action that would banish this blight from their lives. She knew her mission. She was fighting for their survival.

She stayed in her studio until midafternoon devising ways to counter Madeline's cunning. Since Virginia had recovered a healthy skepticism, she no longer questioned the privacy of her own thoughts.

But she could not ignore the probability that Madeline had sensed a change in their relationship. If so, she would be on her guard, alert to Virginia's every move, plotting moves of her own. The battle lines were becoming clearly drawn in Virginia's mind. More important, she had a more rounded picture of the enemy than before. And it was formidable, awesome.

Virginia's priority was to anticipate Madeline's moves and find ways to counter them, in advance, if possible. Was she any match for Madeline? She had her doubts. Nevertheless, just as Madeline had found the weakness in Virginia and her family, she must probe to find the weakness in Madeline.

From the moment she returned from Madeline's apartment, Virginia had avoided her, although she had let Madeline know that she was home. Madeline had made no effort to join her. Virginia was grateful for that but suspected it was cause for concern. It was unusual for the

two women to share the house for any length of
time without contact.

Jack's phone call triggered Virginia's plan.
Madeline's responses to Jack had clearly shown
that she had chosen the killing ground. She,
Virginia, was to be the sacrifice.

Virginia gathered whatever emotional resources she could and took the first step toward
what she knew would be the ultimate show-
down. *High noon for the Sargents*, she thought
bitterly.

Slipping out of the house, she took the car
and drove to the twins' school. They could not
be left out. They had to bear witness. She
needed them with her. Now. Today.

"It's not fair," Bobbie cried.

"We can't miss any more rehearsals," Billie
echoed.

Virginia had told the drama teacher that they
were needed at home.

"But why, Mommy?" Bobbie asked.

"It's very important," Virginia said. She was
about to say "Trust me," but the memory of
that phrase riled her. Instead she said, "I want
you with me."

"But why?" Billie echoed.

"Because it's necessary for you to understand
what's going on in our house. Especially with
Madeline." She coughed into her fist. "And with
you father."

"Daddy?" Bobbie asked.

Virginia could not be totally honest with the
girls. Not yet. But she was determined that they
discover the truth. Nothing less would set them
free . . . all of them.

When she returned to the house, Jack had already arrived. She intended to confront Made-

line and Jack directly, but there was something she had to do first. She told the twins to join them in the den in fifteen minutes while she went into her studio.

"Now where would it be?" she whispered to herself, searching the room. It pleased her when she found that her suspicion was correct. *You're not all that mysterious, Madeline,* she told herself.

Jack and Madeline were in the den, sitting opposite each other. The deadly serious atmosphere in the room was palpable. It was clear to Virginia that they had decided on a course of action between them. Jack's complexion reflected his dilemma; two blotches of red colored his cheeks. The rest of his skin was ashen.

Madeline stared at Virginia with narrowed eyes in an attempt to generate their old magnetism. Virginia was unmoved. She offered a smile of greeting.

"Hi, guys," she said.

Jack and Madeline seemed beyond smiles or good humor.

At that moment the twins came running into the room, stopping short when they saw the expressions on the faces of Jack and Madeline.

"Why aren't they at rehearsal?" Jack snapped.

"I wanted them home," Virginia said.

"Do you think that's wise?" Madeline asked, telescoping the clear message of impending confrontation.

"Very wise," Virginia said.

Madeline seemed confused by her remark. Virginia liked that. Already, she was hampering whatever plan Madeline had in mind.

"I don't like this, Virginia," Jack said, glancing at Madeline.

"Who does?"

"What I have to say will disturb the girls," Jack said. He looked toward the twins and shrugged. "I'm sorry about this, children."

"So am I," Madeline said sweetly. She looked at Virginia and shook her head sadly as if to say: Poor woman ... putting her children through this ordeal.

Virginia sat between the two girls on the couch, her hands joined with each. She squeezed them for reassurance. It was obvious that they were confused.

"Don't be frightened, children. Everything will be fine," Virginia said. She glared at Jack who turned his eyes away.

"Believe me, Virginia," Madeline said, "I didn't want this to happen."

"I made something happen?" Virginia asked, eyes widening, hoping that her feigned innocence was convincing.

"You've deliberately destroyed us," Jack said, his lips curling in anger.

Virginia was taken aback. She had not expected the vehemence. The twins looked at each other, frightened.

"That's a mouthful, Jack." Virginia was determined to keep calm. Despite the anger boiling inside of her, she forgave him. He was totally captured, a willing tool of Madeline's. As she had once been. *Concentrate*, she pleaded with herself. Find the flaws.

"Neither of us can understand your motives," Jack said.

"Not understand? I thought Madeline understands everything. Don't you, Madeline?" Virginia said, hoping the sarcasm would be loud and clear.

"Evil wears strange masks," Madeline said.

"Evil, is it?" Virginia said. "Whatever happened to the unseen beings? I thought they were the troublemakers."

"Mommy," Billie said, squeezing her hand, "you're upsetting Aunt Madeline."

"It's all right, sweetheart," Virginia said soothingly.

"Ginny, we're losing everything. Everything. Compulaser has plummeted."

"And I'm to blame?"

He looked at his daughters. "It's as if something's possessed her," he said, directing his explanation to the twins.

"Possession, too?" Virginia said.

Madeline nodded and glanced toward Jack. So she was letting him carry the ball.

"It was a willful act of jealousy and revenge," Jack said. "A Judas act."

"I thought possession was when another being had control over your will," Virginia said. "Now you accuse me of a willful act."

He hadn't expected the response. Again, he glanced toward Madeline, who nodded.

"Even forgiving you can't change the facts. We're busted." His voice broke. "Finished."

"And it's all my fault?"

He nodded.

She looked at her husband. He seemed utterly transformed.

"What has she told you?"

"The truth," Jack said.

"And what is that?" Virginia asked.

"That it was you who circled those stocks."

It was exactly the way she had imagined it.

So much for psychic phenomena. Anybody could do it with a little reason and a lot of luck. The twins looked at her, puzzled, but said nothing.

Jack was seething. Virginia could see that his mind was clapped shut.

"Why did I do that? Pick those stocks?" Virginia asked quietly.

"To hurt us. To denigrate Madeline."

She turned to face Madeline.

"And you're certain I did this?"

"Absolutely."

"I was possessed by an evil force?"

"Yes," Madeline said, "and it still has you in its power."

Virginia looked at the twins. They were petrified, but she held tightly to their hands.

"Then where the hell were your psychic gifts?" Virginia asked. "Your vaunted telepathy? Your mumbo-jumbo astrology predictions? If I did that, why didn't you know I did?"

"Your allies kept it from me," Madeline said blandly.

"The unseen beings?"

"Exactly," Jack echoed.

"I thought you made money on the first pick," Virginia said, turning to Jack.

"I did. The second was flat. Then came Compulaser. You sucked me in, then you took your shot." He looked at the twins. "I'm sorry about this, kids. All the money I had in the world is tied to Compulaser. That's the stock your mother led me to buy."

"Don't you believe a word of it, girls. He has no idea what he's saying." She pointed to Madeline. "There's the brains behind it all. You are one clever bitch."

"I resent that," Jack said. He sighed and slumped in the chair. "Not that it matters. We're finished. This house. Everything. Gone."

The twins looked at their father, frightened by what they were hearing.

"Not to worry, kids," he said, "I still have my job. I'll be back up there soon ... with Madeline's help."

"You believe that, Jack?"

"Yes."

"And you still think that everything Madeline has predicted will come true?"

"Eventually." His voice trailed off. "Someday," he whispered hoarsely.

Madeline reached out and touched Jack's arm.

The gesture inflamed Virginia. How dare she? But she held her temper. "And what proof has she offered you?" Virginia asked.

"Proof?" He looked helplessly at Madeline.

"He doesn't need proof, he has my word," Madeline said, smooth as silk. She was, Virginia noted, remarkably poised. "Of course, he denied it to himself. That was only natural."

"Only natural?" Virginia turned to Jack. "Also only natural for me to cause my own family's financial demise? Only natural that I wish to destroy my family?"

Jack cleared his throat. "It wasn't your fault. You were possessed," he sputtered.

She glanced at Madeline. "Calling on the demons again, Madeline? No way. No more. I say again, where is your proof? You're a great one for proof. Then show us, show us all."

Behind the mask of calm, she saw Madeline's smugness. Madeline hadn't wavered and Jack was buying it.

Virginia spoke to Jack directly now. "I think you owe it to your children to offer more than just"—she leveled her gaze on Madeline—"that woman's word." From his perspective, she knew, it was sacrilege. Virginia was providing him with even more evidence that she was upsetting the karma. The twins whimpered beside her. Virginia embraced them soothingly.

"They have no right to be here," Jack said, "they've been through enough."

"They have every right, and it's about time, too." She looked at Madeline. "We've had quite enough playacting, Madeline, quite enough lies."

Madeline smiled. "Playacting? You people are under my protection. I've shown you your future."

"You've shown us fantasy, Madeline."

"Be careful of what you say, Virginia," Jack snapped.

"Then ask her for proof, Jack," Virginia pressed. "Surely the great clairvoyant can provide you with proof of my so-called misdeeds." She turned again to Madeline, goading her. "Show him proof."

Madeline maintained her attitude of gracious tolerance. What was her counterploy? Virginia wondered.

"How were these so-called stock picks conveyed to you?" Madeline asked Jack. The question confirmed Virginia's hunch. Now she knew that she had penetrated Madeline's mind-set. *Proceed with caution*, she told herself. No kudos yet.

"Circled in green Magic Marker," Jack responded.

"Come with me," Madeline said mysteriously.

Jack looked at Virginia and sneered. *Poor baby,* Virginia thought, *what have I put you through?*

Madeline led them to Virginia's studio, pausing until they all were inside the room. She did have a flair for the dramatic, Virginia thought, not without some grudging admiration. But how easy it was to see through her now.

Virginia had rearranged the studio that day. She had deliberately turned all the studies of Madeline toward the wall. No longer did Madeline's image dominate the room. The significance of this could not be lost on Jack. Certainly not on Madeline. Behind Jack's facade of strength and calm, Virginia could see the first faint signs of uncertainty. *You ain't seen nothin' yet,* she said to herself.

With the twins cowering next to her, they watched as Madeline stood in the center of the studio. She stroked her chin as if in contemplation, then zeroed in on the center drawer of Virginia's desk, one that she used for nonartistic paperwork. With great self-confidence and satisfaction, Madeline put her hand on the drawer knob.

But before she opened the drawer, she turned to Virginia. "I'm sorry about this Virginia." Glancing toward Jack, she said, "What I predicted for your future is irrevocable. Above all, I want you to know that what is occurring is not your fault. You're an innocent victim and I do forgive you, no matter how it looks. I also want you to know that I still value your friendship and the closeness and love I've experienced in this house. So please, please don't let anything that happens break the bond that we all have between us."

It was a solemn little speech. Jack had a

puppy dog glow of slavish approval on his face. It indicated to Virginia how terribly far Jack had drifted from reality. Still a believer, even in the face of financial disaster. What puzzled her most was how Jack could believe that this so-called revelation was going to relieve that problem. Did he cling to the hope that Madeline would reverse this condition?

Then she remembered her own mental slavery, her mindless puppetlike responses to Madeline's manipulation. For a brief moment, her courage faltered.

Madeline opened the drawer. She stooped, looked closer at the contents, then started to rifle them. With growing frustration, she pulled the drawer out of the desk and upended it on the floor. Kneeling she scattered papers, pencils, pens, paper clips. Flushing deep red, she stood up and glared at Virginia.

"Where is it?" Her face was contorted with anger.

The twins huddled closer to Virginia. Glancing toward Jack, Virginia threw him what she hoped was a look of genuine puzzlement.

"Do you know what she means?" she asked him. Despite her inner turmoil, she managed to sound calm. He shook his head and shrugged.

Coming closer to Virginia, Madeline waved a finger in her face. "It's a trick," she said. She turned to Jack. "She's possessed, I tell you. We're dealing here with the devil incarnate. This is not your wife. Don't be fooled by her appearance." She looked toward the children. Her carefully groomed hair seemed to be unraveling of its own accord. "This is not your mother, girls. I tell you it's the devil."

The twins clutched at Virginia, whimpering.

It took all of Virginia's resources to hold herself back from what she knew she must do. *Not yet*, she begged herself. *Soon*. She looked at Jack, whose expression was flaccid, slack-jawed, pained.

"I don't understand any of this," he said hoarsely.

"They've captured her, Jack." Madeline's voice was rising. "The unseen beings. I may have to channel immediately."

"Not yet, Madeline," Virginia said quietly. "I think it's time to follow me."

Without another word, she left the studio, hand in hand with the twins. "Can't be helped, sweethearts," she whispered.

"Don't go with her," Madeline screamed. "They'll take you as well. Don't go."

"Momeeee," Bobbie squealed, trying to hold back.

"Momeeee," Billie echoed.

Virginia continued her movement, dragging her daughters along. Behind her, she heard Jack's footsteps and Madeline's anxious entreaties. She headed for the guest room. On top of the dresser she saw Madeline's pocketbook. Jack was close behind her.

"Give me that!" Madeline screeched. Beads of perspiration had settled on her upper lip.

Virginia raised the pocketbook above her head and sidestepped Madeline.

"I swear to you, you'll go straight to hell," Madeline seethed.

Virginia ignored Madeline and opened the pocketbook clasp. She threw the contents on the bed.

"Is this what you were looking for, Madeline?" she said, holding up a green Magic

Marker. Virginia was fully aware of her own dramatics, determined to play the role to the teeth.

"She's lying, Jack. She planted it there," Madeline said. She glared at Virginia. "Damn you."

Virginia held up the marker. "Jack, we've been taken," she said. She turned toward the twins. "This woman is a liar. Tell them, Madeline."

Jack continued to stand beside Madeline. Virginia could tell that he had not yet returned to the real world.

"And this little baby?" Virginia said. She picked up Madeline's key chain from the muddle on the bed. She held up the "genie."

"Did you give her this, Jack?"

"What is it?" he asked.

"It opens electronic gates, just a smaller version of ours."

Jack was puzzled.

"Did you give it to her?" Virginia repeated.

"Why no—" Jack began, then stopped abruptly.

"You mustn't listen, Jack," Madeline said.

"Why not?" Virginia snapped. She turned toward Madeline. Virginia's face was flushed, her lips pressed together in anger. "Jack didn't give you our spare "genie," and I didn't, so is this how you opened the gate, Madeline?"

"This is not really Virginia, Jack," Madeline cried. "You must resist her."

"You had it all along, right, Madeline? You needed it to perform the miracle of Basil. Tell us, Madeline, right or wrong?" Virginia said.

Madeline lunged at her. The twins screamed. In what must have been an instinctive reflex, Jack stepped forward and held Madeline back.

"Bitch," Madeline cried, twisting and squirming. Jack held her fast. "You are the devil. I swear she is. The devil."

"Tell us how you did it, Madeline," Virginia said. "Tell us."

Suddenly Madeline closed her eyes. Her body went rigid. She began to shake. From out of her mouth came the same eerie croaking sounds that they had heard during the so-called channeling session.

Jack slowly released her. She fell to her knees. The strange sounds continued. Madeline's face contorted.

Virginia embraced the twins and held them close to her. "Nothing to fear children," she told them.

Jack, bug-eyed, stood transfixed, apparently still convinced that Madeline was a medium, contacting the unseen beings in the spirit world.

Now, Virginia decided. She released the girls after one last reassuring squeeze and knelt next to Madeline. Madeline's eyes were shut tight. The sound coming out of her grew louder. Virginia put her mouth close to Madeline's ear.

"Maybe you can reach your sister Margaret, Madeline," Virginia said firmly, certain that the sound of her voice registered. "Margaret, Madeline, your twin sister."

The sound coming from Madeline's throat faltered.

"You can stop all this nonsense now," Virginia scolded. "We've had enough."

Madeline continued to emit the strange sounds, but their decibel level had considerably diminished.

"Louder, Madeline, maybe you'll scare up

your mother as well." She paused. "Or your father."

Madeline suddenly grew silent. She opened her eyes.

"What are you saying?" she asked, her voice soft now.

"It's all over, Madeline," Virginia said. Reaching out, she grasped Madeline's hand and helped her to a chair. Madeline's face was streaked, her hair totally awry. Deliberately, Virginia kept her eyes averted from Jack. He'd have to work his own way through this, she decided. The twins as well.

"I don't really have to ask the question, 'Why us?' I know 'why us.' We both know, don't we?"

Madeline shrugged. The fight was out of her. Discovery had transformed her.

"Know what?" Jack asked.

"That Madeline is a fraud," Virginia said.

Madeline said nothing. A brief frown passed over her forehead. Her eyes blinked away tears.

"Are you saying . . ." Jack began, then faltered.

"Tell them, Madeline," Virginia said.

Madeline lowered her head. "A little research here, a little luck there, a little guesswork and suggestion."

"Tell us about the great miracle of Basil," Virginia said.

"I never said it was a miracle," Madeline shot back. "I can't be responsible for what you believed."

"Come on, Madeline," Virginia pressed, "show us your cleverness."

"I gave you hope."

"Hope?" Jack asked. He was having difficulty grasping their meaning. He sucked in a deep breath. "What about Bobbie getting hurt?" The fight was out of him as well.

"Lucky guess, right, Madeline? Coincidence."

"I did warn you," Madeline said, making some effort to recover.

"Mumbo jumbo," Virginia said. She turned to Jack. "Bobbie got hurt. It was an accident. Madeline knew how to capitalize on that."

"I predicted it," Madeline said.

"We're all right about half the time," Virginia said. She was without fear, unburdened. "On average." Granted, she told herself, there are mysteries out there. And vulnerable people. Like us.

"I have this gift," Madeline said. But her insistence sounded hollow.

"When did you first know, Madeline?" Virginia asked pointedly. She was following a road map in her own mind.

"I knew," Madeline scowled.

"When your father came home that night? You had sensed it earlier, right? Then when he came through the door, you saw his face and that confirmed everything. It was then that you ran away. Am I right, Madeline?"

Madeline squirmed in her chair.

"Am I right?" Virginia repeated.

Madeline lowered her head again, her shoulders hunched. "Yes. Yes," she whispered. "I knew he was going to kill my mother and my sister. I knew it. I knew it and I should have warned them but I was afraid." She started to cry, quietly now.

Virginia searched within herself for pity. She found none. "How did you pick us, Madeline?"

Madeline swallowed and brought herself under control, then wiped her eyes with the back of her hand. "I . . . I saw you one day, walking along the pier at Santa Monica. Mother, father, twin girls. Like we were. A happy, loving family." She started to cry again. "I didn't mean any harm."

"How many times have we heard that?" Virginia said coldly. She looked at the twins, who were desperately trying to understand what was happening. Then at Jack, beaten now, hope gone. "You owe us this, Madeline."

"I followed you back to your house. If you need to know things, you can find out."

"All you need is bits and pieces, right?"

Madeline nodded.

"You knew my habits. The standing appointment at Mel's. I was going to the dentist then." She laughed. "Improving my smile. You found my "genie" in the car in the parking lot outside my dentist's office, didn't you? It was simple to get the code, I bet. Loosen a couple of screws. Copy down the numbers. Then you had this one made." She jangled the key ring. "Right so far?"

Madeline lowered her head.

"You opened the gate. Got Basil into your car. Dumb dog will go anywhere. Then all you had to do was keep him in the car or your apartment until evening. Right? Of course, he was coming back. You brought him back. Some miracle. If I resent anything I resent having kept him cooped up all day."

"I tranquilized him," Madeline said. "He slept peacefully in the backseat."

"While you went to the beauty parlor."

Madeline shrugged and nodded.

"You did go through my pocketbook that day in the beauty parlor. Is there a more fertile environment for women to become intimate? You

saw my sister's letter. You had already found
out things about my husband. We reminded you
of what you had lost. You wanted to find it
again. Was that it, Madeline?"

"Yes. Yes," Madeline cried.

"Still lying though your teeth, eh Madeline,"
Virginia said. "You wanted more than just being part of our little happy family. You wanted
to control us. You wanted to play God. Is that
it, Madeline?"

Virginia's adrenaline had risen and with it her
sense of outrage. A kaleidoscope of recent mem-
ories flooded her mind, turning the rage inward
as well. How could she have been so gullible,
so naive? No matter what, she thought with bitterness, we'll never be the same.

"We gave you our minds and . . ." She looked
at the twins. "We gave you everything." She
turned to Jack.

"You were right about her. A sleazy fortune-
teller. Her clients were probably all gamblers.
Horses, football, baseball. Anything you can bet
on. Probably the stock market as well."

"I had a damned good average," Madeline
snapped. "All depended on a little luck." Her
nostrils quivered. "Try explaining luck. There's
more out there than meets the eye."

"You called one of your stock market players.
Fished some tips out of him that had, trusting
to luck, some prospects."

"Jesus, Madeline," Jack said as if it were a
cry of pain.

"She needed to hold our interest, prime the
pump. She had it figured to take all of the
credit, but none of the blame. What idiots we
were." She felt ashamed.

"Jesus, Madeline," Jack said.

"Of course, she knew about Compulaser. She had ample opportunity to go through your briefcase. She took a Ph.D. in the Sargent family. Sucked us in."

Jack pursed his lips and shook his head in disbelief. "You've ruined us, Madeline," he said, his voice choking.

"I didn't want you to get hurt. You have to believe that."

"Believe you?" Virginia said with contempt.

"You're all so vulnerable," Madeline said. With her fingers, she brushed back her hair. Exposure had apparently unburdened her as well. "How easily people fall into it. You all want so badly to believe that your dreams will come true. It was an easy guess about both of you. You, Virginia, wanted to become a great artist. And you, Jack, to have your own business. Anybody could have spotted that." She was desperately trying to recover her poise. "I took no money. Remember that. Not a nickel. Maybe that was my big mistake. But . . ." A tiny sob escaped from her. "I just wanted to be part of your family."

"And so you were," Virginia said.

"You can't imagine what it was like. My sister. My mother. My father." A sob erupted in her throat. She fought for control. "You were there. Don't you understand. You were there. I wanted it to be like it was. Is that so terrible?"

"You attacked us," Virginia said, vitriol boiling inside of her. She was playing for sympathy now, falling back to her last line of defense. "You took away our sense of self."

Madeline slowly stood up, drawing her shoulders back, her body stiff, her face tight. "You gave it to me. All of you," Madeline said. "Willingly. You gave me yourselves on a silver platter. All I ever needed was the information and the lingo. I'm damned good at the lingo. I made you do whatever I wanted. I had you in my hands. You believed it all, bought it all." Her gaze panned their faces, the eyes intense with pride, anger and, no mistaking it, regret. "Hell, I was God here."

Virginia would, she knew, always remember this scene. Jack stunned, glaring with simmering anger and frustration, the realization of their folly bubbling to the surface like boiling oil. The twins, struggling to sort out this bizarre episode, searching each other's faces for the answers that might take them a lifetime to find.

But maybe this will teach them to treasure their individuality, Virginia thought. To guard against predators who would and could steal their will and substance. *Be on guard always, my children. Never never never let it happen to you,* she begged them in silence.

After this long pause, Virginia felt suddenly enervated. She turned toward her husband as if handing him the relay stick for the final lap of a race.

Jack moved, picking up Madeline's pocketbook which was lying open on the bed. He scooped up the contents and began to thrust them inside. He paused, opened the key ring and removed the genie, then threw the keys back into the pocketbook. Clasping it shut, he handed it to Madeline. In a reflex motion she took it.

"I want you to leave my house," he said, "this minute."

"My things . . ." she stammered.

"We'll send them to you." He took a deep breath. "Trust me."

Madeline's lip quivered. Her eyes filled with moisture. "Despite everything," she whispered, "I love you all." Fighting to preserve a posture of dignity, she hurried from the room.

Only then did Jack open his arms. Virginia and the twins crowded in. But it was not until she heard Madeline's car leave the driveway that Virginia was able to savor her first real taste of freedom in a long, long time.

·26·

Dawn came over the far hills as Jack stood by the bedroom window watching its arrival. The shock of discovery had worn off and he was left now with the ashes of his gullibility.

The postmortem in his mind was surprisingly without rancor. He was angry at Madeline's treachery, but not outraged by it. Mostly, he was disgusted with himself. Something deep inside of him had reacted to her manipulation. All logic had capitulated. He had surrendered his mind and his body. The remembered image of himself having sex with Madeline, with Virginia's eager consent, filled him with self-loathing.

And so, he told himself, his punishment would fit the crime. With the dawn would come the realization of his financial ruin, retribution for his greed. He chuckled bitterly. The end of the yuppie dream.

"Back to the drawing board," Ginny had said last night in the haze of sexual aftermath. They had made love, but it was more a validation of their marriage than an erotic event. He was not

certain that Virginia had experienced the same
sense of letdown nor did he choose to discuss
it with her at that moment, but something had
blunted his libido. Was it Madeline's departure? Or perhaps it was the thought of his
financial demise. Certainly, that was understandable.

What he seemed to be left with was cynicism
and a sharper nose for analysis. Buyer beware,
he thought bitterly. They had been snookered
both financially and emotionally. Now he would
have to dissect every situation before taking any
action.

The loss of potential adventure saddened him.
It had been downright delicious to live with fantasy and illusion. Mindlessness had its comforts and compensations. Succumbing to reality
was depressing, especially now, facing the prospect of financial disaster.

Earlier, in a long postcoital discussion, he and
Virginia had discussed it. "Without going over
the numbers, which are staggering, our only solution is personal bankruptcy," he had told her.

"People do it all the time," Virginia had responded. "It'll build character."

"We've got a long way to go on that," he had
sighed. "The firm will dump me. No sense kidding ourselves about that. These things have a
domino effect." He had thought suddenly of
poor Jane and Singer, both of whom would
surely go down with his ship. "Probably kill me
in the business. Maybe bar me."

"Then you'll find something else."

"We'll have to move."

"We've done that before."

"And take the twins out of private school."

"They'll understand."

"Dump the fancy cars."

"Big deal."

He had been amazed at how easily she was accepting the situation.

"Well, I'm not going to cut my wrists, Jack. I can still get a job as a commercial artist. And you've never let grass grow under your feet either. Besides, rich is relative. Money, need I tell you, is not all there is."

"Never was," he had agreed. Then why had he been so single-minded in its pursuit? It wasn't only Madeline who had tripped him up, it was his own blind, stupid greed.

"So we'll just have to switch dreams," Virginia had told him. She had grown silent, and when he had lifted himself on his elbow to see her face, she seemed wistful, far away. "I loved the one I had," she said.

"I kind of liked mine as well," he admitted.

"She sure knew what turned us on," Virginia said, "in more ways than one."

"She was one clever lady."

"How did she put it? Lingo. She knew the lingo of hope, all right. All those pseudo sciences that feed on yearnings and provide answers to the unanswerable. Astrology, telepathy, clairvoyance, numerology, channeling, reincarnation, the whole nine yards. God, she was good. Or is that a sop to us, as if it took real skill to take us on."

"Yeah, real skill. We fell like dominoes."

"I fell first. Remember that. You resisted."

"I fell harder."

"It's the kids I worry about most," Virginia had said. The thought had triggered their silence and followed them to a restless sleep.

After Madeline had left the night before, they

had spent time with the twins, mostly answering their questions and reassuring them that Madeline's so-called talents were easily explainable contrivances and had nothing at all to do with the supernatural. She had admitted that in their presence, hadn't she? Virginia had made a wise decision, letting them see for themselves. No verbal explanation could have matched that.

"Put her out of your mind, kids," Jack had told them. "She made up stories. Sometimes she got lucky in her predictions. Sometimes she goofed up badly. Like with your old broke dad."

"Don't worry, Daddy, we'll go to work," Bobbie had said. "We can easily pass for fourteen, can't we, Billie?"

"Maybe even fifteen," Billie had echoed.

He had kissed them both.

"With you guys, I got all the treasure I need," he had told them.

"I still can't figure out about the green Magic Marker," Billie had interjected, just when he felt he had closed the circle on their understanding. He had done his best to explain it, realizing as he did so, that the explanation was not satisfactory, that moral ambiguities would persist.

It was then that Virginia filled in the gaps, telling them abut going through Madeline's things earlier, finding the apartment keys and the genie, seeing the Magic Marker, making duplicate keys, exploring Madeline's apartment, finding the letters.

"Welcome to the real world, kids," Jack had told them, hoping that they would accept their mother's cunning and trickery, accept the concept of lying to catch a lie.

Later, lying in bed, unable to sleep, he lis-

tened to Virginia's soft breathing and watched
her body rise and fall in gentle rhythms. Only
then did a troubling idea come to him. He
stroked her awake, watching her eyes open.

"How could you know?" he asked.

"Know what?" she whispered.

"That she would try to pin you with it, put
the evidence in your studio drawer. How could
you know she had put it there?"

"I knew her game by then. No magic necessary. No mumbo jumbo required. Clairvoyance
is a head game. Precognition flows out of intu-
ition. It's a perfectly human attribute."

"You stacked the deck," Jack said with admiration.

"Fire with fire," Virginia shrugged.

"But suppose she hadn't cracked wide open."
He shivered. "I would really have believed that
you were possessed, that you had done me in."

"I wouldn't have blamed you." She ruffled his
hair.

He was silent for a long time.

"The rabbit stew tasted like shit."

"And I hate the color orange."

At that point they had drifted off to another
fit of restless sleep.

Standing now, watching the quickening dawn,
his depression began to fade. The fact was that
it was rather pleasant to be free from economic
burdens. Being on the verge of bankruptcy had
an oddly tranquilizing effect.

From one perspective, at least, it could be
joyous, an unfettering. He could indulge in profound thoughts about values, the evils of materialism, the silliness provoked by the pursuit of
wealth. Possession-bound was to be enslaved by
the trivial. "What does it profiteth a man if he

gaineth the whole world and loseth his own soul?" How apt, he thought. And reassuring.

In his heart, he forgave Madeline, although he was less forgiving about himself. In a way, he supposed it was a compliment that she wanted to be a part of his family. His family was lovely and loving. He adored his three wonderful ladies. He wasn't afraid of the future. Bankruptcy, after all, wasn't death.

The blinding ball of the sun cleared the distant peaks. Time to face the inevitable, he sighed. He showered leisurely, switching from hot to cold, as if it were a purification ritual. Wiping the steam from the mirror, he prepared to shave, studying his face. No, he decided, not this morning. Better yet, he would grow a beard. He had always wanted to grow a beard. Never had. Too busy trying to conform to the image of the hustling stockbroker on the go, in pursuit of money and power. What else?

"Welcome to the second half of your life," he said aloud to his mirror image, winking and showing a broad smile. Then he saluted and went into the bedroom. He dressed in jeans and polo shirt and brown penny loafers without socks.

Perfect for the guillotine, he told himself. Off with the head of the old Jack Sargent. Then would come reincarnation. A laugh bubbled out of his throat and he saw Madeline's face in his mind. The angel of resurrection, he decided, smiling. He went over to the bed and bent to kiss his wife.

Her eyelids fluttered, then quieted. Unburdened, she was deep in sleep. Maybe the future could be an adventure again, he told himself. He proceeded to the twins' room. They were sleeping together in one bed, two dolls lying neatly in their quilt wrappings. There's a miracle, he said through eyes misted with tears. He touched their golden hair, then bent down to kiss them.

That done, he found Basil folded into a ball in the crease of the quilt at the foot of the bed. He petted him lightly, sensing the need to touch all living things in his circle of life. Dumb mutt, he thought. Tricked as well. Then he quietly let himself out the front door.

But before moving to the garage, he stood outside for a quiet moment, surveying his million-dollar home.

"Sumbitch," he said aloud, enjoying the mimicry, "I'll always love ya." He paused, laughed. "But I can do without ya."

Satisfied with the irony, he got into the Jaguar and drove down the hill. Ten minutes later, he walked past computer banks manned by frenzied colleagues. Occasionally, someone would lift his eyes from the screen and look at him curiously. He hoped he had the look of devil-may-care determination as he walked the so-called last mile with dignity. Show them class, he told himself.

Inside his office, the telephone was ringing. He paid no attention. He found his briefcase, dumped what was in it into the wastebasket and reloaded it with his personal effects, pictures of Virginia and the twins, a pen set that had been a gift from his parents and a paperweight snow scene with a title plaque that read: CONNECTICUT WINTER. Before dropping it in the briefcase, he turned it over, watching the snow fall on a Yankee barn.

As he watched it, a voice interrupted the nostalgic reverie.

"Mr. Conway needs to see you immediately." It was Miss Hernandez, Conway's secretary. "We've been trying to get you on the phone." She sniffed with distaste at his unkempt look.

"You got me," he answered with a smile, snapping shut his briefcase. He followed Miss Hernandez into Conway's office.

"I found him," she said, discreetly leaving the paneled plushness of this inner sanctum.

Conway sat scowling behind his desk. He was a man who showed his emotions, and his rage was a billboard on his face.

"You lost the Singer account, Jack."

"And that's not all," Jack said. He no longer felt the slightest sense of intimidation. His mind felt clear, his motives pure.

"No, it's not, you asshole," Conway continued. "You've ruined Jane Meyers. Poor woman was hysterical on the phone this morning. She was up to her ass in Compulaser and so were her clients."

"Let the buyers beware," Jack said cheerfully.

"A fucking psychic," Conway fumed. "Jane was hysterical. Said you were flimflammed and she fell for it, too." He shook his head. "Who the hell is this woman?"

The question took Jack by surprise. No, he decided. If there were to be legal proceedings he would keep Madeline out of it. The book was closed on that aberration forever.

Conway said, "The ethics of it were atrocious. My ass will be on the line with the front office. How could you?"

"It's a long story," Jack said.

"You realize that you've got to go."

"Look at me." He raised his briefcase. "I'm packed."

"Greed will do it every time," Conway sighed.

"Every time," Jack echoed. "That's what our business is all about."

"I want that woman's name," Conway said, standing up.

"You're not her mark, Conway. She's into happy families."

"What the fuck are you talking about?" Conway sputtered.

Jack shrugged and turned to go. No point in prolonging the abuse. He felt aeons away, as if he were watching the scene from a great distance.

"You could have at least stopped them from selling out," Conway shouted.

Jack stopped dead in his tracks. His heart leaped. He turned to face Conway again.

"You're not making any sense," Jack said.

"You are a cagey bastard, Jack." He took a deep breath. "I suppose you don't know that the stock's up to ten. All in the first hour."

"Compulaser?"

"Asshole," Conway shouted. "They got out at the close last night. Somebody's got their hooks into it. Looks like two buyout bidders fighting it out. The point is . . . you were derelict in not notifying Jane and Singer. It was a shitty thing to do."

"I don't believe it," Jack said flatly.

Conway punched in the computer on his desk.

"Eleven, pal," Conway said. "Worst part is that I've got to face the feds on whether or not you were operating on inside information. Who

the fuck is going to believe this psychic bullshit?"

Jack stood rooted to the spot. His mind raced
with speculation. Another of Madeline's miracles? He felt himself slipping back into the old
mind-set.

"The feds have no case," he said.

"You think I don't know that." Conway's tone
had softened. "You could have at least given me
her name. Let me in on it," Conway said, "after
all I've done for you."

Jack turned and walked out of Conway's office in a trance. Reality seemed splintered. Logic
faulty. Back in his office, he picked up the
phone. Old habits died hard. He knew what he
had to do.

In the next half hour, he settled all accounts.
He sold out his shares of Compulaser and made
arrangements to pay off his loans to his credi-
tors and to return to Jane and Singer what they
had lost on the transaction. He was still left
with a handsome profit.

That finished, he swiveled his chair and
looked out of the window into the bright California sunshine, hoping to still the turmoil rattling in his brain. Elation had dissipated. His
sense of freedom had eroded. The burdens of
financial responsibility crowded in on him
again. For a brief moment, he felt the window
of logic and reality close. With whatever
strength of will he could summon, he raised it
up again. But it never, ever would be opened as
high as it had been earlier that morning.

He would always be plagued by a festering
sense of something happening beyond his range
of reality.

Swiveling back to his desk, he punched in 411

on his phone and got Madeline's telephone number. He called it, waiting for the ring. His hand sweated against the instrument. But when he heard her voice, he hung up.

Perhaps, instead, he would send her a check. No, he decided, that would be an admission of belief in what she herself had publicly rejected. *People are gullible and vulnerable,* she had said. *You all want your dreams to come true.*

He called his home. After three rings, Virginia answered.

"You'll never believe this . . ." he began.